THE GRAVEDIGGER'S BRAWL

ABIGAIL ROUX

RIPTIDE PUBLISHING

Riptide Publishing
PO Box 6652
Hillsborough, NJ 08844
www.riptidepublishing.com

The Gravedigger's Brawl
Copyright © 2012 by Abigail Roux

Cover Art by Reese Dante, http://reesedante.com
Editor: Tiffany Maxwell and Rachel Haimowitz
Layout: L.C. Chase, http://lcchase.com/design.htm

ISBN: 978-1-937551-53-7

First edition
October, 2012

Also available in ebook:
ISBN: 978-1-937551-63-6

THE GRAVEDIGGER'S BRAWL

BRAWL

ABIGAIL ROUX

RIPTIDE
PUBLISHING

For Sara, my grandmother. She passed away nine years ago, but my three-year-old daughter has been talking about her since she could speak.

TABLE OF CONTENTS

CHAPTER ONE

D r. Wyatt Case sat at his desk with his eyes closed, listening for the sound of footsteps in the outer office. His assistant had orders to stop anyone trying to see him with as much fanfare as possible so he'd have time to prepare for the confrontation. Or hide. But she was on her lunch hour and Wyatt was on his own for the moment.

The outer door creaked open and his entire body began to tense as if anticipating a physical blow. There were two voices—one male, one female—discussing his whereabouts. Wyatt slid out of his chair to his knees and crawled into the kick space beneath his antique desk.

He wasn't ashamed, either.

It had been a stressful week and Wyatt wasn't used to that kind of thing. His mind wasn't built for strain, and his museum ran smoothly for the most part. But the trustees had been at him all week, jabbering about how the construction of the museum's new wing was hurting attendance and they needed a fresh exhibit to draw in the crowds.

Wyatt hated to tell them, but the only crowds the Virginia Historical Society would be drawing this time of year were screaming schoolchildren and die-hard history buffs who would come to the museum regardless of construction or new exhibits. In late September, the summer crowds were all gone, and the weather was nice enough that people were still trying to squeeze life and fresh air from the outdoors.

There was a curt knock, and the door to his office opened.

"Now where in the world could he be?" Edgar Reth, the acting president of the society, grumbled.

Wyatt closed his eyes, putting his hand over his mouth. One snicker and he was done for.

"It *is* almost lunchtime," a woman said. Emelda Ramsay had sat on the board since before Wyatt was born. She was old Virginia money, concerned with nothing but the welfare of the museum and the historical society, rising above the politics and financial pressures that many trustees had fallen to over the years. She had been a key proponent of Wyatt's when he'd been brought to Richmond to take over the museum and Wyatt considered her a friend and mentor. It was certainly bad form to be hiding from her beneath the very desk her grandfather had donated, but that was life. He was tired of her having to defend him from Reth, who was a pompous ass, but had clout. If Wyatt couldn't please the trustees, not even Emelda could save him.

Emelda's sensible flats echoed on the hardwood floors as she walked toward the desk. "I'll just leave him a note," she said as her feet came into view.

Wyatt rolled his eyes. This was ridiculous. He crawled out from under the desk, and Emelda gasped as he appeared at her feet.

"Dr. Case!" She pressed her hand to her chest.

Wyatt stood, dusting off his sleeves. "My apologies, Emelda, I didn't mean to frighten you."

"Dr. Case, what in the world were you doing under there?" Reth demanded.

Wyatt glanced at him, schooling his features into innocence. "Pilates."

"You do Pilates under your desk?"

"You don't?" Wyatt asked, eyes going wide.

Emelda cleared her throat and smoothed a hand over her smart blazer. "Indeed."

"What can I do for you?" Wyatt asked as he looked between them.

Reth waved a file folder at him. "Have you seen the most recent numbers?"

"Why yes, Dr. Reth, I believe you emailed them to me. Three times. And had a courier deliver them to me. At my home. Which . . . wasn't creepy at all."

"Dr. Case, do you realize that we're talking about your future here at the museum?" Reth asked. Wyatt could practically see the steam rising from his head.

Wyatt rubbed a finger across his eyebrow and nodded. He'd given them idea after idea, exhausting his mental stores as he laid out plans for all the possible exhibits they could create with the artifacts they had on hand. They couldn't get any artifacts of significance on loan in the short period of time before the new exhibit was due, they couldn't purchase or barter anything new, and they couldn't pull magic out of their asses.

If they had listened to Wyatt and his subordinates when the plans for the new wing had been pushed through, they could have been prepared. Wyatt had tried to show them the cost of the remodel, and not just the monetary cost. He'd been overruled, though, and now they seemed shocked by the drop in attendance.

Reth tossed the file onto the desk. "If a solution is not presented to the board by the end of the week, you're done here, Case. Is that clear enough?"

"Crystal," Wyatt said through gritted teeth.

Reth turned on his heel and stormed out of the office. Wyatt sighed and turned to Emelda, who was shaking her head and frowning.

"He's going to ask for your dismissal next month if we don't have something spectacular to show the trustees."

"I know."

Emelda patted his arm and smiled encouragingly. "I have faith."

Wyatt couldn't help but laugh. "In what?"

She raised her eyebrows and cocked her head, surprised. "In you, Dr. Case."

Wyatt smiled weakly as she walked away. She shut the office door behind her, and Wyatt sank to his chair and held his head in his hands. After a few minutes to compose himself, he glanced up at one of the framed posters on his wall, a copy of an original Thurston show marquee. It advertised "the Great Magician" and pictured Thurston at a desk, bent over a large tome being held up by red imps. The Devil leaned over him, reading over his shoulder and holding his oil lamp for him.

Wyatt glared balefully at the imps. He kind of knew how the man in the poster felt, his work aided and encouraged by evil.

What he needed was inspiration. Or somewhere better to hide than under his desk. As the head curator, such nebulous things as new exhibits, attendance, and public interest were Wyatt's responsibility, and he would take the fall when the numbers showed hard losses over the construction. But every single suggestion he'd brought forth had been shot down as being too staid or not capable of drawing in the younger crowd. Virginia at War. Lincoln's Private War. The World at War! The only one the trustees had really liked was How to Tell Your Curator to Stick It up His Ass.

Wyatt was prepared to tell them that if they wanted a younger crowd, they were going to need a younger curator. At thirty-eight, he didn't consider himself old, but he was out of ideas and out of touch with the target audience.

That was one good thing about his line of work, though; historians never went out of style. In theory. But Wyatt knew you couldn't force an interest in history on people. You couldn't manufacture a love for it out of a few interesting baubles and trinkets being put on display, no matter how cleverly they were presented. It had to be organic, a spark of knowledge put into the mind. All you could do was offer the truth to the masses and hope they found it as fascinating as it was.

Another knock at his door made him wince, but he didn't have time to duck beneath his desk before the door opened.

To his eternal relief, Noah Drake stuck his head in and grinned at him. "You're hiding from the suits, aren't you?"

Wyatt sighed. "They caught me even though I just spent two minutes crouching under my desk."

"Dignified."

"There's a disturbing amount of head room under there."

Noah grinned wider and nodded as he stepped inside. "Some people pay big money for that."

"Wildly inappropriate."

Noah laughed. "Come on. We're going to lunch."

"We are?" Wyatt asked with a hint of dread.

The last time he had let Noah drag him somewhere, he'd wound up in Virginia Beach without a car and mysteriously missing his socks and boxers. Noah rode a motorcycle to work and his long hair was often pulled into a ponytail as he lectured. Like Wyatt, he was openly gay. And God help the poor soul who made a derogatory comment, because while Noah may have had an Ivy League degree, he also had several Krav Maga belts at home.

Noah laughed as Wyatt frowned at him. "Don't look at me like I'm about to eat your canary. Come on, I promise nothing untoward will happen."

Wyatt sighed and then allowed himself a small smile as he stood and grabbed his coat. He was already placing bets on whether or not the bartender was going to have sleeves. "I assume I'm driving?"

"Actually, we're walking. I heard about this great place in the Fan last weekend." They stepped out into the hall and Wyatt turned to lock his office door.

The Fan District was an aptly named neighborhood nestled across the street from the museum, called that because of the way its streets fanned out from its center. The Fan District was one of Richmond, Virginia's lovingly restored historic districts, full of converted condos, restaurants, and used books stores. It was a history buff's dream, an emo kid's hunting ground, and getting trendier and therefore less authentic all the time. He thought they'd hit every restaurant in the Fan, but it seemed like new ones popped up every week. Wyatt had no problem wandering into the area for a little lunch.

He did have a problem with the mischievous glint in Noah's eyes, however.

"What's the catch?" he asked.

"No catch."

Wyatt stopped at the outer door and gestured for Noah to peer around the corner.

"This is escalating quickly," Noah said, but he humored Wyatt and looked around the corner for any trustees on the prowl.

Once he gave the all clear, they made their way to the employee exit. Lately, Wyatt felt like he was in a live action version of *Spy vs. Spy*, and it was only getting worse.

"This is some dive that serves heart attacks, isn't it?" Wyatt asked.

"Wyatt, I promise, there's no catch. Just a nice walk and some lunch. Why," Noah asked with a narrowing of his eyes that didn't camouflage the mischief. "What have you heard?"

"They have a hot bartender or waiter or something and you're dragging me there as cannon fodder so you can flirt with some buff guy in cutoffs."

"Hardly!" They nodded to the security guard at the staff entrance and stepped out into the chilly autumn afternoon. "He's not really buff."

Wyatt snorted.

"And I doubt he wears cutoffs. I like them a little more—"

"Please, spare me any details."

"Closet case."

"Flaming whore."

"Touché."

They stopped at the streetlight and waited to cross the busy street named simply Boulevard. The boundary between the Fan and the boutiques of Carytown, Boulevard was lined on each side with turn-of-the-century houses, most restored, others still languishing as rundown condos with bikes and Christmas lights hanging off their once-splendid balconies. It wasn't hard to imagine it as it had been in its glory days, though.

Wyatt grinned and shook his head as they crossed the four lanes and wide grassy median at a jog. The wind whipped at them and sent dried leaves skittering across the road at their feet. It had been a mild mid-Atlantic summer and was cold now at the end of September. Wyatt wasn't complaining, though. He would much rather bundle himself up in a jacket than suffer through the sweltering summers and warm falls the Eastern seaboard was accustomed to.

They walked down the sidewalk, shoulders brushing. "So, tell me about your latest conquest. And then tell me why you need to drag me along."

"I figured you'd do anything to avoid Reth," Noah said wryly.

"A fair assumption."

"So play wingman for me and stop complaining. I met this guy at the shop. He's got this great World War-era bike," Noah said.

"I see." Wyatt pulled the collar of his coat up against the chill. "One or two?"

"He's only got the one."

"World War I or II," Wyatt asked.

"Oh. Irrelevant to the story, but II," Noah answered. He was wearing a stupid grin, not going into further detail about the bike because he knew Wyatt neither understood nor cared about any more of the particulars. Noah spent a lot of his spare time at the motorcycle shop on the seedier end of Boulevard, the one right next to the tattoo parlor with the checkered floor. Wyatt sometimes suspected he owned part of the place.

"He told me he tended bar at this place in the Fan and that I'd like it, so I checked it out this weekend. It's got great ambience." Noah gave a dramatic flip of his hand.

"Ambience. People only talk about ambience when there's nothing else good to say, Noah."

"No, Wy, you're gonna love it. The food's pretty good too."

"Uh-huh. And since you've already got an in with this guy, you need me why?"

"Because I think you'd really like the place."

Wyatt stopped short and turned to glare at his companion. "This guy doesn't have a friend, does he? Are you trying to set me up?"

"I'm sure he's got no friends. No friends at all."

"Noah!"

"No friends, I swear!"

Wyatt narrowed his eyes and glared for another moment, but Noah's innocuous stare never wavered, so Wyatt turned and began walking again, smiling grudgingly. He had the very distinct feeling that he was being set up with some random guy Noah had found at a bike rally or something. But there wasn't much he could do about it if he wanted to duck the trustees, which seemed the greater of two evils just now.

Wyatt didn't date seriously; he just didn't have the time or interest in it. He had always been happy on his own. But he would have fucked a polar bear if it meant not being bothered by Edgar Reth today.

When they got to the bar, Wyatt found a beautifully restored Victorian with a carved wooden sign hanging outside that read Gravedigger's Tavern. A chalk marquee on the sidewalk indicated the day's specials in a pleasant scrawl, and below that, Olde Richmond Towne Ghost Tours was permanently advertised in paint.

"Fun," Wyatt drawled. "Do you have to be wearing eyeliner to get in?"

"Don't read too much into the façade," Noah said as he took Wyatt's elbow and pulled him to the door.

It wasn't all that crowded because they were behind the lunch crowd, and it looked like the few patrons inside the tavern were regulars. No one sat at the tiny booths that lined the walls of the long, narrow room. Instead, the four people in the establishment were all leaning against the bar that covered the length of one wall, talking with each other and the man serving. One patron wore a long black trench coat. A young woman wore red and black striped tights under a leather miniskirt. Two others wore work vests and had orange hard hats on the stools beside them. An eclectic assortment, to say the least.

Wyatt gave the surroundings a wary glance. It wasn't dirty or greasy like he had expected from a place an acquaintance of Noah's worked, but it looked . . . well-used. In fact, Wyatt liked the vintage feel of the place. The walls were dark and rich, covered with black and wine-colored brocade fabric, and there were antique sconces along the walls that filtered soft light into the room. The ceiling sported tin tiles, and all the woodwork in the place seemed to be original to the old Victorian structure. At night it would probably be quite intimate. The dark wooden floor appeared to be original as well; it was smooth and dull from years of use, any wax or lacquer long worn away.

Noah waved to the bartender and slid into the nearest booth. The man nodded at Noah and smiled as he wiped out a glass with a dishrag.

"Is that the guy?" Wyatt asked as he sat across from Noah and shifted on the leather seat. It was real leather, he was surprised to find, worn and smooth from age and use.

"That's Ash. He's hot, right?"

Ash was a good-looking guy: dark curls, darker eyes, tall and wiry. Wyatt tried not to smile. "Not what I was expecting."

Noah raised an eyebrow.

"Big muscles, braided ponytail, goatee with beads in it."

Noah snorted and rolled his eyes, looking away with a smile and shake of his head.

"Sleeveless leather vest and patches that say 'The bitch fell off' on the back."

Noah laughed, holding out his hand to make Wyatt stop. "You have a low opinion of my taste in men."

"Not low. Just . . . you know, leather-bound and hairy."

"You suck," Noah said as a woman with purple hair came up to take their orders.

She must've caught Noah's words, because she grinned at Wyatt and said, "You'll be popular in certain circles then."

Noah threw his head back and cackled. Wyatt could feel himself blushing, thankful for the low light and the heavy curtains on the windows.

"What can I have Ash make for you?" the woman asked as she rested her hands on the edge of the table.

Wyatt fought the urge to lean away from her. She had piercings everywhere: in her eyebrow, in her nose, one in the side of her lip, and so many in her ear that she probably picked up NPR on clear nights. Her long hair was done in a beautiful array of old-fashioned curls and loose braids, only it had royal purple streaks and white feathers through what appeared to be natural black. She was wearing a corseted dress over fishnet tights, outrageous heeled boots, and velvet gauntlets on her wrists.

"What's good?" Noah asked, unperturbed. They hadn't been given menus.

"Oh, you're fresh meat?" the waitress asked with something like unholy glee as she turned and pointed them out to the bartender. "Hey, Ash, is this the guy?"

The bartender nodded and pointed a dirty glass at them. "1951 tan I.dian Chief. Hey, Noah." He offered them a small smile.

Noah nodded in return, the smile on his face threatening to become permanent.

The waitress whistled and looked back down at Noah, impressed with the mention of the motorcycle. Wyatt felt distinctly out of place, and he took up his customary post in the background as he listened.

"I'm Delilah Willis," the waitress said. She offered her hand to Noah, then crossed her arms over her chest and leaned against the side of Wyatt's booth. "Nice to meet you. You got it with you?"

It took a moment for Wyatt to decide that she was asking about the motorcycle.

"Not today."

"We better make sure your food's good enough to get you to come back. That means I'll be cooking it," Delilah said, loud enough for the bartender to hear.

"We're not up to fire codes right now," the bartender replied.

"Caleb'll cook it then," Delilah said without missing a beat.

Wyatt couldn't help but smile. Noah always managed to find some real characters. God only knew how.

"What would Caleb recommend?" Noah asked.

"You want meat, non-meat, or other?"

"Cheeseburger?" Noah asked.

"Meat, gotcha."

"Club sandwich?" Wyatt ventured.

"Other. Coming right up," Delilah promised, and turned away.

Wyatt frowned at Noah, who was laughing silently. "How is a club sandwich 'other'? What have you gotten me into?"

Noah waved him off and shook his head, still chuckling.

Wyatt watched Delilah as she headed for the little door at the end of the bar that led to the kitchen. Another waiter came almost at the same time, nearly running her over. He was at least a foot taller than she was, broad in the shoulders and lanky. He grabbed her and spun her around to keep from toppling her over, then smacked her on the ass as she continued into the kitchen.

"Dammit, Ryan, every time you do that I end up with a hand print on my ass for a week."

"You love it."

"I know I do," Delilah said before disappearing behind the swinging door.

Wyatt couldn't help but stare. He found the casual attitude fitting in the quirky establishment, but it still shocked him. He was also shocked to find that he was feeling more at ease, despite this not being his type of place.

Ryan the waiter waved at them both. "This the guy?" he asked Ash, and the bartender nodded.

Wyatt would never say anything, but he thought the burly waiter was much more Noah's speed than the man behind the bar. Though both had dark hair and eyes and the same easy way of moving and smiling. Wyatt wondered if they might be related somehow.

Ryan came over and shook their hands. "Ryan Sander, nice to meet you. Talk later." Then he left for the front door and the patio.

Wyatt found Noah looking at him with a crooked smirk. "What?"

"What do you think of the place?"

Wyatt narrowed his eyes. He leaned over the table and pointed his finger in Noah's face. "I don't want to be set up."

"He's your type, though, right?" Noah asked with a glance at the bar.

"Are you kidding? I don't go for guys more than half a foot taller than I am, thanks."

Noah barked a laugh and shook his head, edging closer. "I'm talking about Ash. The tender."

Wyatt's brow furrowed, and he risked a longer look at the man behind the bar. Ash was leaning both elbows on the bar top and talking with one of the men seated there. He wore a long-sleeved white dress shirt, sleeves rolled up to his wiry biceps, with black suspenders and pin-striped black trousers. His eyes were lined in heavy kohl, and when he spoke, Wyatt caught glimpses of metal on his tongue. His black hair was slicked back, long enough that it ended in riotous curls behind his ears and at the nape of his neck. He looked almost like an Old West bartender in his getup. As unusual as the total package was, it was appealing on that particular man in this particular setting. There was something very pseudo-Victorian about the whole thing.

Was it a uniform or just personal style? Ryan had been wearing something very similar, sans the suspenders and tongue ring.

Wyatt studied it for too long, and when he looked at Noah, he once again found his companion grinning. "Your type, right?"

"I don't have a type."

"Yes, but if you had a life, he'd be your type, right?"

Wyatt rolled his eyes. "I thought we came here for *your* eye candy."

"We did."

Sure we did. "If that's the guy you came to see, why are you trying to set me up with him?"

"I met Ash a few weeks ago, just like I said," Noah said quietly, leaning closer. "We hit it off, but he's not my type and I'm not his. He told me he wanted me to meet the guy he worked for and I thought, 'Hey, I'll toss him Wyatt in return.'"

"Real stand-up of you."

"He's a sweet guy. Don't let the gaslight bent throw you off."

"The what?"

"Gaslight. It's like steampunk without the steam. Or the punk. Victorian throwback, gothic without the emo?"

"Are you speaking English right now?"

Noah laughed.

"I have no idea what you're talking about."

"He's quirky and he likes things like suspenders and top hats and riding crops. And I didn't tell him you'd be coming to meet him so you can play it . . . however it is you academic types play it."

"Noah. *You* are an academic type."

Noah waved that off with another mischievous grin. "But I'm the awesome kind who tends to get laid a lot."

Wyatt pressed his lips together, trying not to smile.

"If you don't like him, you don't have to do anything. Just eat with me and we'll go back to work. But if you have the hots for him, then I think maybe you two would get along pretty well. And here's your perfect chance to get to know him."

Wyatt glared at him.

"Did Delilah get y'all's drinks?" Ash asked from behind the bar, and Wyatt and Noah both jumped guiltily. The patrons at the bar had all left.

Noah glanced at Ash and then back at Wyatt, giving his head a jerk as he slid out of the booth. He walked up to the bar and reached over, shaking Ash's hand.

Wyatt followed, uncertain of how he would handle this. If he blew off the informal introduction, Noah would poke fun at him for the rest of the day for being a prude or antisocial or any number of other things that were partially true, and then he would forget it and life would go on. Noah was anything but overbearing or nosy. Usually. But the bartender—Ash—was an attractive man who seemed to have earned Noah's approval. And it took a lot to earn Noah's approval.

"What can I get you?" Ash pulled up two glasses and set them on the lower shelf on the inside of the bar.

Noah slid onto a stool. "What do you have on tap?"

"Sarsaparilla." Ash had a nice drawl that Wyatt thought may have come from the Gulf Coast, dulled by years away from home.

Noah sighed in mock disappointment and shook his head.

Ash filled up one of the beer mugs with what did appear to be root beer, straight out of one of the taps. "You're educating the city's youth, you can't drink until noon."

"It's past noon."

"Semantics."

Wyatt claimed a stool. "Is that really root beer? On tap?" he asked, despite his inner filter telling him to keep quiet and observe rather than interact just yet.

"Best in town," Ash said with a hint of amusement. "Make it two?"

"Sure. What sort of bar serves root beer on tap?"

"The kind that encourages designated drivers," Ash said wryly. He nodded his head at Wyatt. "Who's the critic?"

"Oh! Shit, I'm sorry. Ash, this is my colleague, Dr. Wyatt Case. He's the head curator at the museum. Wyatt, this is Ash Lucroix. Gravedigger extraordinaire."

Wyatt and Ash shook hands, then Ash placed the two glasses of root beer in front of them and smiled crookedly.

"Gravedigger?" Wyatt asked with a hint of wariness. He wasn't certain he wanted to know the story behind the name, but he just couldn't help himself.

Ash nodded. He popped a stirring straw into his mouth and grinned.

"Is this some sort of slang I'm not aware of?"

"As opposed to slang you *are* aware of?" Noah teased.

"Touché. Is it?"

"No," Ash said. He pulled the straw out and gave Wyatt a disarming smile. He had beautiful teeth, save for a small chip in one of his canines that gave him an impish quality. It was the only imperfection on his otherwise stunning face. "The barkeeps are all called Gravediggers here. The current rumor is that it's because we make the best drinks in town."

Wyatt shook his head. "I don't get it."

"Their drinks are so good that people stay until they can't go home," Noah said.

Ash smiled. "Something like that."

"Is that where the place got its name?" Wyatt asked. He could never help it; history always pulled him in.

"No." Ash leaned his elbows on the bar. "It was originally called Fossor's Tavern. This house was built by a family called Fossor." He pointed over his shoulder at the back of the bar. Most of the wall was lined with shelves, but near the center was an old marble fireplace, just like many of the other houses in the Fan.

The mantle was well polished and empty, and Wyatt wondered why they didn't use it as a shelf to store bottles or glasses on, or at least some sort of decoration. The gilded mirror above it was showing signs of age, with black spots and the occasional crack around the edges. It was clean, though, and appeared to be original.

Etched into the marble of the fireplace beneath the mantle was the name Ash had mentioned: Fossor.

"When Caleb bought the place, he called it Fossor's as a tribute."

"And this Caleb person knew that *fossores* were what the Romans called gravediggers?" Wyatt ventured with a knowing smirk.

Ash cocked his head and blinked, his story derailed. "Yeah." He laughed, looking back at Noah. "Museum set, huh?"

Noah shrugged immodestly.

"Well. Anyway, Caleb knew what the word meant and he called us his gravediggers. Most people didn't even get why the tenders were called that, but they went along because that's what people do. It got so popular that we changed the name of the tavern a few years ago."

"Fascinating," Wyatt said in earnest.

Ash smiled and nodded, still looking like he was a little thrown off his game. When he turned to begin putting away the glasses he'd cleaned, Noah waggled his eyebrows at Wyatt. Wyatt snorted.

Delilah stepped back through the narrow door beside the end of the bar and planted her hands on her hips, glaring at Ash as the man restocked glasses on the back wall. The motion drew Ash's attention and he did a little double take that Wyatt found kind of adorable.

"What?" Ash asked when Delilah didn't say anything.

"Did you bang on the wall again?"

"No." When Delilah's eyes narrowed, Ash held out his hands, each clutching the handles of four beer mugs. "No!"

Delilah glanced at Noah and Wyatt and both men shook their heads in silent answer. She muttered and disappeared back into the kitchen.

"What's that about?" Noah asked as soon as the door had stopped swinging.

"I think she's trying to freak me out in retaliation for scaring her with a broomstick last month. She's got the others in on it, I can feel it."

"Scaring her with a broomstick?" Noah asked, laughing.

"It was elaborate and brilliant."

"If you say so."

Ash finished setting the glasses up on their shelves and turned back around. Wyatt admired the way the wiry muscles in his shoulders moved under the thin white shirt. The suspenders were . . . intriguing.

"The place is supposedly haunted, but I've worked here five years and I've never seen anything. They're trying to make me think there's a ghost."

"So, what, October comes calling and they're trying to get you all spooked?" Noah asked with obvious enjoyment.

Ash flopped his dishrag in the direction of the beautiful Victorian glass door. Outside, the chalk sign advertised ghost tours. "October is our bread and butter. Have you heard of the Gravedigger's Brawl?"

Noah nodded, but Wyatt shook his head.

"It's . . . huge," Ash said, obviously struggling to find a better word. "Hottest Halloween party in town every year. Costumes are required; it goes until dawn. Caleb rents all these props and gets pros to come in and do our makeup."

Wyatt nodded, smiling at Ash's obvious excitement but inwardly cringing at the thought of such a crowd. "Sounds . . . awful," he admitted with a laugh.

Ash grinned crookedly. When Wyatt looked into his nearly black eyes, his stomach did a little flip.

"Anyway," Ash said with a sigh. "I think they've got some sort of scheme brewing, 'cause they won't stop talking about hauntings and seeing things and hearing noises upstairs. They're using me as the guinea pig 'cause ghosts freak me out."

"How do you know the place isn't just haunted?" Noah asked.

"Because I refuse to be scared at work."

"Mind over matter," Wyatt said.

"Technically," Noah countered, "it'd be mind over non-matter."

Wyatt shook his head, trying not to laugh.

Ash leaned against the opposite shelf of the bar and began cleaning another glass. The panel that held the mirror above the fireplace lifted up with a swishing sound, and Noah and Wyatt both jumped. Through the hole where the panel had been, they could see the gleaming stainless steel kitchen on the other side of the wall. That explained why they didn't keep anything sitting on the mantel.

The panel hit one of Ash's cleaned glasses that he'd placed on the mantel and sent it tumbling off the shelf. Ash caught the glass as it fell, flicked his wrist, and let the glass roll up his forearm to his elbow, where he popped it into the air and caught it again. He placed it on the proper shelf and then turned around to peer through the open panel.

Wyatt and Noah gaped.

Delilah was leaning over, smirking through the panel from the other side. She pushed two plates of food through the opening. "Soup's on."

"Evil bitch," Ash singsonged. He set the plates down in front of Wyatt and Noah and the panel whooshed shut again.

Wyatt stared, mouth ajar, as Ash walked to the far end of the bar and grabbed some rolls of silverware. He cut his gaze to Noah, who was looking at him with wide eyes.

"Wow," Noah mouthed to him.

Wyatt nodded and glanced back at Ash Lucroix. He wasn't just attractive. He was *interesting*.

Ash pressed his lips together and watched them for a moment. He had the distinct look of someone who wanted to say something but couldn't figure out how to do it. Noah looked up at Ash as he picked up his hamburger and then glanced at Wyatt.

Wyatt poked at his sandwich, wondering if he should excuse himself to go wash up or take a piss or something so Noah and Ash could talk about the man Noah had come to meet.

"It's okay," Noah told Ash. "Wyatt's been oblivious to all things sex-related for like fifteen years, you can talk about it."

"I have not."

"Too *busy* for all things sex-related then."

"Fair point."

Ash looked him up and down and raised an eyebrow. "That's a shame."

Wyatt met his eyes, unable to look away as the heat of a blush crept up his cheeks.

Noah cleared his throat, breaking the spell. Wyatt tore his eyes away and Ash shook his head, then leaned against the bar again.

He looked at Noah and dropped his voice to a whisper. "So? Still want to meet Caleb?"

Noah grinned. "Got nothing to lose, right?" he said with the typical Noah Drake *joie de vivre*.

"Oh, you'll love him," Ash drawled with a hint of mischief worthy of Noah himself. "Come back tonight, he'll be around and able to talk."

"Will do."

Ash smirked and glanced at Wyatt. "Come with him, Wyatt. I'll serve you something besides root beer."

Wyatt smiled crookedly.

Ash looked away and stuck his tongue out of the corner of his mouth, patent disbelief on his face. "I cannot believe I said that. I'm gonna go clean the bathrooms." He gave a mock salute and walked away.

Noah and Wyatt both snickered. Wyatt watched him until he disappeared through the kitchen door.

"So?" Noah whispered.

"I like him."

"I'm a genius," Noah crooned before biting into his hamburger.

It was with great regret that Wyatt found the lunch hour dwindling. He and Noah lingered as long as they dared, chatting with Ash, Delilah, and Ryan whenever the trickling stream of patrons died down enough for them to be able.

They left with promises to return that night, and on the walk back to the museum Wyatt had to bite the inside of his cheek to keep from grinning like a fool the entire way.

CHAPTER TWO

"I don't like being set up," Caleb Biron growled through the opening of the wall. He spoke with a cultured British accent. It was well after the lunch hour and the tavern was empty, save for a few regulars sitting in the booths and reading or doing work on their laptops.

Ash bent over, peering through the opening as he rested his hands on the back bar. "You don't like much of anything."

"I like being left the hell alone."

"Caleb!"

"Ash," Caleb mimicked, his voice high and whiny as if Ash were nagging him.

"Come on, Caleb."

"I won't be nice to him."

"If you can't be nice to Noah, then you can't be nice to anyone." Ash narrowed his eyes and bent closer to the opening in the wall. "Although from what I've seen, that'd be pretty par for the course."

Caleb growled and pulled the stick that held up the hidden panel. It came crashing down on the back of Ash's head with a dull thwack. Ash winced and jerked back, rubbing the back of his head as he glared at the now solid wall. Stars skittered to the edges of his vision and disappeared.

"Fuckwad," he grumbled. When he turned around, Ryan was standing at the bar. Ash huffed at him. "What?"

"You got a grudge against this Noah guy? He seemed pretty all right to me."

"No! I just think they'd hit it off."

Ryan cocked his head and looked at the spot where the partition opened. "Yeah. They're made for each other." He reached over the bar and grabbed Ash's neck, pulling him forward and making him bow his head so he could look at where he'd been hit. "Do you have a confusion?"

Ash swatted Ryan's hands away and straightened back up. "It's a concussion."

Ryan smirked. "Sounds even worse."

"Shut up. Go do something productive." When Ryan turned away, Ash frowned again and rubbed the back of his head.

He glanced at the clock and took a deep breath to settle the nervous flutter in his stomach. It was nearly five o'clock. He hadn't asked when Noah and Wyatt got off work, but he assumed it was around five. But then, he had no reason to think that, other than because it was when everyone else got off work. He didn't even know when the museum closed.

He tried to tell himself that the butterflies were due to the dread of introducing Noah and Caleb now that he was sure Caleb would be a bastard about it. It was partly true, anyway. But the moment he'd seen Wyatt Case walk through the door, he'd been intrigued by the man's aura. Confidence mixed with uncertainty. Intelligence countered by naiveté. Smoking hot swimmer's body camouflaged by khakis.

As the grandfather clock near the entrance began to chime the hour, Ash exhaled slowly. The crowds would be in soon, and then the fun would begin. Gravedigger's had become infamous in Richmond for being the first bar in the state to introduce flair bartending. They added in magic tricks and sometimes even performances on the bar. Other establishments had tried it since, but Ash and Ryan were still considered the best in town.

Hopefully he would be too busy to be nervous or even think about Wyatt Case.

By dusk Ash was up to his elbows in drink orders and laughing, carousing patrons. It was Thirsty Thursday and Gravedigger's was packed, and would remain that way until midnight.

Noah and Wyatt had failed to show, but Ash still glanced at the door every time he heard it open. He didn't want to admit that he was disappointed, but trying to deny it was beginning to get distracting, and it was dangerous to be distracted when you were flairing. Ash had more than once been hit in the head with a flying bottle of booze in the early years.

The door opened again as Ash tossed a bottle of gin in the air and caught it behind his back. He managed to glance over, and a rush of relief and renewed nerves swept through him as Noah stepped into the bar, followed closely by Wyatt.

Ash rolled the bottle over his wrist and held it upside down, pouring as he nodded at the two academics. Wyatt met his eyes, a smile playing at his lips as he gave a bashful nod. Ash couldn't help but grin. The guy was cute as hell. His sandy blond hair was cut short and neat, allowing him to run his fingers through it without mussing it. He had beautiful sea-blue eyes that looked like they could cut glass. He was about the same height as Ash, maybe six feet tall, and had that whole bumbling academic with pent-up sexual frustrations vibe going.

Ash was lucky that what he did was second nature as he watched Wyatt work his way through the crowd. He'd have been sure to get another bang on the head otherwise.

He mixed one more drink to finish out the bottle, let the empty roll down his arm, and then popped it with his elbow to send it flying into a receptacle at the rear wall. He set his other bottle down and held up his hands.

"All right folks, that's all for me!" The people lining the bar, two rows deep in places, waved bills at him and called out; others applauded and whistled. Ash leaned over the bar, taking the tips and nodding his thanks as Ryan set up behind him.

"Thank you, thank you, I'll be here all week," Ryan was saying as the applause for Ash's work died down.

When Ash had gathered all the tips and taken one little bow, he sidestepped out from behind the bar and tried to make his way through the crowd to Noah and Wyatt.

"Hey!" Noah shouted above the din.

Ash took the hand he offered and shook it, pulling their clasped hands to his chest as he hugged the man with one arm. "Thought you'd chickened out," he said into Noah's ear. It was hard to hear above the music and cheering and general merriment. Ash had always loved the chaotic atmosphere of Thursday, Friday, and Saturday nights, but it made it hard to converse.

"We got held up. Museum emergency."

"Right." Ash patted Noah on the back and let him go. Wyatt was looking around and trying not to watch them too closely. Ash stepped toward him and held out his hand. "Wyatt, good to see you again."

Wyatt looked down at his hand in surprise and then gave that adorable, bashful smile as he took it. Ash pulled him close and hugged him in the same manner he had greeted Noah. It was how he greeted everyone he knew, but when he pulled Wyatt closer, it made his chest flutter and his breath catch. When he pulled back, his heart was pounding just a little faster.

It had been a long time since he'd had that reaction to someone he'd just met. He enjoyed the rush of the sensation, the exciting prospect of new territory to explore.

"Y'all want a drink?" Ash offered. He jerked his thumb over his shoulder at Ryan.

"We're good right now. Work in the morning, you know," Wyatt said, just loud enough for Ash to hear.

"Museum emergencies," Ash repeated, amused. He nodded toward the door to the kitchen. "Come on then, it's quieter in the back. Hey," he said as he pulled Noah closer and they began to force their way through the crowd. "Caleb's cranky. If you want to tell him to go fuck himself, I might have to blow you in the alley out back as a thank you."

Noah cackled, his eyes shining with good humor. "Interesting offer, but I'll pass either way. Cranky, huh?"

Ash winced. "You said you like a challenge."

"I love a challenge."

Ash opened the door and ushered them in. The kitchen was much quieter than the outer bar, although the music still filtered in through speakers in the ceiling, and the two evening cooks argued constantly as they worked. Ash looked around and found Caleb sitting on one of several empty crates in the corner near the back door. He was smoking a cigar and letting the fan next to him blow the smoke out the open door.

"Caleb, these are the health inspectors I forgot to tell you about," Ash said, deadpan.

Caleb glared at him and then gave the other two a salute as he blew thick blue smoke out his nose. "I don't want to be set up, and this little git knows it."

"Ash said you were a cranky bastard," Noah said. He stepped past Ash, knelt in front of Caleb, and took the cigar, examining it with a critical eye before taking a slow drag.

Ash watched in stunned silence, holding his breath as they waited for Caleb to respond.

Noah handed the cigar back and blew a perfect ring of smoke past Caleb's face toward the door. "Cubans, huh?" he asked with a cheeky smirk.

Caleb stared at him for a long moment, mouth ajar, the trail of smoke from the cigar slithering up into the air between them as Ash and Wyatt waited, tense and silent.

Caleb finally tore his eyes away from Noah to look up at Ash. "I like him."

"Looks like you have an eye for matchmaking."

Wyatt and Ash sat at a booth in a quiet corner of the bar. The boisterous crowd had died down just before midnight, when Ryan's shift ended. Most of the people in the bar now were there for the calmer, more intimate atmosphere.

Ash raised his glass and grinned before he took a sip. "I'm a freaking magician," he drawled.

"We'll just call you Thurston."

Ash raised one eyebrow and grinned. "Greatest magician to ever live. More popular than Houdini in his time. I'm impressed."

"If that sort of knowledge impresses you, then I like my chances," Wyatt said, and Ash laughed. He raised his hand to call for two more drinks.

Caleb tended the bar for the last two hours of the night most nights to wind people down from the shows Ash and Ryan put on. Tonight, Noah sat at the end of the bar talking to him whenever he was free. They hadn't stopped flirting for five hours, and they were getting along even better than Ash had expected. Most people could only tolerate Caleb for limited periods of time. He was blunt, rude, grumpy, and possessed a rapier-like wit that he wasn't afraid to use, all topped off like a cherry by that damned British accent that made you feel inferior. Ash, Ryan, and Delilah were, as far as Ash knew, the only people he was even marginally civil to.

When Ash had met Noah, he'd known that not only would Noah be able to match wits with Caleb, he'd probably enjoy it.

Ash looked back at Wyatt and smiled. Wyatt was watching him as if the rest of the bar didn't even exist. "You always this ... intent?"

"Only when I'm fascinated."

Ash raised one eyebrow in disbelief. He usually read people well, but he hadn't expected the shy museum curator to be so forward. He liked that Wyatt could surprise him.

Wyatt laughed and shook his head, looking down at the table. "I'm sorry, I don't drink much. It makes me braver than I really am."

"Does it?" Ash planted both hands on the table and leaned forward, pinning Wyatt with his gaze. "I'll just go hurry those drinks along then," he murmured before smirking and sliding out of the booth.

The drinks he brought back were stronger than they should have been, but he was feeling daring tonight.

"So tell me what exactly a museum emergency looks like."

Wyatt groaned and ran a hand through his hair. As he told Ash about his problems at the museum, the playful air faded from him and the worry lines seemed to grow deeper. Despite trying to make a joke of hiding under his desk that morning, Ash could see how deeply troubled Wyatt was by it all.

"So you see my dilemma, right?" Wyatt asked, motioning pleadingly with his hands. Ash was torn between watching those hands and watching Wyatt. "I mean, I'm lost. If I can't come up with something, I'll be fired."

"Doesn't seem right. They should have known construction would hurt business and planned ahead."

"Thank you!"

Ash couldn't help but laugh at Wyatt's sincerity, though he did feel sorry for him. He seemed so stressed now that he'd gotten on a roll speaking about it. Maybe that was why Wyatt had allowed Noah to drag him here when it was so obviously not his scene: he needed a release.

"So you're here researching a new exhibit?" Ash ventured. "Or is it stress relief?"

"Neither," Wyatt said with the honesty of too much alcohol. He gulped down the last of his drink.

Ash cocked his head and bit his lip against a smile. "I could probably help you with one."

Wyatt's blue eyes met his with intense interest, but then his expression softened and he leaned forward. "You already have," he whispered, the sound conspiratorial. They both laughed as if it had been a joke, and continued talking and drinking as the night wound down around them.

Another hour and Ash realized that perhaps he'd made those drinks too strong. He could hold his liquor, but it had been a long week and he was exhausted on top of being drunk. Caleb agreed when Ash tried and failed several times to sit on one of the bar stools, and promptly took his keys from him.

"That's so unnecessary," Ash grumbled as he leaned against the bar.

Noah and Wyatt were the only ones left, and Caleb had already locked the door and turned off the outside lights.

"I don't drive to work, Caleb. Remember?"

"Do I trust you to walk home by yourself when you're sober? No. Do I trust you to stumble home alone tonight? Hell no."

"I could drive him," Noah offered as he flicked his keys in his hands.

"I'm fine."

"I can walk home with him," Wyatt said, voice soft and gruff as he leaned against the bar.

Caleb glared. "You're more sloshed than he is!"

"But less likely to wind up sleeping in the street," Wyatt countered with a goofy grin. Ash smiled at him. There wasn't a chance in hell he'd get through the night without falling into bed with this guy.

"Oh, Christ," Caleb grumbled before ushering them all out of the bar, where they were no longer his problem.

Wyatt wrapped his coat around himself and they turned the corner, walking down the side of Gravedigger's and away from the heart of the Fan. "How far is it?"

"About six blocks. It's usually not such a bad walk when you're going in a, y'know, straight line." Ash waved his hand in front of him, trying to illustrate said straight line without weaving.

Wyatt glanced at him and smiled. Ash was wearing a black pea coat and a lime green scarf, the only bit of color on him. He was hunched against the wind, head resolutely down to watch his footfalls. Wyatt reached out and slid his arm around Ash's waist. The contact sent a thrill through him.

"Two drunks are better than one," he said to excuse the brazen move.

Ash snorted and slid his hand into Wyatt's coat pocket. Wyatt bit his lip to hold back a foolish grin. They were both unsteady on their feet, but leaning against each other did have its benefits. It kept them warm in more ways than one, stoking that hint of excitement that came from the touch of someone new.

And it kept them from falling over.

The walk to Ash's building on the very edge of the Fan wasn't a short one, but when they reached it, Wyatt found himself regretting that it hadn't been longer. He stood with Ash at the massive glass door to his building and searched for something even mildly appropriate to say. He wanted to come in with Ash, wanted to spend more time with him, wanted to see what sorts of things he held dear in the condo upstairs, ask if maybe he could see him again. But it had been so very long since Wyatt had even had a passing interest in someone else, he couldn't decide how best to vocalize any of those desires.

"You don't think I'm going to let you walk back to the museum alone, do you?" Ash asked as he slid his key into the lock, flicking his wrist and pushing in with practiced ease as he opened the door. He stepped into the foyer and reached for Wyatt, pulling him by the lapel of his coat. Wyatt glanced around the building distractedly, his nerves making it hard to meet Ash's eyes as the man helped him down the couple of steps into the building's foyer. The walls were exposed brick and the stair railing was ironwork that looked like it might have been original.

"Eighteen twenties?" he asked.

"Yeah, how'd you know?" Ash sounded breathless as he let the massive door fall closed behind them with a loud clank.

"Museum," Wyatt grunted. He realized that Ash was taking much of his weight, and he straightened up and cleared his throat. He overcompensated and almost lost his balance.

Ash grabbed him, but he pushed at him instead of pulling, slamming him against the wall at the base of the stairs to keep him from falling. Wyatt couldn't tear his eyes from Ash's; their dark brown depths were nearly black in the low light. He could feel Ash's breath on his lips, the scent of beer and something more earthy, like sandalwood, assaulting him. Wyatt's entire body tingled.

Then they began to laugh. They tried to remain quiet so as not to disturb the neighbors, but it swiftly degenerated into the simultaneous snickering and snorting and hushing that always manifested when drunks tried to be quiet.

"Please tell me you can walk up the steps," Ash said with a hushed giggle.

"How many floors?" Wyatt looked up the narrow, winding stairway.

"One little flight," Ash whispered, his voice low and tantalizingly intimate. He slid his arm around Wyatt's waist again and pulled him away from the wall.

Wyatt turned into him and kissed him hard. Ash stumbled, and his back hit the wall as Wyatt pressed into him, his body thrumming as Ash returned the kiss.

The bang of a closing door several floors above them forced them apart to look up. They stood frozen, panting against each other's mouths as they waited. The door closed again and all was silent.

"Okay," Ash whispered, nodding as if he were agreeing with something. "Okay."

"Stairs," Wyatt murmured against Ash's lips. Ash nodded once more before Wyatt kissed him again.

They climbed the stairs together, staggering and gripping the railing. As they neared the top where the stairs curved around, Ash bent over and began crawling. Wyatt leaned against the wall and laughed as Ash reached the landing and sprawled on his back in front of the first door, but his laughter died away as he let his eyes drift appraisingly over Ash's body.

"That your door?"

Ash managed to nod without lifting his head from the floor, and held up his keys as he lay on the landing, his legs still on the steps. Wyatt leaned over him, bracing his hand on the floor as he took the keys. He pressed his body down onto Ash's and kissed him.

Ash's arms wound around his neck and Wyatt growled low in his throat, rolling his hips against Ash's groin. He couldn't quite believe he was being so reckless, but the combination of the drinks and his intoxicating companion was too much for his inhibitions or common sense to combat.

With a great deal of effort, Wyatt pushed himself back up and stood, pulling Ash to his feet. Ash took the keys and hastily unlocked his door.

They said very little as they made their way across the living room. Ash shed his outer layer of clothing as he led Wyatt toward the bedroom, and Wyatt gave the condo a cursory glance as he followed. It was clean and neat, with large pieces of dark wood furniture that had the strange effect of making the small rooms look bigger.

The bed in Ash's bedroom was large, too, and unmade—an endearing quirk amidst an otherwise tidy home. Wyatt was sure he'd appreciate it later, when he didn't have more pressing things on his mind.

He reached for Ash's suspenders and used them to pull the man closer. Ash grinned as Wyatt looked him up and down.

"These things come in handy," Wyatt said as he slid his fingers up the coarse material.

"They do have their uses," Ash purred. He slid his thumbs under the suspenders and pulled them off his shoulders, backing away from Wyatt's grasp with a wicked twist to his lips.

Wyatt followed, entranced.

Ash flopped onto the end of the bed, pushing his trousers to the floor as he slid up into the middle of the bed and lay out on his back. Wyatt dropped his jacket and reached for his belt.

"Do you make this a habit, Dr. Wyatt?" Ash asked as he pushed his boxers down his hips.

Wyatt took a deep breath, enjoying the free show. "Not really."

Ash smiled in the half-light that filtered through the blinds, his eyes shadowed and unreadable. "Me either."

"Good to know." Wyatt pushed his own pants to the ground, yanked his shirt over his head, and climbed onto the bed.

Ash reached for him. Wyatt settled between his spread legs as they kissed messily, and Ash pulled a knee up and slid his leg over Wyatt's hip. He grinned as Wyatt gasped against the kiss. "You like the tongue stud, right?"

Wyatt nodded.

Ash kissed him again, then whispered, "Kissing's not the only thing it makes more interesting."

"Oh, Jesus." Wyatt's cock jumped against Ash's thigh, stirring an intense desire deep in his gut.

Wyatt loved the way Ash writhed and whimpered when he stroked his fingers down his thigh, the way he curled around Wyatt in an impressive display of flexibility. He loved the way Ash's skin smelled of cigarette smoke, liquor, sweat, and sandalwood, a heady combination that evoked thoughts of taboos and forbidden territories. He loved the way Ash tasted like something new and unexplored, how Ash's tongue ring made each kiss something he'd never experienced.

Ash's hands dragged over Wyatt's skin, tugging at him, digging in as they rutted against each other, nails leaving burning trails as Wyatt kissed him. Finally, he pushed at Wyatt to make him sit back on his knees. Ash was stunning, spread out on the bed, legs wrapped around Wyatt's waist.

He was even more stunning when he had Wyatt's cock in his mouth a few moments later, lips sliding against skin, tongue doing unspeakable things that made Wyatt curl over him and grab a handful of his hair in warning.

When Ash pulled back and smirked up at him, Wyatt could hardly breathe. Ash made sure to lick him up and down one last time, leading the way with that piece of metal that seemed designed just for this sort of thing, before crawling across the bed to stretch for a nearby drawer.

Ash tossed a condom and lubricant to Wyatt and turned over to his hands and knees.

Wyatt rolled the condom on, his entire body thrumming for more intoxicating exploration. Ash moaned, long and loud, when Wyatt gripped his hips from behind and worked his cock into him.

Wyatt lowered his head and groaned, his entire body swamped by lust and alcohol and an unusual feeling of being in a different atmosphere. He promised himself he would analyze that feeling later, when he didn't have his cock buried in the most fascinating, alluring man he'd ever met.

When he began to move, he groaned again, louder this time. His thrusts were slow at first, to give Ash a chance to adjust, but Ash gasped and pushed back into him demandingly. Wyatt bit his lip and sped his movements, unable to close his eyes for the need to watch the way Ash's lithe body moved against his, the way his cock spread Ash apart and pushed inside him.

Ash reached up and grabbed the headboard of the old wrought-iron bed, preventing it from banging against the wall as Wyatt thrust into him harder and harder. As orgasm threatened, Wyatt bit his lip and stopped moving, gasping as he fought it. He pulled out of Ash with the greatest of care and crawled backward, yanking at Ash's hips. Ash rolled onto his side, and Wyatt slid off the bed, standing at the edge and holding Ash's hips, forcing himself to wait, letting the pressure in his gut die down as his cock throbbed.

"Come on."

"Wait," Wyatt gasped.

"I don't care, I just want you back in there," Ash said as he arched his back and pushed up with his hips.

Wyatt slid his hand down the middle of Ash's back and pulled on his hip, pushing into him again. The mattress recommenced its creaking as Wyatt thrust into him, but the headboard didn't complain any longer. Wyatt grabbed Ash's shoulder, fingers digging into the skin as he held Ash still and pounded into him. Ash gasped desperately, threw his head back and arched, pushing into Wyatt's thrusts. Wyatt reached with his other hand and grabbed a handful of Ash's damp hair, panting as he rode him.

Ash cried out again and Wyatt released his hair and reached around to fist his cock. Ash bucked against him, writhing wantonly, groaning as he spilled himself into Wyatt's hand. Ash's pleasure seen to, Wyatt pushed him all the way to the mattress, holding him down flat and fucking him without mercy until he came with a stifled shout.

He continued rocking until he was spent, his breath coming in gasps against the back of Ash's shoulder. He made certain the condom came with him when he pulled out, and he flopped onto the sheets, rolling onto his back, gasping for breath.

Ash grunted and turned his head. He was breathing heavily, skin damp with sweat, hair mussed and eyes still lined with the heavy kohl. How it wasn't spread all over his face by now, Wyatt would never know. He looked completely debauched with the rumpled cognac-colored sheets as his backdrop.

Wyatt stared at him for a long time, breathing hard and letting his body recover, stunned by how such a sordid night could feel so fucking beautiful.

Ash closed his eyes. "Jesus, that was fun, Wyatt."

Wyatt kissed him, a long, languid play of lips and tongues that banked the residual heat between them.

When they finally parted, they sprawled sideways across the bed. Wyatt stared at the ceiling as uncertainty and incredulity flooded in with the cool air of the open window. What had he been thinking? He didn't even know this man, had spent a mere five hours with him getting drunk and pretending not to be intimidated by his perfect face and his unfamiliar lifestyle, and now here he was in his bed? He never behaved this impulsively.

"I need water," he grunted as he pushed himself off the bed.

Ash didn't move or open his eyes.

Wyatt huffed as he padded into the tiny bathroom, his mind spinning with thoughts of his next move. He stayed in the bathroom long enough to calm his racing heart. The encounter had been incredible, but rather than tiring him, adrenaline was racing through him, burning away any remnants of the drinks that had fueled his initial bravery and foolishness.

He looked at himself in the mirror. What the hell should he do now? Was he brave enough to face someone like Ash in the morning, when all the liquor and sexual tension was gone and there was nothing left between them but an awkward morning after?

When he poked his head back into the bedroom, Ash hadn't moved. One arm cradled his head and one knee was cocked to the side. His other foot hung over the far edge of the bed, just as Wyatt had left him when he'd come inside him. He was sound asleep.

Wyatt licked his lips and swallowed hard, letting his eyes linger. Then he began quietly gathering his clothing.

Ash cracked an eye open and managed a tortured groan as the morning light streamed through the blinds of his bedroom. He was still sprawled sideways on his bed, naked and freezing despite the blanket that covered him.

The place was silent as a grave. Not even the floor above creaked with the footsteps of his neighbors yet. He raised his head carefully and looked around, pleased when it didn't make his head hurt or make his stomach revolt. He knew instinctively that he didn't have to waste his breath calling out for Wyatt Case. Wyatt had covered Ash with a blanket before he'd left, but he was long gone.

Ash pushed himself up and winced at sore muscles and a crick in his neck. "At least it was a good time," he grumbled.

Despite his attempt at a cavalier attitude, he couldn't help but be disappointed. And pissed off. He knew better than to bring someone home from the bar. For some reason, a sweet museum curator who had spent the entire night talking to him hadn't struck him as the type to fuck and duck.

Ash sighed and shuffled into the bathroom. He stood in front of the toilet and looked out at the street through the bathroom's window. It was the last week of September, but the house next to his building was already flying a Halloween flag at its stoop. A ghost with goggle eyes grinned stupidly at him as orange and red leaves fluttered across the road behind it.

October at Gravedigger's meant big business, and Ash would need to go in soon to help with prep. He had no time to mope about being left alone in bed by a virtual stranger. He huffed and looked down, muttering as he flushed the used condom left in the bowl.

CHAPTER THREE

"So, tell me about the hot doctor," Delilah said as she and Ash prepared the tavern for a busy Friday.

Ash looked up from the napkin he was folding. An unpleasant mixture of embarrassment, anger, and lust settled in him. "Maybe later."

"Oh, come on! Please? I'll tell you all the details of my night," she bargained, waggling her pierced eyebrows.

"If I wanted to hear about what Ryan does in bed, I'd ask him."

"Hey!"

"I'm sorry, was that still a secret?"

"Shut up," Delilah said, blushing. "Did you take him home?"

Ash rolled his eyes and looked up again. She was smiling, looking at him expectantly.

"Yeah, I did."

"And? Museum curator: untapped source of impressive lovemaking, or deserving of the dusty shelves?"

Ash couldn't help but smile, though he tried to hide it as he looked down at the napkin again. "Definitely the former."

"Stellar. Are you seeing him again?"

"No," Ash answered immediately, losing the smile.

"What? Why? You two were really cute last night. I thought you liked him."

"I did." Ash picked up the stack of silverware he'd just prepared and met Delilah's eyes as he rounded the bar. He was about to tell her what had happened when a loud thump from upstairs interrupted him.

Delilah jumped, and Ash almost dropped his carefully rolled bundles of silverware as he looked up.

"What the hell was that?" Delilah asked.

Ash shook his head, and there came another thump from above, followed by a rattling and skittering that sounded like something scurrying across the floor.

"If we have mice up there, Caleb is going to hit critical mass," Delilah said.

"That's a really big-ass mouse."

Delilah propped her broom against the nearest table and headed for the door to the upstairs. "I'm going to go check it out."

"Hold on! What are you doing?" Ash hurried to unload the silverware and follow. "You don't know what's up there, it might be dangerous. Hold on."

"Ash, I don't need a big bad man to protect me, okay?"

"Do I look like a big bad *anything*?" Ash asked, laughing as he put a hand on his chest. "Seriously, though, hold on." He went behind the bar and knelt to pull out the locked box that Caleb kept under there. It held an old .22 Colt revolver. Ash took it out and checked to see that it was loaded, then stood again.

"Maybe it's a ghost," Delilah said with relish.

"Yeah, that's the most logical explanation," Ash muttered as he walked back over to her.

"You know we've been getting tons of people saying they saw a face in the mirror in the bathroom? Creepy stuff."

"I refuse to acknowledge what you just said. There's been some weird break-ins around the neighborhood lately, Caleb was telling us about them the other night."

Delilah frowned. "Oh."

"You can't just go heedlessly charging into danger, you need to know these things," Ash admonished, smirking as he handed her the gun. "Take this when you go."

"What?" She laughed and smacked his chest, ignoring the weapon. "No, now you have to go with me."

They both jumped as something slammed against the locked door right beside them. Delilah put Ash between her and the door, her hands on his arms as she peered around him.

"Who's there?" Ash called out, the gun hanging uselessly in his hand.

The only answer was a chilling scratching sound on the door, like stiff fingers trying to find purchase on the smooth wood.

"I'm so out of here," Delilah whispered, and Ash felt her step away.

He shook his head and stepped forward to reach for the doorknob, clutching the .22 like the small caliber might do more than just piss off whatever he shot with it.

"No, no," Delilah hissed, clutching at Ash's suspenders as he gripped the glass doorknob and turned it.

There was a flurry of movement from the other side of the door, brushing and thumping and scratching, and when Ash pulled the door open and pointed the gun into the darkness, a bird shot out of the stairwell into his face.

Ash screamed. Delilah screamed. The bird screamed.

Ash's world became a confusion of feathers in his face, shouting in his ear, being hit by a broom whenever Delilah missed the bird, and the overwhelming urge to duck under a table. When the dust and feathers cleared, the bird was perched on the decorative molding on top of the front window, and Delilah was laughing hysterically as Ash pulled pieces of straw from the broom off his clothing and out of his hair.

He grumbled as he looked up at the bird. It was large and black, its feathers an almost iridescent indigo. It had a black bill and yellow eyes that blinked rapidly at them as its chest heaved.

"Poor thing." Ash moved slowly as he went to the front door and propped it open, looking up at the bird as he did so.

"He's a grackle," Delilah said as she helped him open windows.

"Huh?"

"My dad was a bird enthusiast," she said with a shrug. "That's a grackle."

"What do I care?"

"I love the way that word sounds. Grackle."

Ash laughed. "Are you high already?"

Delilah grinned and gave him a wink. "At least it wasn't a ghost."

It was only Monday morning, but Wyatt Case was sitting and staring at the vintage Thurston poster on the far side of his office, unable to concentrate.

He had never had a one night stand before. Never. He had never dealt with the aftermath, such as it was. He had never left a person he'd just had sex with, drunk, in bed without even a word of good-bye. Hell, he hadn't even said thank you. Were you supposed to say thank you? Would that be insulting? Wyatt didn't know. He knew you weren't supposed to leave without telling the person you'd just screwed that you were going, though.

The knock at his door didn't even register. It wasn't until Noah stuck his head into the office and said his name that Wyatt tore his attention away from the poster and blinked at him, trying to get his eyes to focus.

"You're in early," Noah said with a frown.

Wyatt's first instinct was to be ashamed. He wondered if Ash had told Noah over the weekend about their little rendezvous. He shrugged.

Noah slipped into the office and closed the door behind him. "What's up?"

Wyatt rubbed his hand over his face and closed his eyes. "I'm a complete bastard, you know?"

"Wow, news flash." Noah swiped at some dust as he sat in the only empty chair in the room. Everything else was stacked high with books and frames Wyatt had never gotten around to putting back up after the office had been painted over the summer. The Thurston poster was the only thing he'd hung.

Noah furrowed his brow as he studied Wyatt. "Wanna talk about it?"

Wyatt stared at the poster over Noah's shoulder and shook his head. He had liked Ash, really liked him. How trivial his reasons for leaving seemed now.

"Well. If you change your mind, you know where to find me."

Wyatt thumped his head on the back of his chair. "Yeah, hiding from the trustees in the basement like all the rest of us."

"That's why I dropped by. They're all here. They're on the prowl this morning."

"Oh, fuck me." Wyatt stood and looked helplessly around the office. "I've got to come up with something or they're going to have my head."

"Wyatt, calm down. Look, why don't you take a sick day, go home, spend some time relaxing. Maybe something will hit you when you're not expecting it."

"I'm not so sure that will help."

"Neither is sitting in here brooding. What's up with you, anyway?"

Wyatt shook his head stubbornly.

Noah huffed. "Fine, don't talk to your best friend. Hey, I never asked you what happened with you and Ash. Did you hit it off?"

Wyatt stared at him. He would have to tell him or drown in the guilt. "Yeah," he said. "Yeah, we got along okay."

"Think you'll see him again?"

He swallowed against the tightening in his throat. The hell of it was that he really did like Ash. He'd just panicked over the oddity of what had happened—and ruined any chance of something more.

"I doubt it," he said. Noah frowned and gave him a questioning look. "I mean, I liked him and all, but . . . Noah, he's not really the type of guy I usually—"

"Wyatt, you don't *usually* anyone. Give him a chance!"

Wyatt held up a hand. "Just drop it, all right?"

Noah stared at him for a stunned moment, and then nodded. "Sorry."

They sat in awkward silence for another long moment. Finally, Noah stood and stepped toward the door. He was still looking at Wyatt when he put his hand on the doorknob.

"Think about some time off, huh? It's not the end of the world if you can't get this exhibition rolling. Even if they fire you, you can always turn to making porn."

Wyatt laughed despite himself. He waited until Noah was almost out the door before calling to him. "Thanks," he said when Noah turned back. "And I'm sorry for being a prick."

"That's okay. We're all used to it by now."

Wyatt realized as the door shut that he hadn't even bothered to ask Noah what had happened between him and Caleb Biron.

He stood stock still in the middle of the office, frowning. He wasn't used to being an asshole. He wasn't used to feeling guilty. He wasn't used to looking his friends in the eye and wondering if they'd found out what he'd done. He didn't want to keep feeling like this.

He grabbed his jacket and slid into it as he made for the door.

"I'm heading out," he told his assistant as he walked through the office. "Back soon," he said over his shoulder before she could question him.

When he stepped through the door, he saw Edgar Reth stalking down the hallway, followed by Emelda Ramsay and Stuart Lincoln, another of the trustees who might as well have been on his knees for Reth at all hours of the day.

Reth jutted his chin out. "Dr. Case."

Wyatt had to work hard not to groan. "Mr. Reth," he said instead, making sure to drawl out the name in imitation of Reth's nasal, condescending voice.

They stopped in front of him, and Wyatt reached out to take Emelda's elbow as she leaned toward him and kissed him on the cheek. She knew it ruffled Reth's feathers when she showed such unabashed favoritism toward him, and Wyatt loved her for it.

"Dr. Case, what progress have you made in your plans to boost attendance?"

Wyatt looked at him for a long moment as he tried to restrain himself from telling Reth the only progress he'd made was getting laid by a man with a tongue ring.

"Mr. Reth, I believe we've discussed, at length, the fact that Dr. Case is not solely responsible for this matter," Emelda said with a stern glare. "If the board had taken his warnings more seriously when construction was being planned, we would not be here."

"May we step into your office to discuss this?" Reth asked as he started toward Wyatt's office door.

"No," Wyatt said curtly. Reth turned to look at him as if he'd been slapped. Wyatt raised an eyebrow. "I'm busy."

Lincoln stepped forward, a whole head shorter than Wyatt, and put one bony finger on Wyatt's chest. "What could you possibly have to do that's more important than speaking with us?"

Wyatt looked down at his finger, then up at him with a clenched jaw. "It's more important to me to sweep the bathroom floors than it is to sit and listen to you recount *your* shortcomings."

Lincoln responded with a series of rapid blinks. Wyatt picked up his finger and pushed it away from his chest.

Emelda stepped between them, holding her hands up in a graceful display of class and propriety. "Gentlemen."

"You have some nerve, Case," Reth said. "You're only here because I haven't moved to get rid of you yet."

Wyatt met his eyes, valiantly resisting the urge to stab them with the ink pen in his pocket.

"Museums across the country are closing down due to lack of funds. Do you want us to be next?"

"If we are, your name will be emblazoned across the annals of history with the failure," Wyatt said. "If you cared anything for history, that would terrify you more than losing that hefty stipend you get every year."

Reth bristled, sputtering. "End of week!" he finally said through his teeth. "I'll bring the matter of your termination to the board by end of week and be rid of you for good!"

He stormed past Wyatt and Emelda, Lincoln on his heels like a trained puppy.

"Oh, Wyatt," Emelda said with a sigh.

"I'm sorry, Emelda, I just . . ."

Emelda clapped her hands together. "I've been hoping you'd do that for weeks now!" Wyatt wouldn't have called her matronly; she was far too elegant and proper for that. Perhaps it was that cool propriety—her impeccable dress, her perfectly coifed silver hair, her expensive jewels and perfume—that made her approval so rewarding.

Wyatt grunted and huffed a laugh.

"I won't be able to save you now, Wyatt, not unless we come out with something brilliant in the next day or so." She looked off down the hall at the retreating backs of her colleagues. "But you will be emblazoned across the annals as the man who finally told that prick where to stick it."

She patted his cheek and walked off. Wyatt watched her, mouth agape.

When he was finally able to shake off the surprise, he realized his fingers were trembling. He'd basically just gotten himself fired, because he knew inspiration wasn't suddenly going to strike him in the next day.

He looked at his watch, indecisive now. It was barely nine o'clock in the morning. The odds of Ash being at Gravedigger's at this time on a Monday were very small, and he should probably start packing up his belongings in preparation of being given the old penny loafer boot. But he set out for the bar anyway, knowing he needed to see Ash more than he needed to sit in his office and feel sorry for himself.

The walk seemed somehow longer as he made it alone. His mind was heavy with the impending loss of his job, but that wasn't what he lingered on. He paged through every possible permutation of what he might be able to say when he saw Ash. None of it sounded even remotely acceptable.

Far too soon, he was standing on the opposite corner from Gravedigger's, staring at the unassuming establishment with dread. He shoved his hands in his pockets and told himself to just do it. Take his medicine and start down the road of no longer feeling like a prick. He crossed the street and shuffled up to the door, peering through a pane of glass at a hint of movement within. To his simultaneous relief and dismay, he could see Ash inside, sitting cross-legged in the middle of the floor with his back to the door. There was something large on the floor in front of him and he was hunched over it, fiddling with it.

Wyatt took a deep breath and tapped on the door.

"We're closed," Ash said without turning to look at the door, never ceasing his fiddling. "Come back at eleven."

Wyatt pressed his lips into a thin line and tapped again.

Ash flopped his hands in exasperation, and Wyatt saw a screwdriver in one of them as Ash twisted to glance back at him. The look on his face told Wyatt this might not go well, not that he had expected it to. Ash seemed surprised to see Wyatt standing there, but then his jaw tightened and his warm eyes hardened. He twisted back around and shook his head, then rolled his shoulders before pushing to his feet.

He walked to the door and rested his forearm against the doorjamb, leaning close to the glass as he looked Wyatt over. Ash was wearing charcoal gray trousers and a sleeveless undershirt. Burgundy suspenders highlighted the outfit. Again, it was a quirky ensemble, even without the kohl around his eyes this morning. But it suited him. Wyatt admired him through the glass door, feeling that same heat kindle in his chest.

"We're closed," Ash said.

Wyatt nodded, but he pointed at the deadbolt. "Can we talk?"

Ash chewed on the inside of his cheek and scowled, and for a moment Wyatt thought he would refuse. But finally he reached out and flipped the deadbolt, then stepped back so Wyatt could open the door. By the time Wyatt pushed through the doorway, Ash had already turned and was walking away.

"I owe you an apology," Wyatt said as he let the door fall shut behind him.

"I know you do." Ash turned around and took a step toward Wyatt. "You know what flushing a condom can do to your pipes?" He was still holding the screwdriver, and Wyatt's eyes were drawn to it for a moment before he looked back up at Ash.

"What? That's not why I—"

"Well, it should be. You know how much a plumber costs?"

"You had to call a plumber?"

"No, but if I do in the future, it'll be your fault." Ash placed the tip of his screwdriver at his temple and tapped. Wyatt watched him, dumbstruck.

"I . . . okay," he managed.

"Fuck you, Wyatt," Ash grumbled. He turned around and dropped gracefully to the floor. "It's no fun to bitch at you if you don't argue back."

He resumed his position and began loosening the screws on the back of what Wyatt now recognized as a window air conditioning unit.

"I . . . I came to—"

"I know why you're here," Ash said without turning his head.

"I'm here to apologize." Wyatt walked around to stand in front of Ash again. It was hard to talk to someone who was sitting on the floor. He felt stupid for standing, but he couldn't just drop to the floor alongside him.

"You're here for seconds," Ash said.

"What? No! I—"

"You're not here because you feel guilty, you're here because you liked it."

"That's not true. I mean, it is, I did, but . . . that's not why I'm here. I shouldn't have walked out. I panicked and . . . I just needed you to know I'm sorry."

"I know you are."

Wyatt sighed in exasperation and knelt down to meet Ash's eyes. "Look, I came here to make it up to you."

Ash glanced up at him and then away. "I didn't tell Noah you skipped out on me, if that's what you're here to find out."

"That's not why I'm here."

"Sure it is. If you're not here for seconds, then it's guilt. You were probably talking to Noah right before you came here and you were wondering if he knew and what he thought of you. Am I right?"

Wyatt blinked and nodded as his mouth went dry. How did he know that?

Ash shrugged and held out a hand as if to say, *See?*

"I was also thinking about you," Wyatt said, voice hoarse.

That gave Ash a moment's pause. He stared at Wyatt for a long time and then shook his head and looked away.

"Ash—"

Ash glanced back at him and raised an eyebrow. The look in his eyes cut Wyatt off. "You're not the first one-nighter I've had bail on me, okay?" Ash sighed as he rested his hands on the unit. "You're the first to try and carpet bomb my plumbing, but whatever. It stings for a day or two, I get over it, I move on. Let's just call it a great screw and leave it at that, okay? Not ruin it with all this." He waved the screwdriver between them.

"But . . ." Wyatt sighed and looked the man over. Here in the light of day, Ash was almost better looking than Wyatt remembered, if that was possible. The sleeveless undershirt suited his lithe frame, showing off the definition of his wiry muscles, and for some reason the suspenders were growing on Wyatt. The only thing that marred the picture was a bruise on Ash's shoulder, just at his collarbone and neck.

"What happened?" Wyatt asked as he reached out and brushed Ash's shoulder.

Ash swatted his hand away and scowled at him. He turned his head and peered down at his shoulder with difficulty, pushing aside his shirt and suspenders to see. When the material moved, Wyatt could plainly see four thin marks on the front of Ash's shoulder.

"Looks like a hand print," Ash answered grudgingly.

Wyatt's stomach gave an unsettling twist. "I did that." He remembered grabbing Ash's shoulder just there and holding him in place from behind. "Did I hurt you?" he asked with a wince. "I mean, are there more bruises or . . ."

"I didn't even know about that one. Don't worry about it." Ash gave a lopsided shrug as he readjusted his shirt. "That's not a first either. Lets you know you had fun when you can't remember what happened."

Wyatt frowned, wondering how often that particular scenario happened.

Ash went back to dismantling the A/C unit. When he concentrated hard on something, his tongue seemed to find its way out and curl around the corner of his mouth. It was endearing. Even with the tongue ring sticking through it.

Wyatt noticed with a slight stirring in his gut that it was a different stud than the one Ash had been wearing before. He'd been intimately acquainted with the previous one.

"Different tongue ring, huh?" he asked before thinking better of it.

"It's left over from Saturday."

"Left over?"

Ash huffed at Wyatt's look of consternation, then cupped his hands around his mouth and nose, opening his mouth so Wyatt could see the stud in shadow. It glowed a very faint purple. "I change them out. We entertain as we mix. People get a kick out of it."

Wyatt nodded, but said under his breath, "I liked the other one better."

Ash gave a derogatory snort. "I bet you did."

Wyatt squatted there for another moment, trying to think of anything to say that could convey his regret. No words came, though, and he admitted to himself that Ash was done with the conversation and he should be as well.

He stood with a sigh. "I am sorry."

Ash pursed his lips and nodded without looking up.

"Take care, huh?" Wyatt said as he trudged to the door. It sounded so weak that he instantly regretted saying it.

"Hey, Wyatt," Ash said as soon as Wyatt reached for the doorknob. Wyatt turned around. Ash was still sitting with his back to the door. "You know what I always do in the morning with someone who's slept over?"

Wyatt's stomach flip-flopped. "What?"

"I fuck them again."

Wyatt closed his eyes as a jolt of lust shot through him. He reached for the knob and lowered his head. "Wish I'd stuck around to see that."

"Yeah," Ash said. "So do I."

Wyatt exited the bar before he could subject himself to any more abuse, no matter how much he deserved it. He stood outside and peered up into the crisp blue sky for a long time, trying to reconcile that he'd probably screwed up what could have been a good thing. When he looked down again, his eyes landed on the chalk sign that was chained to the front of the building. He frowned. The specials had been erased, but the bottom still advertised the ghost tours.

Wyatt's body lurched as an idea hit him like a truckload of Acme anvils. He turned back to the door in time to see Ash stand and viciously kick the A/C unit. He banged on the glass. "Hey!"

Ash jumped and turned around. He frowned when he saw Wyatt standing there, then he tossed the screwdriver aside and stalked over to the door.

"What the hell, man?" he said through the glass.

"Those ghost tours, do they start from here every night?" Wyatt asked as he pointed at the sign.

"What?" Ash frowned.

"The ghost tours!"

"Yeah. Monday through Saturday. They start around eight this time of year. When it's good and dark."

"Are they popular?"

"Yeah. They bring in about twenty percent of our business." Ash crossed his arms over his chest, obviously confused by Wyatt's sudden change of interest. "Why?"

"What sort of things do they show you?"

"I don't know, man, ghost stories and shit. I've never been on one. Are you done?"

"No! I need to know what sort of stories they tell!"

Ash flopped his hands in exasperation. "Why?"

"The October exhibition!" Wyatt shouted back, pointing in the direction of the museum. "Ghost stories! A history of ghost stories! That could save my job!"

Ash stared at him, then shook his head and shrugged. "The state is full of ghosts and myths and legends, man. You could make an exhibit about them, but you'd be pandering if you went that route without some serious research and truth behind it."

"Hell, pandering's what they want me to do. My life is research!"

"Then take a couple ghost tours. Present the stories as they're believed to be and then tell the truth behind them. Make it worthy, at least."

Wyatt rapped his knuckles on the glass. "Thank you," he whispered before turning and jogging away.

Ash stood at the door, frowning as he watched Wyatt jog down the sidewalk toward the museum.

"Why is it always the wackadoos who're so good in bed?" he said sadly.

A loud bang from upstairs seemed to answer him, and he jumped and turned, looking up at the ceiling as his heart rate skyrocketed.

He stayed silent and still, holding his breath. But all he could hear was his own heart pounding in his ears. He exhaled shakily. Heard a faint noise. Like someone drumming their fingers on a wooden table in the distance.

Ash took a tentative step forward and licked his lips. "Hello?" he called out, surprised at how shaken he was. Houses this old creaked and groaned all the time. Not that he'd ever heard this particular house make that particular noise, but still . . .

The drumming seemed to fade into the echo of his voice as it filtered through the bar. Had he really heard it, or was it just his imagination? He'd been listening to that damned broken A/C unit bang and clang for so long he'd be hearing things for days.

When no other sounds presented themselves, he leaned back against the glass of the door and let his head hang. He snorted and laughed—

Then hopped away and shouted at a loud banging on the glass beside his head. He whirled and staggered back from the door, his hand over his heart as Caleb, on the other side of the door, chuckled.

"Morning!" Caleb called as he slid his key into the lock and opened it. "Little skittish this morning, are we?"

Ash glared at him, still holding his hand over his heart. "Asshole," he huffed. "Scared the shit out of me."

"I can see that." Caleb shrugged out of his jacket and hung it on the coat rack beside the door. "What's going on, Sir Yipsalot?"

"Shut up." Ash patted his chest and then ran his hands through his hair in embarrassment. "Just . . . thought I heard something upstairs right before you got here."

Caleb's smile vanished. "You the only one here?"

"Yeah, I got here about thirty minutes ago. I swear, if Ryan's up there with some girl, I'm going to kick his ass."

Caleb raised a dubious eyebrow and smirked.

"I'd put up a valiant effort, at least!" Ash turned away and went in search of the screwdriver he'd chucked into the unknown earlier.

Caleb circled the unit Ash had set in the middle of the floor. "Air conditioning's broken again?"

"And that's not the only thing," Ash grumbled. "It's just the only thing I couldn't fix."

Caleb sighed as he frowned down at the broken unit. "Well. It's not like the upstairs really needs it anyway. We just kept it running to keep the wood from warping with the humidity."

"Yeah, I know, I've been here," Ash said with a little more acid than Caleb deserved. "It should be okay 'til spring. Over the winter we can get someone to come in and extend the central system to the upper floors."

"That'll cost an assload of money."

"But then we could use the upstairs and expand," Ash said. It wasn't the first time they'd had this discussion.

"I suppose. We could just buy a new unit." Caleb waved a hand at the A/C. It popped at his feet, sizzling. "Or not."

The unit popped again and then sparked. Caleb hopped back as Ash dove for the bar. The unit spit sparks again and began to sputter flames from inside as Ash pulled up onto the bar and reached over, stretching and grabbing a dirty dishrag. He pounced on the unit with the damp rag, beating out the flames as Caleb scrambled for the fire extinguisher.

They managed to get it out before it did any real damage, and more importantly, before the smoke reached the detectors on the ceiling and set off the sprinklers.

"Wow," Caleb said as they stood side by side, looking at the charred unit warily and waiting for more flames.

"Yeah," Ash said, panting as he held the singed dishrag in his hand.

"Good bloody thing you took it down when you did."

Ash didn't want to imagine what would have happened if it had caught fire while in the window upstairs. "Kicking it may have hastened its self-destruction," Ash admitted.

"Huh."

"Glad it didn't do that while I was screwing it," Ash said distantly. Caleb turned to look at him, and Ash glanced back and blinked. "What?"

Caleb just shook his head and turned away.

Ash frowned, pulling at his ear as he heard the odd drumming sound echoing from somewhere above. It was probably just adrenaline, but as he peered toward the ceiling, a feeling of dread seeped into him. He looked away as a shiver ran through his body, determined not to let the ghost stories get to him.

"That's sort of near brilliant, Wy," Noah said. He popped open a bag of Cheetos and scooted his chair closer to the lunch table.

Wyatt had laid out his tentative plans for the October exhibition, including Ash's suggestion that they display the popular myth to draw people in, then tell the truth behind it with artifacts to suit their goal of actually educating.

"It's going to take some hellacious research, though. It's already the first. Do we have time to have it up and running by the weekend?" Noah asked.

"If we know where to start, I think we can get it outlined in a few days. Then we can enlist some students to help put it all together. It should be ready by then. It's perfect. It has the pandering aspects the Trustees seem to want, it'll have a low artifact count, and it'll bring in crowds that wouldn't usually look twice at a museum. And we can actually put some real history into it to keep it respectable. Maybe even convert some interest in places."

"Ash helped you come up with this?" Noah asked, smirking as he leaned back in his chair.

"Um, sort of." Noah raised an eyebrow, and Wyatt sighed and lowered his head. "The other night . . ."

Noah grinned cheekily. "Do tell."

"I went home with him. We slept together," Wyatt blurted, looking around to make sure no one had heard him.

"I figured. And?"

"I didn't . . . really stick around 'til morning," Wyatt admitted.

Noah's smile fell and his brow furrowed. "Oh."

"I just panicked a little about—"

Noah held up a hand and shook his head. "Happens to the best of us, man. Don't explain."

"I went to see him this morning. Tried to apologize."

Noah's eyebrows shot up. "How'd that go?"

"Not too well. Hey," he added, eyes narrowing as Noah's lips twitched. "It's not funny." But his voice trembled with a laugh.

"No, not at all." Noah snickered a little, leaned back in his chair, and covered his mouth with his hand.

"I feel awful, okay? I really liked him."

Noah's smile faded. "What exactly did he say when you talked to him?"

"He seemed more pissed about my flushing the condom than about me actually leaving."

Noah threw his head back and laughed, rocking back in his chair and sliding both hands over his face.

"Noah!" Wyatt hissed as several heads turned and looked at them. Wyatt leaned closer to Noah, frowning. "It's not funny."

Noah was still snickering as he shook his head. "It really kind of is. So wait, you discussed your one-night stand and his plumbing, I assume you did so heatedly because Ash has a little bit of a temper on him, and then you . . . what, sat down and fleshed out ideas for the exhibition over a latte?"

"Not exactly."

"So Ash didn't *exactly* offer to help," Noah said, eyes narrowing.

"Not . . . exactly. I figured we'd go do the ghost tour and see . . ."

"So. You want the two of us to traipse over to the bar where the guy you screwed over is working and nance around until the ghost tour starts tonight? What, you're rubbing it in his face?"

"No! I wouldn't do that!" Wyatt stopped short and frowned. "Is that how he'll see it?"

"I don't know. I know I'd be kind of pissy."

"Goddammit."

Noah was silent for a long time as Wyatt mulled over the issues. The last thing he wanted to do was hurt Ash even more or, God forbid, piss him off. But his job was the most important thing in his life and he took it very seriously. Sure, it was an unusual way of working, but so was trying to put together a major exhibit in less than a week.

Noah pushed his Cheetos bag aside and leaned forward over the table. "You really liked him?"

Wyatt met his eyes.

"And I don't mean you really liked fucking him, 'cause I can see how that would be fun for both of you. I mean you liked *him*."

Wyatt swallowed hard, and thought about the hours he and Ash had spent talking that night before they had ever gone the step further. Wyatt had been comfortable with him even in the middle of a crowded, rowdy gaslight bar. "Yeah."

"Okay." Noah nodded and sat for a while, studying Wyatt. "Well, you're a bit of a dumbass. And it probably won't work anyway 'cause Ash doesn't seem the type to take shit from many people. But if you're serious, I might be able to talk to him. Convince him it would be a favor to me to help out on this, get you two to spend some more time together. Without fucking!" he said, pointing his finger in Wyatt's face.

"Deal."

Noah sat back and nodded. "And I'll ask Caleb tonight about any ghost story type things he or his crew might know."

Wyatt raised an eyebrow and smiled. "Tonight, huh?"

To Wyatt's surprise, Noah blushed. He shrugged and shifted in his seat and grinned. "We may have really hit it off."

It was so rare to see Noah being coy, Wyatt was tempted to prod for more details just to watch him squirm.

But then Noah glared. "Unlike you, however, we didn't fall into bed together quite so hastily. You slut."

"Couch and floor still count as falling into bed together."

"Shut up." Noah gathered his Cheetos and stood. "I'll meet you at the staff door at five, okay? Quit looking at me like that! Go do your job!"

Wyatt chuckled as Noah walked away. He didn't have much hope of Ash changing his mind, but the mere prospect was enough to get him through the rest of the day.

At ten minutes to five, he stood outside the staff entrance, basking in the weak warmth of the sun as he waited for Noah to show. Roughly fifteen minutes after five, Noah came tumbling out of the building, the strap of his leather satchel snug against his chest and his hands full of papers, his coat, his umbrella, and another large black bag.

"What is all this?" Wyatt asked as Noah piled some of the things into his arms and grunted in greeting.

"I did some preliminary research," he said as he dug in Wyatt's pocket for his car keys.

"Hey!" Wyatt twisted away from Noah's groping hand. "Private property, asshole."

"That's not the current rumor, you whore."

"Shut up," Wyatt laughed. Noah snagged his keys and nodded at Wyatt's car.

"Let's stash this shit in your backseat. Does that stupid freaking tin can even *have* a back seat?"

"Yes." They trekked over to the staff parking lot where Wyatt's car sat in the space reserved for the head curator. They stacked all the files Noah had been carrying in the backseat, and then Noah hefted his satchel into it as well. His coat and umbrella went next, and then he set the black bag down on the trunk and unzipped it.

Wyatt peered over the car at Noah's bowed head. "What's that?"

"Camera." Noah grunted as he extracted a large SLR digital camera and inserted a memory card. "Signed it out for research."

"Nice."

"I know, I'm a freaking genius." Noah straightened back up and slammed the car door. "You ready?"

Wyatt eyed the tailored shirt Noah was wearing. "Did you change?"

Noah flushed. "Had an incident in the preservation room." He jerked his head and turned to start walking.

"We could just drive," Wyatt said as he jogged around the car to catch up.

"Yes, but this way you have more time to think about what you're going to say when we get there."

"True." He grinned slyly at Noah. "Is Caleb going to be there?"

Noah smiled. "Maybe."

Wyatt plucked at the shirt Noah had changed into. Only when he was lecturing did he wear nice clothing like that. "That why you look good?"

Noah huffed but shook his head. "I really did have a spill. Even got all over my shoes." He pointed down at feet; his boots were stained dark on the toes. "This was all I had in my office." He stopped short and turned. "Should I change? I mean, I could go home and get—"

"Noah." Wyatt took Noah's arm. "You look good, you don't need to change. Wow, you really like this guy, huh?"

Noah flashed a silly grin. "Yeah."

Wyatt smiled, but he soon began thinking about Ash and the look in his eyes when Wyatt had tried to apologize. The exasperation and the annoyance, the way Ash had so easily shrugged it all off as a non-event. What if he'd been able to write it off without angst because he didn't care? What if he'd been relieved that Wyatt had been gone when he'd woken and really was just pissed about the plumbing?

Wyatt slowed to a stop. Noah continued on for a few feet before he realized Wyatt had dropped back, and he turned to look at him questioningly.

"I don't think I can do this," Wyatt said.

Noah nodded in understanding and walked back beside him. He reached up and smacked Wyatt on the side of the head. "Did you leave your balls in his toilet too?"

"Ow! What? No!"

"Then get the lead out, Case," Noah said as he grabbed Wyatt's elbow and began pulling him along.

"I hate you."

"I hate you too."

When they got to Gravedigger's, the patio out front where the porch had once been was already full of laughing patrons. Several dogs were tied to the iron fence, sitting with their masters as they ate. The festive lights strung over the patio acted as a ceiling of sorts, and were already on and winking in the shade of the building.

Wyatt hesitated, but Noah, unyielding, dragged him to the door and shoved him unceremoniously inside. It wasn't as crowded as the patio. People were probably trying to drain the last dregs of warmth out of the day. The show in here was impressive, though.

Ash hadn't changed his clothing since Wyatt had seen him that morning, but he looked different. The heavy eyeliner was back, accenting his dark eyes, and his wavy hair had been gelled, appearing jet black and perpetually wet. Ryan was dressed similarly, right down to the suspenders and tight white undershirt, and they were both standing on top of the bar, juggling bottles of alcohol and tossing them back and forth to each other in perilous arcs.

Wyatt stood gaping as he realized that not only were they tossing the bottles around, but they were also mixing drinks as they did it. The music that played along with them was so loud that Wyatt felt it more than heard it as a steady, rhythmic beat in the pit of his stomach. It had a distinctly Old World Gypsy feel to it, very fitting as the crowd clapped in rhythm, watching in awe as the bartenders performed what was essentially a circus act.

"Wonder why they're doing this today?" Noah shouted to Wyatt over the noise.

"I don't know. Ash said they only flair on weekends. Maybe they're practicing for that big tournament they're going to." Wyatt shrugged. "Well hell, we're not going to get to talk to them like this."

"They can't do that forever."

Wyatt had yet to take his eyes off the two men. Noah was right. It was all very athletic and involved. Surely they couldn't go for more than a few minutes at a time.

Caleb, who was standing behind the bar, tossed a new bottle into the air at Ryan's waist, and Ryan caught it, juggling three bottles so high that they almost grazed the ceiling. All three bottles were open, Wyatt realized, but somehow they didn't spill as Ryan tossed them around. They seemed to have mastered the angles and the centrifugal force it required. Wyatt was beyond impressed.

Ash began tossing the glasses he had been juggling at Ryan, and Ryan tossed his bottles at Ash. The bottles spun in slow circles, and the lights caught the cuts of the heavy highball glasses. They mixed as they juggled, somehow managing to pour the liquor as they held the bottles in odd places: the crook of an elbow, sitting atop a shoulder. Ryan caught the first glass and then tossed it to Caleb, who caught it without ever turning it upside down. The next glass Ryan caught and held in his left hand as he tossed the last bottle to Ash.

In the end, Ash was juggling all three bottles and Ryan was holding two glasses of amber liquid. Ash caught the bottles and held them all in one arm like a pageant winner would hold a bouquet of flowers, and Ryan tossed him a glass. He caught it, and they turned in unison, holding up the glasses triumphantly, and then all three men kicked back the shots that had been poured and bowed.

The little crowd cheered. Noah and Wyatt stood staring in patent disbelief as Ash and Ryan climbed down off the bar.

"That's inhuman," Noah said as the music died down and returned to the slower, more intimate tunes Wyatt remembered from the other night.

"There's got to be a trick to it," Wyatt said. He was reminded of the Thurston poster in his office. He wondered if Ryan and Ash were using the same sleight of hand that the master magicians had used.

"Still pretty cool," Noah said as he began making his way to the bar.

Wyatt hesitated, dreading the look on Ash's face when he saw him. Finally, he sucked it up and followed, figuring he deserved what he might get.

Noah knocked on the scarred wood of the bar and got Caleb's attention.

"Hello, lad," Caleb said, smiling warmly as he walked up and leaned his hands on the bar. They greeted each other with the sort of flirtatious intimacy of a new couple. Wyatt looked away to give them some privacy.

"What can I get you?" Caleb asked as he nodded in greeting to Wyatt.

Wyatt smiled uncomfortably, wondering if Ash had told his friends what had happened.

"We want information," Noah growled.

Caleb laughed and inclined his head, waiting for Noah to explain.

"We're prepared to bribe."

"Now, that's interesting." Caleb smirked. "What sort of information? And more importantly, what sort of bribe?"

Noah leaned in closer, telling Caleb what they were thinking with the museum exhibit as Wyatt looked around for Ash. He'd disappeared after hopping off the bar. He saw Ryan, though, who waved at him and smiled as he made his way through the thinning crowd. Delilah was there too, delivering food and taking orders.

Ryan shouted as he got closer. "Hey, Wyatt. How are you? You come to see Ash? He's out on the patio whoring himself for tips." He shook Wyatt's hand and patted his shoulder distractedly. "Good to see you, man. Talk later." He stepped away and slid through the little swinging door that let him behind the bar.

Wyatt snorted in amusement. A hand came to rest on the small of his back as someone slid by him, and Wyatt turned to find Ash standing right beside him.

"Hey," Wyatt managed to say, though his heart had just jumped into his throat.

"Back for more, Dr. Case?" Ash asked in a flat, low voice that still managed to carry through the noise.

"Yeah . . . I mean no!" Wyatt said, flustered as he got a close-up look at Ash. The kohl around his eyes was an amazing way to enhance them. Wyatt had never thought he would find such a thing attractive. The tips of Ash's gelled hair looked like they could probably pierce armor, but it somehow suited him. "I mean . . . sort of."

Ash met his eyes, looking like he was fighting a smile.

"Hey, Ash," Caleb said before Wyatt could stutter through any sort of explanation. "Tell these two what happened to you this morning."

Ash looked between Wyatt and Noah. "Why?"

"They're researching ghosts."

Ash peered at Wyatt again, and when Wyatt shrugged, Ash walked around Noah and stepped behind the bar to stand beside Caleb. "You want ghost stories?"

"What happened to you this morning?" Noah asked.

"Nothing," Ash huffed curtly as he picked up a clean towel and draped it over his shoulder. "Why are you asking us?" he asked without looking at Wyatt.

"We were thinking about taking the ghost tour to get some ideas," Noah answered. "We were wondering if maybe you guys knew some stories or something to tide us over."

Ash turned to Wyatt. "You're running with the ghosts and legends idea?"

"We'll make it worthy."

Ash pursed his lips. Beside Wyatt, Noah smirked and pulled himself closer to the men on the other side of the bar. "We'd be more likely to make it worthy if we had help. You're a Child of the Night, right?"

Ash glanced at him and snorted in amusement. "Extortionist."

"You know it."

"Child of the Night?" Ash added.

"What?"

"Children of the Night are prostitutes and vampires, numbnuts."

"Oh."

Ash moved out from behind the bar again. "Come on," he said with a long-suffering sigh as he headed for the kitchen.

"Well it sounded all . . . gothy," Noah said to Caleb before turning.

Caleb grinned. Wyatt couldn't help but smile as he followed.

Ash was speaking to the evening cooks when Noah and Wyatt pushed through the door. He finished hearing their complaints about the stove that continued to refuse to work and promised he would fix it before turning away.

"Either of you know how to fix shit?" he asked in annoyance. They'd remodeled the entire kitchen just a few months ago and already things were going wrong. He gestured for them to move toward the back door, where he set up several milk crates and sat on one of them with a groan. How it was possible to be sore three days later and still have enjoyed it, he didn't know. His guess was that the alcohol had helped.

"Not as such, no," Noah said. He took one of the milk crates and gestured for Wyatt to sit as well. Wyatt hesitated.

Ash looked between them with narrowed eyes and then sighed. "You told him, didn't you?" he asked Wyatt in exasperation. "I told you I wouldn't say anything."

"Wyatt's conscience is fairly pervasive, makes him do all sorts of stupid shit," Noah said as Wyatt opened his mouth and closed it again without speaking. "We're really not here for that, though."

Ash looked between them suspiciously, but then decided Noah wouldn't bullshit him. "Okay. So you want ghost stories."

Noah nodded. "Ghost stories, unexplained happenings, urban legends."

"And you want the truth behind the popular story?"

"If you have it," Wyatt said in his soft, gruff voice. Ash fought the urge to be attracted to it. "If not, we'll research it and see if we can find it. We're only using stories we can tell the real history behind."

"What if the real history is unexplainable?" Ash asked.

"History doesn't have to be explainable," Wyatt responded, looking confident for the first time since he'd been in Ash's bed. "The real history states the facts. We make from those facts what we will. If the events are unexplainable, that's not history's fault."

Ash stared up at him, intrigued with the man again despite himself. Finally, he nodded and waved his hand at the third carton. "Sit down, huh? You're making me nervous hovering."

"Sorry," Wyatt mumbled. He pulled the carton closer and sat.

His knee brushed Ash's, and Ash looked at him from under lowered brows, wondering if he was really as ingenuous as he seemed or if it was just a very good act. Ash didn't like to think he'd been played. Wyatt had seemed sincere. He still did, which was why Ash still found himself attracted to him.

Ash cleared his throat and looked away, meeting Noah's eyes and frowning as Noah smiled at him sympathetically.

"Okay. I've been working here about five or six years now," he said. He leaned against the wall behind him, trying to ease the ache of his muscles. "Working in a place like this, you hear things. People tell us stories trying to impress us, thinking we're all obsessed with death and stuff." He sighed as he ran his hands through his hair and belatedly realized it was practically plastic tonight. "Ugh," he muttered as his hand came away with a sticky combination of sweat and reanimated hair gel.

Noah chuckled and Wyatt bit his lip against a smile. Ash reached out and wiped his hand on Noah's arm as he tried to remember some of the things he'd heard over the years.

"A lot of the stories have to do with disaster and mass deaths. You know about the Richmond Theatre fire of 1811? And the Church Hill Tunnel collapse in 1925?"

Wyatt and Noah both nodded. Noah was smirking at him.

Ash rolled his eyes. "Of course you do, you're historians. Well, Byrd Theatre is supposed to be haunted as all hell. The former manager, I think. The ladies bathroom does all sorts of weird things. And there's a vampire story that goes with the tunnel collapse."

"Vampire story," Wyatt repeated.

Ash nodded. "You've heard of the Richmond Vampire?"

"I thought he was supposed to be in Hollywood Cemetery," Noah said.

"He is, along with a dog statue that comes to life at night. But the Richmond Vampire story started with the tunnel collapse."

"How so?"

"Story goes that, after it happened, as workers were rushing to help the men trapped by the collapse, a creature crawled out from the wreckage. Legend says its mouth was covered in blood and its teeth were pointed. Strips of decomposing skin were hanging off its body."

Wyatt exhaled. "Lovely image."

"Family exhibit, woo-hoo," Noah singsonged. Wyatt snorted.

"Anyway. The story says that the creature ran away from medical attention, toward Hollywood Cemetery. He hid himself in a crypt that had a date of death chiseled into it but no birth date, and was never seen again. After that, the Richmond Vampire sightings started."

"Creepy," Noah said.

Ash shrugged. "Now, to me the possible truth behind that one is pretty plain. When the tunnel collapsed, a lot of people were injured. There were fires, people were bleeding. Someone crawling out of the tunnel with blood all over them and their skin falling off from severe burns sounds pretty reasonable, right? Being in shock and running off into oblivion only to keel over where your body gave out sounds like it might be reasonable too."

"Yeah, that one's a good anecdotal one," Wyatt said with a nod. He was jotting notes down on a pad of paper. Ash watched the pen move for a few seconds before snapping out of it.

"There's all kinds of stories about the Dismal Swamp area. And all of northern Virginia. Arlington, especially. Are you doing all of Virginia or just the Richmond area?"

"Anywhere that's viable, really. The whole state."

Ash clucked his tongue and closed one eye to peer at Wyatt through the other. "I have a few books at home that talk about the state. I'll hunt them up for you."

"I'd appreciate that," Wyatt said, sounding so sincere and grateful that Ash sort of wanted to smack him.

"Another rare one I've heard is about the DuBois family. You know them?" Ash asked.

"Sounds familiar," Noah said as Wyatt frowned and nodded.

"Well. It's kind of like the LaLaurie family from New Orleans. I grew up there."

"Now, the LaLauries I know," Wyatt said. "They were a wealthy Creole couple in the early 1800s. Eighteen-thirty maybe?"

"Yeah." Ash nodded. "There was a fire in their mansion in the French Quarter one night, supposedly started by their cook to escape their cruelty. When the firemen got the flames put out, they found a hidden room in the house, full of the mangled bodies of slaves. They'd been tortured and experimented on, stuff that would have given the Nazi doctors pause. Some of them were still alive and begging to be killed."

"That's . . . really horrible, but what does that have to do with Virginia?" Noah asked.

"The LaLauries escaped New Orleans just ahead of an enraged mob. They were never brought back to New Orleans. Some rumors say that they stayed in New Orleans, but others tell that they went as far as they could get. France. New York. One rumor says they came here to Richmond briefly before moving on, under the name DuBois."

Wyatt shifted on his carton. "Really?"

"You'd have a hard time researching that one, I'd bet. I've heard they died in France, but not much about the interim. All those records you have access to, though, you might solve a historical mystery," Ash said with forced cheer.

Noah smirked. "What else have you got?"

"There's a bigfoot and/or werewolf near Lake Chesdin."

Wyatt smiled and Noah barked a laugh.

"There were Indian ghosts spotted out on the Pocahontas Parkway a few summers ago. I remember newspaper articles about it. The whole town of Occoquan is haunted. The plantations down on the James are all said to be haunted and Civil War stories and ghosts are all over the state. You could also do a section on how to handle all the things you're talking about. Like how to get rid of ghosts, how to repel them, that sort of thing."

Noah was nodding, but Wyatt just kept gazing at Ash and smiling wistfully as he talked. Ash was both enjoying the attention and worried by it. He would just have to remember to stay away from the drink tonight, to make sure he didn't end up in the same position he had found himself in four mornings ago. But if Wyatt planned to stick around . . .

Ash shook his head, having distracted himself into forgetting what he was saying.

"You okay?" Noah asked.

"Yeah." Ash rubbed at his temple. He'd had a dull headache for the last couple days that he couldn't get rid of.

Noah leaned in closer. "Caleb told me you hit your head the other day."

"What? *I* didn't hit it. *He* hit it for me!" He pointed over Noah's shoulder, where Caleb was walking toward them. "Asshole. And I'm fine."

Caleb approached, lighting a thick cigar behind his cupped hand. "How's storytime going in here?"

Noah grinned. "Your bartender is a veritable font of creepy information."

Ash smiled as he watched Noah's eyes light up. At least he'd gotten one thing right over the weekend.

"His shift is also about to start and Ryan is getting antsy," Caleb told them.

Ash looked at his watch and cursed.

"Your shift?" Wyatt echoed. "I thought you worked early and he worked late?"

Ash shook his head and clenched his jaw. "We take two hour shifts, normally, but we split them when we flair. If we didn't, we'd both fall over from exhaustion after two days. He covered for me the other night when you were here."

"Oh," Wyatt said.

Ash sighed and stood up. "Look, I'm not going to be able to talk at all for the next two hours or so. After that, I'll be taking the tables when Delilah gets off. If you want to go on that ghost walk thing and then come back and have a late dinner or something, I'll be around. But you're going to be better off getting this somewhere else, you know? I've pretty much told you everything I remember off the top of my head."

"Do you work tomorrow?" Wyatt asked as he stood.

"Yeah." Ash looked from Wyatt to Noah and felt his resolve faltering. Damn the man, why did he have to be so cute and enigmatic? He hit every one of Ash's buttons. "But . . . call me, I guess. If you have more questions. Noah's got my number. And I'll let you know if I can dig up that book."

Noah reached out and took his hand, pulling him into a one-armed hug. "Thanks, Ash."

"No problem." Noah patted him on the back and then released him. He turned to Wyatt with a sudden blast of nerves and didn't let himself think before he offered his hand to Wyatt as well. He hugged him awkwardly, pulling him close and acknowledging the attraction he still felt as he put his arm around him. Wyatt smelled like leather and vanilla, and flashes of sultry kisses played through Ash's head.

"Thanks," Wyatt whispered into his ear.

Ash shivered and released him. "Yeah." He sidestepped Caleb and grabbed up the flashlight that sat near the door. He clicked it on and opened his mouth, shining the light onto his tongue as the others watched him.

"What the hell are you doing?" Noah asked.

Ash removed the flashlight and gave them a sheepish smile before opening his mouth to reveal the tongue ring. "It needs light to glow."

Wyatt was grinning crookedly, but Noah just stared at him with a raised eyebrow, his mouth ajar.

"What? Shut up," Ash grunted. He put the flashlight away and retreated to the bar where he knew he and his pride would be safe.

He tried not to notice an hour later when Noah and Wyatt left with the ghost tour. The sense of simultaneous relief and disappointment was disconcerting, and Ash chastised himself before he could get too distracted.

He lost himself in his work, giving the patrons the top-notch show they expected when they came to Gravedigger's. The lights were low and several of the bottles Ash used glowed in the dark. Patrons were getting well-lubricated and loose, having a good time and tipping well. It was with relief that Ash stopped noticing when the door opened.

Hours later, as Ryan, Ash, and Caleb ushered the remaining patrons out the door and called them cabs, Ash finally had time to be disappointed that Wyatt and Noah hadn't returned.

They stood in the middle of the floor after Caleb locked the door, numb and exhausted like they always were at this point in the week.

"Clean up tomorrow?"

Caleb looked at him dubiously, but then nodded.

A loud bang from upstairs accompanied his answer and they all jumped and staggered closer to the door.

"What the shit was that?" Ryan asked. "Did someone get up there?" He began stalking toward the door that led to the upstairs.

A rush of stark fear flooded Ash's body. "Ryan!"

Ryan turned and eyed him in confusion as a gentle tapping began to sound from upstairs.

Ash realized he was close to panicking. He had no idea why, other than something instinctive in him that desperately wanted to leave.

"But what if someone's trapped up there?"

A low, insistent thumping began to echo across the ceiling. It crawled up Ash's spine and into his body, sending icy chills through him. He swallowed hard, trying to fight the panic.

Ryan continued toward the door.

"You okay?" Caleb asked.

"I'm fine. Sort of. No."

"It's the refrigerator," Caleb said, voice surprisingly soothing. "Is that what you heard earlier? It's just the fridge dying. It's been on its last legs for weeks."

Ash took a deep breath, trying to calm his pounding heart while attempting to analyze why he was so terrified. Ryan disappeared through the door, and Ash heard his footsteps on the stairs.

Ash closed his eyes and exhaled as Caleb put a hand on his shoulder. A few moments later, the thumping stopped abruptly, and Ash held his breath, waiting to hear Ryan's returning footsteps. They heard nothing for a few tense moments. Ash's lungs began to burn.

He blew the air out in a puff as Ryan called to them that the beer was all warm and thumped back down the steps.

"What's wrong with you, lad?" Caleb asked.

Ash shook his head. The terror was gone just as suddenly as it had struck. He rubbed his chest. "I have no idea."

"Panic attack," Ryan said.

"Is that a real thing?" Ash asked.

Caleb nodded. "Definitely."

"What causes them?"

"Anything; they're pretty common when you're under stress," Ryan answered. "You okay to get home? What the hell's going on?"

Ash nodded, embarrassed and irritated. "Fuck if I know. I'll be so glad when shit starts working around here again."

Ryan grunted. "That's not fair. I work."

Caleb rolled his eyes and gestured them both toward the door "Go away."

CHAPTER FOUR

Wyatt barely made it through his mid-week presentation to the board without vaulting over the conference table and strangling Reth, but the trustees grudgingly approved his idea. Reth still had Wyatt's head on the chopping block, and if the exhibit wasn't a success, Wyatt would still be put up to a vote.

The stress was starting to morph into something that threatened Wyatt's sanity, but at the same time he was distracted, still focusing on his weekend tryst with the enigmatic bartender from Gravedigger's.

As the flurry of activity that had led up to the presentations wound down, Wyatt found himself once again staring vacantly at the Thurston poster in his office, tapping his pen against his knee. Even Howard Thurston, with his mastery of sleight of hand and his tenuous connection to the macabre, reminded Wyatt of Ash Lucroix.

Ash's world that had nothing to do with Wyatt's. It was darker, richer. There was something familiar and comforting about the old-fashioned aspects, countered by the sharp excitement of something new and different. Wyatt thought maybe that was why he was so drawn to the man.

He'd promised Noah he would stay away from Ash for a little while unless it was about the exhibition, though. And he had done it, both for the sake of his friendship with Noah and for the sake of his own sanity. It would never work if he fell for someone like Ash. The man coordinated his outfits with his tongue rings, for God's sake.

Wyatt closed his eyes and snorted, rubbing his hands over his face. All the reasons he tried to tell himself that Ash was all kinds of wrong for him wound up being things that Wyatt found fascinating or endearing or just plain sexy. He had never thought that walking past a photo of a man wearing suspenders would remind him of the best sex of his life.

Wyatt was a man of his word, though. But now he had a legitimate reason, flimsy though it might have been, to go and see Ash. It was just a question of whether he had the nerve to take what he had found during his research to the bar and talk.

He rested his head on the back of his chair and opened his eyes, looking up at the ceiling. It was past closing time. The interns he'd been supervising as they set up the new exhibits had all gone home. Noah had left early to "take his baby to the doctor," which meant his vintage motorcycle had something wrong with it again.

Wyatt had no excuse not to walk the four or so blocks down the street to the bar. Nothing but the very real terror of rejection was keeping him here.

He growled and stood, gathered the copies of the documents he had collected, slid them into protective sleeves, and placed them in his satchel.

He was out of the museum and walking toward Gravedigger's before he could think better of it.

It was nearly six when he got there, and the after-work crowd had materialized. The bar wasn't very busy, though, and Wyatt found out why when he stepped through the door. The music wasn't blaring like it had been Monday, and Ash was merely mixing drinks rather than performing. The ambience was different. It seemed intimate and almost mellow, in a strangely dark and antiquated way. He liked it, though. It felt like stepping into a different world.

It was the same feeling, he realized, that he'd had that night in Ash's apartment. There was a sense of history here—in the bar, in Ash's condo, even in the way Ash dressed. But it wasn't the same sense the museum gave off, like history on display. It was like stepping into a portal, back to a world that had never been. Like Ash had come out of the past and put a modern twist on it. Wyatt couldn't quite explain it, but it was just one more thing about Ash that appealed to him.

As Ash leaned out and swiped a towel over the scarred surface of the bar, he happened to look up, his eyes meeting Wyatt's. He stopped his wiping, as if Wyatt had somehow frozen him, and stared for a long moment before moving his arm again. He nodded at Wyatt, then looked away as someone requested a drink.

He wasn't wearing suspenders today, just a pair of casual black trousers and a bright red tuxedo vest over a V-neck T-shirt. Wyatt was almost disappointed. But then, he supposed a man could only have so many pairs of the things. The kohl was still there, though. Wyatt was relieved. He had grown very fond of the kohl.

He looked around the room as he walked over to the bar. Delilah was in the far corner, taking an order. Ryan and Caleb were nowhere in sight.

Wyatt set his bag on the bar top and chewed on his bottom lip as Ash mixed a drink. As soon as Ash set the finished product down, he glanced over at Wyatt and then looked around as if searching for the others, just like Wyatt had done.

He walked over, wiping his hands on the towel he had draped over his shoulder. "What's your poison?"

"I have something to show you," Wyatt said.

Ash's eyes darted down to the bag where Wyatt's hands were resting. "Okay."

Ash's distrust was obvious, and Wyatt wanted to reassure him. "It's about the history of this house."

Ash's brow furrowed, and he looked back down at the bag. "Weeknights we take turns at the tables. Tonight's Delilah's go and it's Ryan's night off, so I've got the bar all night. I can't really look at anything unless it gets real slow."

"I understand." He could wait; he had nowhere to be.

Ash looked at him expectantly, then seemed to realize that he wasn't going to leave. "You're going to hang around?"

"If you don't mind," Wyatt said as he reached into the bag and extracted a document. He laid it aside and pushed the bag away from him. "Can you put this behind the bar?"

Ash nodded and stowed the bag under the bar. "Can I get you anything while you wait?"

"I'd love some of that root beer you have on tap." Wyatt met Ash's dark eyes. "I don't do so well with the alcohol, I've found."

Ash stared at him for a long moment, his expression unreadable. Then he nodded and turned away, reaching up to the shelf behind him for a beer mug and letting it roll down his arm. He used his elbow to pop it into the air and caught it with his other hand as he turned back to the taps. The entire movement seemed second nature to him. Did he even know he'd done it?

Wyatt watched him the entire time, unable to deny the attraction or the fascination. Ash filled the mug and set it in front of him with a nod. Then he glanced up and down the bar and leaned against it, coming closer to Wyatt with a sigh.

"It's only going to pick up," he said as he looked down at the copy of the old newspaper clipping Wyatt had encased in protective plastic. "Go ahead."

Wyatt watched him almost longingly, and when Ash glanced up, their eyes met.

Ash hummed. "I know that look."

"I'm sorry," Wyatt said, but he didn't look away. "I was just wondering what color it is tonight."

Ash blinked at him, nonplussed, but then he smirked. He opened his mouth and stuck out his tongue, revealing a tiny red whistle sitting there.

Wyatt leaned closer and peered at it. "Is that a real whistle?"

Ash laughed, looking away. "It takes some practice to get it to actually blow. But it's good for getting someone's attention."

Wyatt gaped as Ash stuck his tongue half out of his mouth and placed the tip of the tiny whistle at his lips. The thing emitted a high-pitched shrill. Delilah jerked her head up and looked over at them, and outside, a dog tied to the iron fence began to howl.

Ash laughed as Delilah flipped him the bird and went back to work.

Wyatt smiled. "How many of those things do you have?"

"Tons."

"They come in all kinds?"

"You have no idea," Ash drawled, his smile growing more evil. "Some of them vibrate."

"Really." Wyatt stared, completely lost for the moment.

Ash grinned wider, displaying that adorable smile with the chipped canine. He was less defensive now. "Okay, show me."

Wyatt swallowed hard. He could sit there all night and just watch Ash work, but he tore his eyes away and turned the news article toward Ash. "This is about this address," he said.

Ash bent over it, scowling. He was probably trying to make out the antiquated print in the low light.

Wyatt sipped at his root beer. The article, in all its early-twentieth-century journalistic relish, detailed the discovery of a veritable charnel house on this very lot. The structure that stood here now had been built in 1909. When the ground was being cleared for the laying of the foundation, the workers had found evidence of burnt timbers and scorched layers of dirt. Then they'd struck something solid beneath the topsoil, and when they broke through a layer of buried mortar and stone, they found an old root cellar, every nook and cranny nearly overflowing with human bones.

Ash inhaled deeply and pushed the article away, frowning at Wyatt. "That's a tad disturbing."

"A tad."

Ash pressed his lips into a thin line and examined Wyatt, obviously unsettled. "So why tell me?" he finally asked.

"It got me thinking. That story you told us, about the house fire in New Orleans?"

Ash's frown deepened. Finally, his lips parted and he inclined his head. "The LaLauries and DuBois legend. Yeah, it's similar, and it really did happen in New Orleans. But the Richmond connection was just urban legend, man. There's no real evidence that the LaLauries ever stayed here for any amount of time, or even came here at all. It was just hearsay."

"All urban legends are based in truth. Why would the legend pick Richmond? There's no connection to New Orleans here. It wasn't even a main port in the 1830s. Why here? Why not Charleston? Why not Boston or New York?"

"I don't know."

"This area, the Fan area? It was mostly untouched farmland until after the Civil War."

"Wait a minute." Ash held up one hand. "Are you trying to tell me you think the LaLauries really fled to Richmond after they left New Orleans and then started it all up again here? That's a bit out there."

"So is thinking that they just up and stopped their experiments after they were caught the first time."

Ash stared at him. A woman at the other end of the bar called his name, and he glanced down and nodded. "Let me think," he said to Wyatt as he moved away.

Wyatt watched him, sipping his root beer as Ash prepared the woman's order. Several more followed, and Wyatt passed the time by just admiring the way Ash worked. The graceful way he moved, the easy way he interacted with the patrons, the way he danced to the music a little when he became too distracted.

A half hour later, Ash slid back up in front of Wyatt. He flopped his towel over his shoulder and leaned on his elbows. "So why are you really here?"

"What?"

Ash tapped the plastic-covered article and met Wyatt's eyes. "It's very interesting. And you may very well be right, even though the leap in logic is like Evel Knievel caliber."

Wyatt laughed and shook his head.

"But I still don't see why you had to come here and tell me about it."

Wyatt's smile fell as he stared at the well-polished bar. Then he met Ash's eyes, and his stomach tumbled. "You were the only other person I could think of that might find it interesting."

"But Noah—"

"Found it interesting." Ash frowned. Wyatt smiled. "Come on. You telling me this information won't bring crowds into the bar in droves?"

He was unable to admit that it had been the only way he could come back in here and see Ash again.

"We're not really hurting for business."

Wyatt shrugged. "I'm sorry. I figured every little bit helped."

Ash studied him as if he were trying to measure him up for a painting. "Yeah, okay."

"There's more," Wyatt said with a smirk. Ash raised an eyebrow, and Wyatt pointed at the bar. "Get my bag, will you?"

Ash knelt and retrieved the bag, setting it on the bar with a grunt. He excused himself to fix several orders, and Wyatt took the time to find the rest of the documents. They outlined the history of the Fan, and Wyatt had retained copies of anything that supported or refuted his theory.

He had the land records from when it had been parceled up to create a town that had never materialized, and the deed for the block now occupied by Gravedigger's, and for roughly four blocks around it.

When Ash returned to him, Wyatt showed him the papers. "All of the lots were bought by the same person. A French doctor."

Ash raised an eyebrow at him.

A man came up beside Wyatt and leaned over the bar. "Got a light?" he asked Ash suggestively.

Wyatt turned his head toward the flirting patron as Ash reached into his pocket and produced a lighter. He tried to analyze his jealousy as he watched Ash light the man's cigarette.

"You'll need to take it to the patio," Ash said with a jerk of his head toward the door. The man thanked him and left, looking downcast for having his advances ignored.

Wyatt peered at Ash and tried to hide his smile.

"Go on," Ash said, completely oblivious.

"Where was I?"

"The French doctor. You think it was LaLaurie?"

"Dr. Louis LaLaurie, yeah. I mean, in the 1830s, if you have a medical degree, you're not just going to close up shop and thumb your nose at the income, you know?"

"Especially if they had to leave all their possessions and wealth in New Orleans."

"You're beginning to see my point."

"Grudgingly," Ash said, his lips twitching into a smile.

Wyatt grinned, unable to hide his excitement. Not only was Ash tolerating his presence and listening to him, but he also seemed to be enjoying it a little.

"So, what, he built a practice here?" Ash asked. He glanced over to see Delilah holding the house phone and signaling frantically. "Hold that thought."

Wyatt nodded and watched him go.

Ash strolled to the other end of the bar and Delilah put the phone to his ear. She didn't relinquish it, so they stood holding the receiver together, looking like little kids sharing a set of headphones.

They listened for a few moments, then began talking animatedly with each other and into the phone. Delilah finally shook her head and began backing away, leaving the phone dangling in Ash's hand. Ash reached for the towel on his shoulder and used it to swat at her.

Wyatt frowned as he watched the little comedy unfold. Their actions were amusing on the surface, but he got the feeling that the phone call wasn't all good news.

Ash talked for several more moments, holding the phone to his ear with his shoulder as he went to the cash register and scrounged up a pen and paper. He began writing, glancing up at Wyatt as he did so. Wyatt's stomach wrenched; he knew by the look in Ash's eyes that their night was over.

Ash soon hung up the phone and tore off the note he had written. He walked back to Wyatt and placed the note in front of him. "That was Noah. He said he needs a ride home, his bike is a no-go."

"I can get him," Wyatt said with a reluctant nod. He began gathering his documents.

"He's on the Pocahontas Parkway. He said it was dark and scary and he's freaked out about ghost Indians getting him," Ash said with a smirk.

Wyatt laughed. "Are these directions?"

"Yeah." Ash huffed. "I also put the number to the bar there, in case you get lost. You got a phone?" he asked as he took out his cell phone.

Wyatt contemplated saying he didn't, just so he could take Ash's and have a reason to come back. But he couldn't do it. He nodded instead and patted his pocket. "Shouldn't be too hard to find him." He folded the note and slid it into his pocket.

"Thanks. Tell him I'm sorry; Caleb's not here tonight so neither of us can really leave."

"He'll understand." Wyatt placed the documents into the bag and looked up, freezing when he met Ash's eyes.

Ash gave him a small smile. "When you have time to finish your story, give me a call."

Wyatt blinked at him. "I uh . . . I don't have your number."

Ash met his eyes for a few tense moments before taking Wyatt's hand and pulling it across the bar. He wrote a number on Wyatt's wrist. His grip was warm, and Wyatt knew Ash could feel his pulse racing. He didn't know if this was a second chance or just a peace offering, but either way it felt good.

Wyatt was still staring at Ash when he released his hand. "Thanks," he whispered.

Ash nodded, a smile playing at his lips as he began clearing up the glasses. "See you around," he said, and moved away.

Neither Noah nor Wyatt ever called the bar to tell them what happened, and Ash was annoyed and worried by the end of the night. He was also annoyed by the fact that despite everything, he still found himself thinking about Wyatt.

He had to admit, if given the chance again, he would still take Wyatt home. Likely tie him to the bed this time to make sure he didn't bolt, but take him home nonetheless.

"Hey!" Ryan called from across the room.

Ash looked up, startled out of his thoughts and embarrassed to have been caught staring into the void. Ryan had come in late that evening to help out after he'd called and learned that Caleb wasn't there. Where Caleb was, no one really knew. But as the boss, it was his priority to not show the fuck up for work whenever he wanted.

"What?"

"Closing time, bitch," Ryan said with relish as he sauntered over to the door and turned the handmade wooden "Closed" sign around.

Ash snorted and opened the hidden electrical panel next to the back mirror. He switched off the power to the outside lights and the sound system, then closed the panel door again. It made a hollow sound as it secured.

Delilah was stacking chairs on the tables. "Caleb told me that someone's coming tomorrow to take the fridge upstairs away."

Ash nodded, wiping down the bar distractedly. That damn refrigerator had been more trouble than it was worth. They had to have one upstairs, though, to store all that beer. Ash was glad it had died, regardless. He had been questioning his sanity. Ever since Ryan had unplugged it, they hadn't heard any tapping or banging from upstairs.

"They having a new one delivered?" Ash asked as he tossed some used napkins into the trash.

"A big one. They're doing all the lifting, so you guys don't have to worry about anything but letting them in," Delilah answered. She began sweeping up half-heartedly.

"Oh, thank Christ," Ryan grumbled as he gathered glasses. "I could just see myself hauling that thing up those steps on my back."

Ash snorted and shook his head. He heard the "clink" sound of the panel closing again and looked over at it with a frown. It was still closed, and when he stepped over to it and gave it a poke, it didn't move.

"What are you doing?" Ryan asked.

Ash shrugged one shoulder and reached for the broom in the corner, staring at the panel a moment longer. "Nothing."

They cleaned up quickly and efficiently, their routine well-practiced, all three of them ready to go home and sleep—or whatever it was Delilah did with her time because she was a hopeless insomniac. When they were done inside, they gathered their belongings, shrugged into their coats, and went outside to tilt the chairs on the patio against the tables.

When they finished, Ryan surveyed the façade of the building to make certain everything looked closed up and suitably spooky. He nodded in satisfaction. "Lilahbelle, how far are you parked?"

"Far enough I won't turn down a big strong man to walk me there," Delilah said with a wry twist to her lips. Ash rolled his eyes. He knew she could take care of herself because he'd seen her do it, but she enjoyed playing the maiden every now and then. And the furtive dalliance Delilah and Ryan had been trying to hide for the last three months was old news. She looped her arm through Ryan's.

"Lead the way then, milady. See you tomorrow, Ashcake," Ryan said. They shook hands and hugged, then Ash gave Delilah a kiss on the cheek. Ryan and Delilah began making their way around the corner of the building toward the small parking lot behind the bar.

Ash started to walk away as well when he heard the faint, eerie sound of classical music coming from inside the bar. He stopped short and looked up at the darkened windows, frowning.

"Hey guys!" he said, his voice coming out a harsh whisper. Ryan and Delilah stopped and turned, and Ash pointed to the door.

"What?"

"Shhh! Listen."

Ryan cocked his head and frowned.

"What is that?" Delilah whispered, breath frosting in front of her. "Music?"

"What the hell?" Ryan dug into his pocket for his keys and unlocked the door. Ash and Delilah were right on his heels. Gravedigger's wasn't often the target of pranks or vandalism no matter what was going on in the neighborhood, mainly because everyone knew that Caleb wouldn't bother going to the police to resolve incidents. He and his staff took care of things on their own. But occasionally a stupid kid would think he was brave and try to get in.

They all stopped short and stared into the dark room. It was creepy in here without lights or people. It didn't look like a tavern, full of life and personality. It just looked like a creepy old house. The music was louder inside, but it didn't seem to be coming from the speakers. Ash knew he had turned those off. He thought he had, anyway. Hadn't he?

The sound of a tortured violin seemed to be filtering up from the floor and through the walls, but it was distant, as if it were coming from very far below. It began to fade as Ryan took another tentative step into the room.

Ash realized he had heard the song before, but he couldn't remember its name or where he'd heard it. The haunting melody still somehow retained a quick tempo.

"You turned off the sound system, right?" Ryan asked as the music grew weaker.

"Yeah, I cut the power to it."

The music faded until it was gone and Ash and Ryan were left standing there, frowning and unsettled.

"Well?" Delilah asked from behind them, and they both jumped at the sound of her voice.

"Don't do that!" Ash said.

"Do what?"

"Sneak up on us."

"I've been right here!"

"Get in here," Ryan said.

"Fuck no."

"What?"

She pulled her coat sleeve up and held out her arm to show them the hairs standing on end. "This is some freaky shit."

Ash nodded. Ryan groaned at both of them.

"Should we check it out?" Ash asked.

Ryan inhaled noisily and seemed to hold his breath as he listened. "Yeah."

"Really?"

Ryan gave him a look and Ash shrugged. He didn't mind admitting that he was freaked out.

"Wait, don't leave me here alone," Delilah said as she hopped into the room and grabbed the back of Ash's shirt.

"Oh, now you're the helpless girl?"

"The smart ones are scared when necessary. Shut up."

They moved together into the bar, staying close to each other. Everything was as they'd left it, though. Ryan went to the power grid and checked to make certain the power was off. The distinctive sound of the panel shutting made Ash shiver.

"Off?"

Ryan turned around "Off."

Ash moved to the door that led to the kitchen and pushed it open, flicking on the lights. It was empty and spotless. There had been a fire in the kitchen over the summer that had prompted the extensive renovations. Ash was relieved to see all that stainless steel gleaming in the light. There was nothing eerie about stainless steel.

He walked to the back door and checked it, noting that the dead bolt was still turned and the chain was still latched. He turned to find Ryan watching him. He shrugged, and Ryan peered around the room. Delilah followed, scowling at everything.

"It's a ghost," she said.

Ryan sighed. "Seriously, Crazytrain, that's not helping." He walked over to the long stainless steel shelf above the stoves and tapped the old radio that sat there. It began blaring classical music. Ash and Delilah jumped and grabbed each other as if they might be able to save themselves by clinging. Ash grunted and looked away in exasperation as the music stopped again. Ryan gave it another tentative poke and it blared to life once more before shutting off.

Ash wriggled away from Delilah and walked over to put his finger on one of the speakers, nudging it. The DJ's soothing nighttime voice emitted from the radio, vibrating Ash's finger.

"And you've been listening to 'La Danse Macabre' by—"

Ash removed his finger and the radio silenced once more. He and Ryan looked at each other. "The dance of death unites us all," Ryan said.

Delilah smacked him on the arm as she stomped out of the kitchen.

"What? It's not my fault!"

"It's always your fault!" Delilah called from the other room.

Ryan reached up and removed the radio's batteries. He tossed them into the trash and growled at them, then flicked off the lights as he left the kitchen.

Ash took a step to follow out of the kitchen, and from the corner of his eye he caught a shadow moving, as if someone had stepped onto the back porch and was looking through the door.

He whirled around, but found himself staring at his own opaque reflection in the glass of the door. He was breathing hard once more and his heart was pounding, but he knew he was just letting himself get carried away. The streetlight outside flickered and then returned to full power as he stood there trying to calm himself.

"Goddamn you, Wyatt. Fucking ghost stories," he muttered as he turned to go back to the main room.

Ryan was heading for the locked door that led to the upstairs.

"What are you doing?"

"Going to check upstairs," Ryan said as he unlocked the door.

"But we found the radio," Delilah said.

"We're here, we might as well." Ryan pulled the old door open by its glass doorknob. Ash jogged to catch up to him.

The floorboards creaked under their feet with every step, and when they got to the landing, they both stopped and searched around. Ash wondered if Ryan felt as uneasy as he did.

"If anyone was up here, we'd hear them," Ryan said as he looked over his shoulder at Ash.

"Yeah." He was surprised to find his voice was hoarse.

"Why's it so cold up here?" Delilah asked.

Ryan and Ash both jumped again.

"Don't do that!"

"What?" She shivered and glanced at the front windows. They were closed. The A/C unit that had killed itself earlier this week was long gone, and they had never replaced it. "It's freezing up here."

"Ghosts," Ryan said with a grin.

"Shut up," Ash said.

"Scared?" Ryan teased.

Ash glared at him. A loud bang from the far side of the landing made them all jump, and Ryan grabbed Ash and turned around, hiding behind him. Ash held his breath, frozen as he tried to make his eyes pierce the darkness. He was too scared to even question the fact that the bigger, supposedly braver man was hiding behind him.

"Is the fridge still unplugged?" Delilah asked in a small voice.

"I don't know. Go check." Ryan prodded Ash in the back with a finger.

"Fuck you, man," Ash whispered, his voice embarrassingly high-pitched as he backpedaled into Ryan.

"Okay, we'll both go check," Ryan whispered as he pressed Ash from behind.

Ash took a tentative step forward and reached for the light switch. The lights flickered on, revealing the foyer of the upper level. They'd left it mostly untouched during the renovations downstairs, and it could almost be called decrepit. Old furniture was stacked here and there, the floorboards were creaky and unpolished, and the heavy scent of mothballs and old wood hung in the air. The only thing used regularly up here was a room Caleb had converted into an office, and he only used it maybe once a week.

Caleb had plans for the upper level, but they had to wait until their down season. The refrigerator they used to store all the extra beer sat opposite the head of the stairs, beside one of the front windows. Ash edged closer to it, feeling Ryan and Delilah behind him as he moved. Halfway across the landing, they could see the plug in the socket.

"Caleb must have plugged it back in," Ryan whispered.

"Huh-uh," Ash grunted. "I heard him up here calling its mother a cunt. He was done with it."

The refrigerator gave another loud bang and then began to grumble rhythmically. Ash jumped and backed toward the stairs, not caring that Ryan was still behind him. The lights flickered, as they were known to do when the refrigerator was sucking power from them, and then went out.

"I want to go home now," Ash said, unashamed as they stood in the dark.

"Me too," Delilah said, voice small.

"Yeah," Ryan said hurriedly. None of them moved, though, unwilling to turn their backs on the dark room and unable to descend the steep, narrow steps without looking.

"Can you give me a ride?" Ash asked after a tense moment of silence.

"Yeah. Move your ass," Ryan said as he pulled Ash back and turned to hustle down the steps after Delilah.

W yatt stepped into the large lecture hall, taking up a spot in the back.

"Some duels over the course of history have been rather out of the ordinary," Noah was saying to the large audience. "Because duelists would pick their locations with the particular goal of not being disturbed, some of them got interesting. In 1808, there's a documented case of two Frenchmen fighting a duel from hot air balloons."

A murmur of laughter went through the crowd, and Noah grinned. "It's true, you can read that in *Smithsonian*," he said with a rakish smile.

Wyatt smiled as his friend walked around the lectern. He wasn't your typical lecturer, but his talks had the highest attendance by far. Detractors would blame his off-color topics or his good looks and charming personality, but Wyatt firmly believed it was his skill and charisma as a speaker and his stellar reputation as a scholar.

"The men shot at each other's balloons with pistols until one of them was hit so many times the balloon crashed, killing the duelist and his second." Noah pressed a button and the picture behind him changed. It was a cartoon-like drawing of two men in balloons, pointing muskets at each other. "By the late nineteenth century, the act of dueling was becoming somewhat passé. Gentlemen were beginning to think it barbaric, and when challenged, many were known to pick outrageous methods of dueling to show their disdain. Howitzers, crowbars, sledgehammers, forks full of pig dung."

Another ripple of laughter went through the crowd. Wyatt chuckled as Noah clicked through his graphics. Some of them were very graphic indeed.

Noah glanced up into the darkness of the audience and Wyatt waved the papers he had in his hand under the red glow of the Exit light. Noah gave him the barest of nods and continued.

Wyatt slid out of the lecture room. He almost regretted not hearing the end of the talk, but he drew the line at forks full of pig dung. He waited outside, leaning against the wall, trying to look innocuous in case any of the trustees happened to wander by. He could hear the low murmur of Noah's voice, and the occasional laugh as the talk wound down.

Wyatt stood where he was and smiled and nodded as the attendees filed out of the room.

Several minutes later, Noah emerged. "Lunch?"

"Forkfuls of pig dung?"

"It's documented." Noah grinned and turned to head for the cafeteria.

"Is dung the proper term for that?" Wyatt asked. "It doesn't change with different animals?"

Noah laughed. "What?"

"You know, like in terms of collectives: a herd of wildebeest or a murder of crows. Guano versus manure versus dung?"

"It does change, actually. Wild carnivores have scat, while domesticated animals have dung. Birds have droppings, but sea birds and bats have guano."

"Jesus, Noah."

"What? I know things."

"I'm sorry I asked."

"Only horses produce manure, unless another animal's waste is used as fertilizer, and then it's all called manure. And for some reason, otters have their very own crap that's called spraint."

"Noah."

"There are also different names for individual versus bulk. Meadow muffins versus dung."

"Meadow muffins? What the hell does that have to do with dueling?"

"Nothing, why?"

Wyatt just looked at him, and Noah stared back as they both tried not to smile. "Are we eating lunch?"

"Of course," Noah said, and they continued on to the staff cafeteria as if they'd never paused. "Collective names are fascinating, have you ever studied them?"

"I can't say that I have."

"Some of them are pretty self-explanatory. A prickle of porcupines, a cackle of hyenas, a pounce of cats, a slither of snakes. But it's a nest of vipers, a quiver of cobras, and a rhumba of rattlesnakes. They also have a parliament of owls and a congress of baboons, which I find insulting to baboons myself."

Wyatt sighed.

"And solitary animals are given collectives regardless of the fact that you'll never see a group of them. Groups of people have collectives too. A den of thieves. Even things that don't exist have collectives. Unicorns, sasquatches. Sasquatches?" Noah stopped walking. "Sasquatchae. Sasquatch," he tried instead. He looked at Wyatt and shook his head, a furrow creasing his handsome brow as he held up one hand.

Wyatt pressed his lips hard together. He waited for Noah to work out the ramble. It was perhaps his favorite aspect of Noah's personality.

"Anyway," Noah said as he began walking again.

"What are they called?"

"What are what called?"

"A collective of sasquatch . . . es."

"Oh. A pungent. Creative, huh? My favorite is a smack of jellyfish."

"How do you get laid as much as you do?"

"I don't know. I know things. Lots of things. Lots of dirty things. What were we talking about?"

"Dueling," Wyatt said.

They chose a table in the far corner, where they ate and talked about Noah's vast and weird knowledge of collectives.

"So," Noah finally said as he crunched a Cheeto.

"Yes?" Wyatt sat back and placed his half-eaten sandwich on his tray. He'd known Noah would broach the subject sooner or later.

"Wyatt!" Noah looked up as if appealing to the gods, and flopped his hands, closing his eyes and sighing. "You were at Gravedigger's last night!"

"And aren't you glad, because you *and* Caleb would have been walking home if I hadn't been there."

"And that's why I didn't bawl you out last night. But I rode the Shadow today and I know I'll get home safe so I can bitch slap you a little and it'll be okay."

Wyatt laughed and shook his head.

"Wyatt," Noah said, leaning forward and pinning Wyatt with a glare. His entire demeanor had changed. His voice was lower and just this side of offended. "I asked you nicely."

Wyatt closed his eyes. "I didn't go to get him into bed." He glanced around and then scooted his chair around the edge of the table so they were closer. Hell, most of the museum staff thought they were screwing anyway. "I was showing him those documents I found, okay? Completely innocent."

"Caleb said Ash could barely stand still when he showed up for work this morning. He said he was spooked by something."

Wyatt frowned and leaned back. "I was well-behaved, I swear."

"Just stay away from him, okay? It's not so hard."

Wyatt hesitated, looking at Noah with a mix of pain and relief. "It is, actually."

"Oh, Christ." Noah smacked his forehead. "Are you telling me you're falling for him?"

"I just . . . He's—"

"I know what he is. I know what you are. And I never would have introduced you if I thought you were going to do what you did!"

"I know!" Wyatt hissed. "And if I could change that, I would. But I like this guy, Noah, I really do. And he wasn't upset to see me, I swear."

"Then what's wrong with him?"

"Why don't we go ask him?"

Noah narrowed his eyes, then grabbed his bag of Cheetos without looking away and stood up. "Very well, then," he said, affected and regal, sticking his nose in the air. How he managed not to smile through the performance, Wyatt didn't know.

Wyatt stood as well, inclining his head to match, and grinned. They stood staring at each other for a moment until Noah broke into a smirk. "We only have ten minutes left to lunch."

"Meet you at five?"

"And bring your fork, sir," Noah drawled in a horrible British accent as he turned away.

Wyatt ran late, supervising the preparations for the new exhibition. He was making frantic phone calls to anywhere and everywhere trying to collect artifacts. He'd even been in contact with a local Wiccan and a group of ghost hunters, much to his chagrin. They had mere days to get the exhibit hall in order, and Wyatt had rolled up his sleeves early on.

At five, Noah wandered into the hall and began helping when he saw how much work remained. It was well past seven when they called it a day.

They stood surveying the pieces they had finished. "These things are turning out pretty creepy, man," Noah said.

"That's what happens when you have too many cooks in the kitchen."

The exhibit had veered into the overly dramatic, Wyatt knew that. There were cases with mannequins made up as monsters, antique and vintage clothing floating on wires as ghostly figures. There were pictures taken from around the state showing unexplainable images, or as Wyatt liked to call them, camera flares.

The last empty cases were confounding Wyatt, and he had no idea what to put in them. But he had fought to keep the rest of it tasteful and he thought they were doing a good enough job. The trustees wanted it scary, though. And Wyatt had to admit, after closing, with the museum still and quiet around them, it *was*. Noah's next words echoed his thoughts.

"The museum is creepy enough at night." He poked at one of the mannequins and watched it like he thought it might poke back.

An idea dawned on Wyatt, so sudden and brilliant that it made him grunt in annoyance. "That's how we should advertise it!"

"What? Museums are creepy, stay away?"

"No, we make the opening an overnight stay in the museum."

"Oh God, the security," Noah groaned. He put his palm to his forehead.

"We do sleepovers for school classes and birthday parties. It's worth a thought, anyway."

"Whatever, Wy, it's disturbing in here." Noah glanced askance at the mannequins one last time. "Still want to head to the bar?"

"Yeah," Wyatt said, staring up at the lifeless eyes of the mannequin for just a little too long. He shook off the shiver that ran down his back and let Noah drag him out of the hall.

They opted to drive Wyatt's car rather than walk in the chilly night. When they got close to the corner on which Gravedigger's sat, flashing blue and red lights were holding up traffic and crowds of people stood in the street, heedless of the cars trying to get by. Gravedigger's was at the center of the action. Wyatt's heart dropped into his toes.

"Fuck, man." Noah pointed to an empty spot on a side road and said, "Park."

Wyatt was already turning, and he illegally parked as he tried to see what was happening. Noah lurched out of the passenger's side before the car even stopped moving. Wyatt threw it in park and jumped out, jogging to catch up, and they forced their way through the crowd to see what the commotion was all about.

Caleb and Ryan stood on the sidewalk in front of the patio of Gravedigger's Tavern. People stood around, murmuring to each other and gawking as two cops held a man against the hood of their car and patted him down. An ambulance was parked in front of the police cruiser, half on the sidewalk, with its lights blinking.

Wyatt looked around almost frantically for Ash.

"Caleb!" Noah called as he stood on his tiptoes. He was several inches taller than the people around him, and Caleb spotted him. He motioned for them to come closer and they began to push their way through all the people. The sun had just set and twilight cast the scene in an eerie blue half-light. As they broke through the crowd, the timed lights over the patios flickered on as if announcing their grand entrance onto the scene.

"What happened?" Noah asked.

"Guy went batshit," Caleb said with a snarl. He nodded his head at the man the police were now handcuffing.

"Where's Ash?"

"Inside," Ryan said, expression grim. "Paramedics are checking him out."

"What happened?" Noah asked again. Wyatt looked at the door, trying to see inside, but the reflection of the lights was all he could make out.

"Ryan had the bar," Caleb said. Noah moved closer to hear his gruff words. "He cut a guy off, told him he was going to call him a cab 'cause he'd had too much. The guy went off, started shouting, threatening the customers, refusing to leave. Ash went over to help escort him outside and the cunt grabbed one of the flair bottles from the bar and hit him in the head."

"Jesus!" Wyatt whispered.

"Those flair bottles are thick. They're meant not to break when you drop them, you know?" Ryan said. He ran his hand through his hair.

The bell on the door dinged, and Wyatt turned to see one of the paramedics coming out of the bar.

"He's doing okay," he said before any of them could ask. "He's refusing to come to the hospital, and we can't force him." He held up the waiver Ash had apparently signed, foregoing the trip.

"Yeah." Caleb sighed and nodded. "He's got a thing about hospitals. Unless he's dying or unconscious he won't be caught in one."

"Well. He's lucky. Someone needs to pay special attention to him, though, for at least seventy-two hours. Make sure he's not suffering from confusion or visual disturbances. If he has ringing in the ears, excessive drowsiness, or vomiting, get him to a doctor so they can check him out. He may experience some memory loss over the next day, and it's my suggestion that he have a follow-up in a few days."

"Memory loss?" Ryan asked.

"Nothing long-term," the paramedic said. "He might wake up in the morning and not remember what happened tonight. That's why I'm telling you all this as well as telling him."

Wyatt frowned and stared at the police car. This was unbelievable.

"Thank you, I appreciate your speed in getting here," Caleb said as he shook the paramedic's hand. A second paramedic exited the bar and held the door open for Ash, who trudged out, holding an ice pack to his head.

"Asshole," he muttered as he watched the police car edge its way through the crowd with its new detainee.

Ryan placed a hand on Ash's shoulder. "You okay?"

"No," Ash said, frowning. He pulled the ice pack away and looked at it. Wyatt saw the blood-spotted bandage it had been covering, and his stomach turned. Ash faced Caleb and scowled. "Do I have to finish my shift?"

Caleb gave a weak laugh and shook his head. "I think you can fuck off tonight."

"We'll take him home," Noah told them. He slid his hand around Ash's waist. Ash leaned against him and looked down at the sidewalk. They led him away, asking people to move aside as they headed for Wyatt's car. People parted immediately, some of them speaking to Ash and others wishing him well.

Ash kept his head down, smiling weakly to a few people. He got into the back of Wyatt's car without a fuss and closed his eyes as soon as he was seated. Wyatt looked at him in the rearview mirror and could barely keep his eyes on the road as he pulled out and drove away from the crowd.

Noah turned around in the front seat and peered back at Ash. "Had to go and play the hero, huh?"

"Yeah, I'm a real fucking superstar."

Ash woke with difficulty, fighting his way out of sleep as if he'd been drugged. When he opened his eyes, he wasn't alone in bed. He squeezed his eyes closed and tried to remember the night before.

Not a thing came to him, though.

He groaned and opened his eyes again. He turned his head, groaning louder at Noah, curled up asleep beside him.

"Oh, God," he moaned when he sat up too quickly. His head spun, but the panic overrode it. He reached over and shook Noah. "Noah. Noah, wake up."

Noah shot up, looking around wildly and then reaching for Ash as if he thought he was falling off the bed. "You okay? Feel all right?"

"No! What . . . did we . . . what are you doing here?"

"You don't remember?"

Ash pushed up onto his hands and knees, looking around the room. His head began to pound and he turned to sit with his back against the headboard, holding his head in his hands. He stared at Noah with growing apprehension, still not quite comprehending why he was here.

To his continued horror, Wyatt appeared in the doorway to his bedroom, hair mussed, frowning. Ash gaped at him, shaking his head.

"It's okay," Wyatt said, holding out a hand. "You were hit in the head, do you remember? They said you might lose some time."

Ash blinked at him, his mouth still hanging open. He looked back at Noah, who had pushed up off the mattress to rub his eyes. "You really need a guest bed, man."

Ash grunted.

"You okay?" Wyatt asked in the same careful tone. "You feel nauseous? Ears ringing?"

"No." Ash glanced from Wyatt to Noah again and began to relax. He huffed and pointed at Noah. "All I could think was that Caleb was going to kill me."

Noah snickered and rolled out of bed. He hadn't even been under the covers, and he still had all his clothes on. If Ash had noticed that before, he could have saved himself the panic. He groaned and rubbed his fingers over his temples. "Wow. Okay, I remember the flair bottle to the head now," he said, words measured. "God, that sucked."

Wyatt chuckled, a low, pleasant sound that sent a slow thrill through Ash's body. Now that he was over his panic and thinking somewhat clearly again, having Wyatt in his place like this was not a good thing.

"Uh . . ."

"We'll leave as soon as we're sure you're not going to bleed out of your ears," Noah said. "Want us to fix you breakfast?"

"No." Ash drew the word out uncertainly. He looked from Noah to Wyatt again and licked his lips, then glanced at the clock. "Oh, shit. I'm late." He threw the covers off and swung his feet out of bed.

He stood and was immediately hit with a bout of lightheadedness. He wavered, closing his eyes and reaching out to steady himself. The others moved toward him.

"I'm okay," he whispered as he held out a hand to stop them and opened his eyes again.

He had stayed on his feet, at least.

Noah held his hands out as if he thought Ash would fall over. "Caleb said not to worry about work."

"Screw that," Ash muttered. He searched around for his clothing.

"It's Friday, Ash, you don't really think you can—"

"Maybe I can't flair, but I can at least wait tables." He stripped off the shirt he'd slept in and went to the closet to retrieve clean clothes for work. He didn't remember taking anything off last night. He reached up and swiped a finger under his eye. It came away clean, no trace of kohl. He frowned at Noah and Wyatt.

"You took a shower when we got home last night," Wyatt said. "You were completely lucid."

"As opposed to all the rest of the time," Noah grumbled.

"Shut up." Bits and pieces of the previous night were beginning to filter through his hazy memory. He tossed his shirt into the basket in the corner, glancing at the two men again as he reached for the closet door. They were both watching him with the same dubious expression. "I've got to go to work."

"Okay," Noah said with a pacifying nod.

"Aren't you two supposed to be at work too?"

They both nodded. Ash winced. They'd gone to a lot of trouble to stay with him, and now they were here suffering from a bad night's sleep instead of at the museum, where Ash knew they were scrambling to get that exhibit done in time.

"Christ, guys, I'm sorry."

Wyatt averted his eyes as Ash stripped off the rest of his clothes and changed. "It wasn't a problem. I'm sort of the boss, so . . ."

Ash stepped into a clean pair of boxers and watched Wyatt. He nodded and glanced at Noah, who was scowling at Wyatt.

"We'll give you a ride to the bar if you insist on going," Noah said, still frowning.

"Thanks."

It was odd getting ready with Noah and Wyatt hovering over him, but he managed to dress, apply the kohl to his eyes, and run a minimum amount of gel through his hair with little fuss. He was changing the stud in his tongue when Wyatt leaned against the bathroom doorframe.

"Never really wanted to see someone do that," he said. "But now that I have, it's quite fascinating."

Ash glanced at his reflection in the mirror and secured the back of the stud, then closed his mouth and cleared his throat.

"Which one is it today?" Wyatt asked.

Ash turned around and leaned against the sink, opening his mouth to show Wyatt. It was called a French tickler, usually used for more nefarious purposes than tending bar. It resembled a Koosh ball, with black and lime green silicone spikes all over it. It matched his lime green suspenders.

Wyatt laughed. "Do I even want to know where you find this stuff?"

Ash smiled. Why Wyatt seemed so fond of the tongue rings, he couldn't guess . . . other than the obvious reasons, of course. But Wyatt didn't really seem turned on by them so much as charmed. Mostly. Mention of the vibrating one had certainly stopped him in his tracks.

"What's it feel like to have one of those in your mouth all the time?"

Ash pressed his lips together and then pushed away from the sink. "Want to see?" he offered.

Wyatt straightened, his arms uncrossing and falling limp to his sides. Ash stepped closer and raised an eyebrow. Wyatt opened his mouth to say something and then closed it again, swallowing instead.

Ash grinned crookedly, enjoying Wyatt's obvious discomfort. He took a last step and pressed his mouth to Wyatt's. Wyatt's lips parted and Ash ran his tongue along Wyatt's as his hands slid around Wyatt's waist.

"Y'all want eggs for breakfast?" Noah called to them from the kitchen.

Wyatt jerked away and gasped. Ash licked his lips and smiled. "Guilty conscience," he whispered.

"And you have a head injury," Wyatt said before turning to go.

"You still liked it."

"Not the point," Wyatt hissed as he left.

Ash snickered and turned to check once more that he looked okay before he followed Wyatt into the other room.

Wyatt sat in the car and watched Ash walk toward Gravedigger's. He waited until Ash had reached the door and entered before he drove away.

The draw of Ash Lucroix was far too tempting. If he was being honest with himself, he didn't know if it was Ash or if it was merely Ash's eccentricities that Wyatt found so fascinating. Not being able to differentiate between the two was even scarier than the feeling of being drawn.

He knew one thing for sure, though: Ash didn't deserve to be hurt because Wyatt was stressed to the gills and couldn't make up his mind.

"I'll stay away from him," he told Noah as he made a turn and started heading back toward the museum.

Noah examined him. "What happened?"

"Nothing. Just . . . I'll stay away from him."

"Uh-huh."

"He kissed me."

"And it was bad?"

Wyatt rubbed his eyes and grimaced. "And it was really good."

"Yeah, that's always my first warning sign."

"Noah. I just . . . something about him turns me into a selfish asshole or something. I don't want to hurt him."

Noah was silent for an entire block. "Okay," he finally said.

Wyatt glanced at him, and Noah was watching him.

"Look. Despite my knee-jerk reaction to protect him, I saw the way he looks at you. He likes you, Wy. Even after what you did, he still likes you. He can see the real you when he looks at you, just like I do."

Wyatt sighed heavily as some of the weight lifted from his shoulders. He'd never been happier to have a friend like Noah.

"Don't make any big decision until next week," Noah advised. "Let it all settle."

"Yeah," Wyatt whispered. "Yeah, okay."

"The only thing that could go wrong for you now is if his plumbing goes haywire," Noah added, snickering.

Ash tried, before the bar opened, to juggle three of his flair bottles as Ryan and Caleb watched. He dropped one of the bottles twice before giving up.

He sedately tended the bar until almost seven, when the Friday night crowd grew larger, and then he and Delilah split the waiting duties as Ryan took on the entire heavy night of flairing with Caleb to back him up. Ash knew they were straining with the added load, but by the end of the night his head hurt so badly that he couldn't even be bothered to feel guilty about it. He was just glad the night was over.

"The new fridge is working," Ryan gleefully announced as Caleb flipped over the closed sign on the door.

"No more ghostly banging," Ash said flatly, waving his damp rag in celebration.

"Why don't you go on home, lad?" Caleb said.

Ash pursed his lips and looked up from the bar top. He knew the answer to that question: Because his couch smelled like Wyatt. Because his bathroom mirror would have a hint of Wyatt's reflection in it. Because his bed was lonely. Because he'd fallen for the asshole even though he hadn't wanted to.

"I'll help," he said instead.

"Okay," Ryan said, tone measured and suspicious. "Well, the new fridge is working but it's also in the middle of the floor up there, so I need some help moving it."

"I got that," Caleb said before Ash could offer.

Ash huffed at him. It'd be no problem if he never had to go into that damn upstairs again. There'd been too many unexplained noises coming from up there.

He heard Ryan and Caleb's footsteps shuffling up the stairs and across the floor, and then the heavy, tortured scraping of the refrigerator as they moved it. Delilah was in the kitchen, checking their inventory and singing. Ash turned around and began placing glasses on the shelves, shivering as the heat in the room began to seep out. All those bodies in such an enclosed space for so long made it perpetually warm. It usually took longer for the bar to grow chilly again, though.

Fall truly was here in all its glory, but despite Ash's love of the season, he felt none of the usual elation as he shut down the bar.

He glanced around to see if a door or window was open, still tracking the dragging of the heavy refrigerator from upstairs. Nothing appeared out of the ordinary, and he turned back to place another beer mug on the shelf. In the mirror above it was a reflection of a man standing behind his right shoulder, pale and drawn with dark, lank hair and black, angry eyes meeting Ash's.

Ash shouted and whirled around, throwing himself backward against the shelves that lined the mirror.

No one was there.

He remained plastered against the back wall of the bar, panting for breath as his entire body flushed with cold terror. His eyes darted around the room, trying to locate the man.

He'd been standing so close, nearly touching Ash, and yet Ash hadn't felt or heard anything but the chill. He grabbed one of the heavy flair bottles and held it up high, peering over the bar to see if the man was crouching there.

Nothing.

The room was empty, and Ash could see from where he stood that the door was still locked. There was nowhere to hide in the large, open space, and there was no one there.

Footsteps pounded down the stairs, and Ryan hopped through the doorway, looking around. "You okay?"

Caleb ran into Ryan's back like two characters from the clown parade. Delilah came hurtling through the kitchen door with her broom at the ready. "What happened?"

"There was a guy," Ash gasped, the flair bottle still held up like a weapon.

"What guy?" Caleb asked.

"I don't know! I saw him in the mirror, he was like . . ." He gestured behind his shoulder to show where the man had been standing. "Right there! When I turned around, he was gone. I can't breathe." He put a hand to his chest and tried to gasp for air. He realized there was shattered glass all around him. He'd knocked all the glasses off the shelves.

"He's having a panic attack," Caleb whispered to Ryan, and hurried around him toward Ash.

Delilah reached for the phone at the end of the bar.

"Don't!" Ash said as she picked up the receiver. "Don't do that. No hospitals, no 911. Please. I'm okay."

"You sure?" Ryan asked.

Ash nodded and met Caleb's eyes, then looked at Delilah, waiting until she replaced the receiver before he broke eye contact. "Just . . . can one of you drive me home? I think I need to get out of here."

Ash woke slowly, curled in his tangled sheets and sighing when he remembered that Caleb had forbade him to come to work today. He didn't have to move at all for the next forty-eight hours if he didn't want to.

His head was pounding and his muscles were sore and not at all happy about having spent the entire night tense and hiding under the covers. He stretched and turned his head to look out the window, wincing as the pre-noon sunlight streamed through the blinds onto his face.

He pushed up on his elbows and peered groggily around his bedroom. The vintage-inspired iPod dock alarm clock on the windowsill said it was nearing noon. The time clicked over and the alarm began to blast music meant to roust him out of bed.

If he'd been planning to disobey Caleb's very specific order not to come to work, he wouldn't have made the lunch crowd. He hadn't even bothered to shower the night before, too exhausted and freaked out to do anything but crawl into bed and surround himself with pillows as if they would protect him.

In the light of day, he was embarrassed over just how close he'd come to panicking the night before. Delilah had dialed a 9 and a 1 before he'd calmed himself to a respectable point.

The sheets pooled in his lap as he sat up and rubbed at his face. His fingertips came away smudged with kohl. His pillowcases were covered with it as well.

"You're such a freak," he said as the frenetic music of the alarm continued to echo through his condo. It looked like a beautiful day, and the way the leaves on the trees lining the street swayed in the wind made him think there might be a chill in the air. Just as he liked it.

He shivered when he remembered the chill in the bar before he'd seen the man in the mirror. The hairs on his arms raised and he had to rub them vigorously to shake off the feeling.

What was he supposed to do with an entire weekend off? This was the first time he'd lain out of work in nearly a year, and it was definitely the first time he didn't feel guilty about it. Just the thought of going back to Gravedigger's made him shiver again. He couldn't get the memory of the face he'd seen out of his mind. Everyone was convinced that the knock to his head had caused his imagination to go into hyperdrive. Maybe he did need a weekend off, just some time to lie out in the grass and stare at the sun and be safe in bed before nightfall.

He reached over and smacked the alarm clock, and the music cut off abruptly. It was time to get some daylight hours under his belt.

An hour later he had showered, foraged through his kitchen, and was dressed in a pair of black track pants and a hooded LSU sweatshirt. He grabbed his keys and left, heading across the way to pick up his neighbor's dog for a walk. Anyone who saw him in the next couple of hours would never recognize him as the man who tended bar at Gravedigger's. His unfettered hair was curly and still damp. There was no eyeliner in sight. The only possible hint of his "true identity" was the tongue ring he'd been too lazy to change out.

He walked along the pond at Byrd Park, head down as the dog tugged at the end of its leash bounced along the sidewalk and yipped at the squirrels in the trees. Finally, he grunted at the dog to stop barking. His headache wasn't quite gone yet, and the sunshine seemed to be doing weird things to his eyes, causing lancing shafts of pain every time he looked up for too long.

"Ash!" someone called from across the large pond.

Ash stopped short and looked up, shielding his eyes against the sun and squinting. He frowned when he saw Wyatt Case standing beside his blue Civic, holding up his hand.

Ash swallowed down a sudden knot of nerves and an annoying burst of excitement. He motioned for Wyatt to start walking and continued on the way he'd been going, closing in on Wyatt at the head of the pond.

"Hey," Wyatt said when they got close enough to speak.

"Hi." Ash wound the leash around his wrist to keep the dog from jumping on the man.

"I don't remember you having a dog," Wyatt said after an uncomfortable moment of silence.

Ash looked down at the mutt and shrugged. "The girl across the way broke her leg," he said, not certain why Wyatt's sudden presence was making him huffy. Perhaps it was Wyatt's non-reaction to his last advance that had hurt his pride just a little.

Wyatt slid his hands into the pockets of his khakis, looking from the dog to Ash uncertainly.

"What do you want?" Ash asked, deciding to just be blunt about it.

His hostility was poorly concealed, and Wyatt shifted his weight and shrugged. "I went by the bar to check on you. Ryan said you were having a psychotic break; I thought maybe it'd be fun to watch."

Ash blinked at him, his cheeks growing warmer. "Oh." He and Wyatt looked at each other for a long moment, and Ash finally just laughed. "I'm sorry. I just . . . It's been a long week."

Wyatt offered a tentative smile. "It's okay. Honestly, if you speak to me at all at this point, I consider it a victory."

Ash frowned. "That's not what I wanted when I first met you."

"Me either. It's what I deserve, though."

Ash wasn't certain how to respond to the self-effacing honesty, so he looked away and released a bit of the leash so the dog could reach the grass.

He cleared his throat. "So how's the exhibition going?" he asked.

"It's going great," Wyatt answered with what sounded like relief. "Noah and I did the heavy research and then put a bunch of undergrad interns on it. They're much more creative with the spooky stuff than we are."

"That's good." Ash smiled. "Spooky stuff, huh?"

Wyatt gave a long-suffering sigh. "Tasteful went out the window when the Board took over. I tried."

"Well, I'm sure it'll bring in some new interest and offend some people who need to be offended. I guess I should come by and see it."

"You should," Wyatt said, his voice low and gruff, sending a thrill of pleasure down Ash's spine. "It was really your idea, you know."

"That's because I'm a genius."

Wyatt laughed, looking back over his shoulder at his car. Ash recognized him as a man with something else on his mind. It hurt a little, knowing his well-being wasn't the main reason Wyatt had sought him out.

They didn't fit in the same sphere; they'd never be able to parse the differences between the worlds of the museum and Gravedigger's. Ash sighed. "Wyatt?"

Wyatt turned back and blinked as if he were surprised Ash was still there.

Ash smiled. The absent-minded professor part of Wyatt was charming. "Was there something else besides witnessing my mental breakdown that you wanted?"

"Oh! Yeah, I . . . I was wondering if you'd . . ." He sighed and shook his head, looking at Ash in defeat. "Actually, no. I was going to ask you to have a look at some of the other documents I have about Gravedigger's, but that's just because I promised Noah that I wouldn't get near you unless it was about the exhibition and I couldn't think of another reason to come that wouldn't get my ass kicked."

Ash stared at him, both dumbstruck and elated by the honesty. "Really?"

"I'm sorry." Wyatt's cheeks colored and he looked out over the pond. "I just . . . I really wanted to see you."

"Have you eaten?" Ash asked. The dog strained on the leash and Ash tugged back to calm him.

Wyatt smiled tentatively. "What did you have in mind?"

Ash grinned and shrugged. He nodded across the street in the direction of his building. Home was about eight blocks away, and there were several restaurants and cafés between the park and there. "I could probably scrounge up something at home," he said, not mentioning any of those convenient eating establishments. "Have to get Bullseye here back to Katie before she thinks I ran off with him."

"You sure?" Wyatt asked with a bigger smile.

"Just don't sneak out while I'm in the bathroom or something, and we're good."

Wyatt had the good grace to look ashamed, but he nodded.

"Better go get your car," Ash added. "The only people that park there for extended periods of time are hookers, dealers, or undercover cops."

Wyatt raised an eyebrow as he extracted his keys from his pocket. "Extended periods of time?"

Ash just gave him a suggestive smirk and headed for Wyatt's car.

Wyatt had been determined to keep his word. Right up until he woke that morning already thinking about Ash and wondering how he was. He'd discussed it with himself while driving to work, and he knew in his heart that he could make it up to Ash and then some.

There was no reason to panic again. He'd seen what sort of person Ash was and he'd overcome the intimidating strangeness of Ash's lifestyle easier than he'd thought he could. The fact that Ash changed his tongue ring to match his outfit and exuded an odd Victorian charm and held almost rock star status among the denizens of the night didn't mean that Ash was scary. All that, in fact, just made him more intriguing. And on top of all that, Ash was interested in *him*.

Wyatt thought they at least deserved to give each other another chance.

The decision to be stand-up about it hadn't kept him from sneaking away from Noah, though. He'd begged off early, saying he had a dentist appointment. He knew Noah had an unnatural aversion to dentists and wouldn't ask any questions about the trip before or after.

Deciding to do things right also didn't keep him from feeling guilty as he followed Ash up the stairs to his door. It had the air of an illicit affair, right up to when Ash handed him the key and nodded at the door.

"I'll take him home," Ash said as he gestured to the dog. "Be right there." He turned and went to the door opposite his and knocked. The dog was sitting patiently, its tail wagging. Wyatt stood watching Ash as he tilted his ear to the door, as if listening for a call, and then reached out and opened it.

Wyatt looked down at the keys in his hand and waited.

Soon Ash emerged from the other door and raised an eyebrow at Wyatt as he strolled across the landing toward him. Wyatt handed the keys back to him, and Ash took Wyatt's entire hand in his. He looked from their joined hands to Wyatt's eyes with a crooked smile. Wyatt stared at him, mesmerized.

"Would it be inappropriate to kiss you right now?" Ash asked.

Wyatt licked his lips and inhaled deeply. "Depends, I guess."

"On?"

"What color is it today?"

Ash's crooked smile grew and he opened his mouth to show Wyatt his tongue. The lime and black Koosh ball from the previous day was still in, and Wyatt raised one eyebrow dubiously. "No Saturday special?" he asked, trying to sound disapproving but failing spectacularly.

Ash took a step and laid his hand against the door behind Wyatt. Wyatt's back hit the door as Ash pressed against him. He reached for Wyatt's wrist and brought it up, pinning Wyatt. The kiss was almost chaste, if the presence of a French tickler could be classified as that. Ash slid Wyatt's hands up the door until he held them over their heads as they kissed, Ash brushing Wyatt's lips with the tip of his tongue but pressing their bodies together hard.

The odd dichotomy of the actions sent an instant pang of lust through Wyatt's body. When Ash eased away, Wyatt exhaled shakily and opened his eyes.

"I'll see what sort of special I can come up with," Ash murmured before kissing him again and extracting the keys from his fist. He continued to kiss Wyatt as he unlocked the door, getting more heated as the door clicked open.

"I didn't come here for this," Wyatt said breathlessly.

"No?" Ash pushed Wyatt through the door and nudged it shut with his foot. "You came for lunch?"

Wyatt stared at him, unable to answer honestly for fear of saying the wrong thing.

"We can do lunch, Wyatt," Ash said with a smile. He reached out and hooked a finger through the belt loop of Wyatt's khaki pants and pulled him near. Their lips almost touched as Ash brought his head closer to Wyatt's, and then he moved away again and smirked as he backed up. Wyatt realized that the man was teasing him. Cruelly. Skillfully.

Wyatt met his eyes, frozen as he tried to decide how to react. Then he offered a rueful laugh. "I may need a minute if we're going to eat food."

Ash laughed, the sound deep and rich and lovely. Wyatt cleared his throat.

"I don't make promises I don't plan to follow through on," Ash said, voice low. "But you said you were hungry."

"I forgot."

Ash bit his lower lip and reached out to pull Wyatt near. Wyatt gripped his arms tightly and held him as they kissed. He got another tantalizing taste of that French tickler and groaned into Ash's mouth.

Ash's hands were sliding into his pockets as Wyatt guided him toward the bedroom. They missed the doorway and Ash slammed against the wall beside the doorjamb. Wyatt pulled back with a gasp and Ash moaned plaintively. The sound went straight to Wyatt's groin, and Ash tugged at him, twisting with him as they sidestepped into the bedroom and toppled onto the bed together.

Wyatt held Ash by his upper arms, and Ash arched his back and writhed under him, managing to wrap one leg over Wyatt's hip.

"What was this about vibrating tongue rings?" Wyatt asked.

"Vibrating tongue ring is a third-date device," Ash said, giving Wyatt a breathy laugh as he tried unsuccessfully to move. "You've really got a kink about restraining, huh."

Wyatt raised an eyebrow and loosened his grip.

"Don't hold back on me," Ash said. He ran his teeth over his lower lip and grinned. "Might go faster with you holding me down, but I'm willing to risk my pride for it."

Wyatt closed his eyes, letting new waves of lust pass through him as Ash's words sank in.

"Let me up first," Ash whispered.

Wyatt rolled onto his back as Ash got up and hit a button on the iPod dock on the windowsill. Music began playing, just loud enough to fill the bedroom with dark, melancholy strains.

Ash tossed a condom and a small tube of KY on the bed, then disappeared into the bathroom.

It wasn't long before he appeared in the doorway again, and he slid his fingers into his mouth and twisted them around his tongue. Wyatt knew he was doing something to that ring, but he couldn't imagine what.

When he was done, Ash slid out of his shirt and tossed it to the ground. The music playing seemed to reach a crescendo as Ash undressed.

Wyatt had trouble catching his breath. "You are fascinating," he said as he sat up on the bed.

Ash grinned and toed off his shoes, then pushed his track pants to the floor, stepping out of them and toward the bed. "You're clothed." He undid the fly of Wyatt's khakis and pulled them off him. Wyatt unbuttoned his shirt, afraid to take his eyes off Ash.

Finally, Ash had him disrobed and pushed him back to the bed, hovering over him.

Wyatt watched in fascination as Ash bent and licked the head of his cock. He groaned, and his hips jerked when a vibrating piece of metal hit his skin. His toes curled and his fingers twisted in the bedcovers. The vibrations enhanced Ash's natural ability, and Wyatt fought against the curl of pleasure in his groin as Ash went down on him, lost in the warm slide of his cock into Ash's mouth.

He reached down and gripped Ash's hair, not wanting this to be over before it had begun. "I thought that was a third-date thing."

Ash ran his tongue ring along the underside of Wyatt's cock one last time before he glanced up and smirked. "Turns out I'm sort of easy."

Wyatt laughed and reached for him. He sat up as he pulled, desperately needing to taste that vibration. He groaned into Ash's mouth and gripped his hips, pulling him into his lap. Ash straddled him, hands resting on either side of Wyatt's face as he kissed him. He was warm and solid against Wyatt's body, all hard muscle and soft skin.

Wyatt could think of nothing but being inside him. Taking him for his own. Fucking him until he screamed. It was a more violent notion than his usual lustful thoughts, but it didn't disturb him. The way Ash moved his hips against Wyatt's groin and bit at his lip told Wyatt he was on the right track. He remembered the way Ash had cried out in pleasure when he'd yanked at his hair and left deep bruises on his shoulder. He wanted the same thing.

Ash's hand left Wyatt's face and reached behind him, grabbing for the condom he'd thrown on the bed. He broke their kiss long enough to tear the wrapper open with his teeth, and then the vibration returned to Wyatt's lips and tongue and Ash's hand was between them, sliding the condom on Wyatt's cock.

Wyatt dragged his fingers up Ash's back as Ash covered him with lube. The hand Ash placed on Wyatt's shoulder to steady himself was slick and warm. Wyatt could only stare into Ash's dark eyes as he raised and then lowered himself. Ash grinned evilly, shimmying his hips and rubbing against Wyatt's cock.

Wyatt dug his hand into Ash's shoulder and pulled him down. Ash fought against the pressure but still lowered himself slowly. Wyatt's cock pressed against him, and with a roll of his hips he was spreading Ash apart. Their eyes never left each other. Ash groaned wantonly and Wyatt slid further and further into him, staring almost desperately into the black depths of his eyes. They both gasped, Ash crying out and clutching hard at Wyatt's arms. He bent to kiss him, and as it grew more heated he began to rock back and forth, working Wyatt into him as Wyatt's fingers dug into his skin. He broke the kiss with a shout and threw his head back. Wyatt reached for him, his fingers on Ash's face. He could see that chip in Ash's canine as Ash bit his lip and whimpered. Ash put both hands on Wyatt's shoulders and rode him faster, his lithe body moving sinuously against Wyatt's.

He was amazing in every way Wyatt could imagine.

Ash met Wyatt's gaze, a challenge in those dark eyes as he raised himself back up, letting Wyatt's cock slide almost out of him, the swollen head caught in tight muscles, pressing and spreading, making Ash tremble. Wyatt bit his lip and yanked Ash back down hard. Ash cried out as Wyatt's cock rammed deep.

Ash rocked and curled down, his teeth scraping against Wyatt's shoulder as Wyatt thrust into him. It was difficult to do while sitting like that, but Wyatt's body moved of its own accord. Everything about Ash compelled him like nothing he'd ever experienced. It was like being possessed.

He restrained Ash's movements just as he'd requested, rocking up into him slowly, holding him tightly as the man wrapped around him and cried out again. His entire body jerked in Wyatt's arms and he leaned away to take himself in hand. Wyatt watched, enthralled, as Ash brought himself off, biting his lip against the pleasure. He eyes were on Ash's face as Ash's muscles convulsed around him and cum slid down his chest and stomach. The best thing, though, was Ash's voice, low and wanton, as he put on his show.

Wyatt couldn't take it any longer. He held Ash tight and rolled them over, pinning his arms and thrusting into him with no regard for carefulness. Ash shouted his name, legs wrapping around him as he writhed under Wyatt's restraining hands. Wyatt pounded into him, seeking his own release, using Ash's willing body to his own ends.

He roared as the orgasm hit him.

Head bowed, Wyatt rocked his hips, eking out the last moments of pleasure. Only when the spasms stopped did he loosen his grip on Ash and pull out of him.

Ash's head was tilted back, eyes closed as he breathed harshly though his mouth. "Head rush," he panted.

Wyatt laughed and touched Ash's face.

Ash opened one eye. "You're awful butch when you really get going," he said with relish, and Wyatt laughed harder.

Ash reached into his mouth, turning off the vibrating tongue ring and then curling his nose up and grinning. "Makes my nose itch," he said with a rueful laugh. "Tongue's numb."

"My whole body's numb," Wyatt said. He bent to kiss Ash once more. Then he rested his forehead against Ash's and listened to the music for a moment as he tried to catch his breath. "I thought you Goth types looked down on Marilyn Manson," he said.

Ash blinked up at him and turned his head to listen. "Do I look like a Goth, man?"

"Well not right now. You look naked and sweaty."

"Shut up." Ash pushed at Wyatt's chest. "It's the radio, Dr. Case, I can't help what they play."

Wyatt pressed him into the bed again and kissed him roughly, unable to explain the sudden need to do so.

As soon as Wyatt climbed off the bed, Ash sat up and held his hands out like he was explaining something to a small child. "Okay. I'm going to go into the bathroom. You are going to stay here," he said with an emphatic gesture toward the ground.

Wyatt rolled his eyes and gave him a rueful smile. "Got it."

"You sure? None of this, 'Oh yeah, I had to be at work three hours ago,' or 'I thought it was the kitchen door and then there were stairs' nonsense?"

Wyatt pulled Ash to his feet to kiss him. "I'm sure," he said against his lips. Ash seemed to waver, and Wyatt stepped back and held him by his shoulders. "You okay?"

Ash opened his eyes wide and then blinked rapidly. "Yeah. Apparently orgasms and head injuries go *real well* together." He closed his eyes again. Wyatt held him until he seemed more certain of his feet. "Okay, I'm good," he finally said, nodding. Wyatt let him go and he made his way to the bathroom.

He stood looking at the half-open door for a long moment, wondering about the details of the "psychotic break" Ryan had half-jokingly told him about and just how okay Ash was. He wasn't going to allow himself to feel guilty about this encounter, though, even if Ash did still appear to be suffering from the after-effects of his head trauma.

After Ash indulged in a shower—taken with Wyatt to conserve water, of course—they sat down at Ash's table to eat.

"How did you get into . . . what did you call it? Flairing?"

Ash laughed. He loved that Wyatt was completely comfortable with his lack of urban knowledge. It was refreshing. "Yeah. Um, well it was a fluke, really. When I was a kid, this traveling circus came through town, and I was obsessed with the jugglers." Ash laughed, biting his lip as he met Wyatt's eyes. "I'd practice for hours, trying to imitate the tricks I'd seen. I got pretty good at it. Then the teenage years hit and I started doing it at parties to impress people, got even better. Started making my own routines. Caleb saw me in a bar in New Orleans one night, offered me damn good money to come here."

Wyatt smiled.

"There's a huge competition in a few weeks. I'm trying not to think about it too much or I get nervous."

"Is it here?"

Ash shook his head and pulled one foot up onto his chair. "Las Vegas."

"Wow." Wyatt looked disappointed. "That would have been fun to see. Is the flairing part of the . . . subculture of the bar?"

Ash laughed. "You just can't turn it off, can you?"

"What?"

"The scholar part of your brain. You're always researching, I love it."

Wyatt's cheeks flushed, but he was smiling too.

Ash tapped Wyatt's shin with his toes. "But no, it's not. The flairing. You called me a Goth earlier, but I'm nowhere near. Gravedigger's is more what people call gaslight."

"Gaslight," Wyatt repeated. "Noah told me something about it. And I . . . may have looked into it. Pseudo-Victorian. Gothic cousins."

"True Goths are closer to me than pale kids in trench coats and chains, and Caleb is an elder."

"I don't know what that means."

Ash grinned. "A Batcaver. You know what the Batcave is?"

"I assume you don't mean Bruce Wayne."

"No."

Wyatt shook his head.

"The Batcave was the original club in London where they first started hosting glam and then gothic rock crowds. Caleb was there at the start."

"You're kidding," Wyatt said. Ash laughed and shook his head. "But I've never seen him wearing the . . . you know . . ."

"Threads?"

Wyatt snorted.

"Their clothes are called gothics," Ash said, then shrugged. "The gothic subculture is pretty fascinating. I've done some observing. What you museum types might even call research."

Wyatt smiled that adorable, goofy smile, and Ash couldn't help but enjoy the warmth that stole over him.

"There are stereotypes," Ash said. "You know, dark clothes, white makeup, obsessed with death and all things dark and spooky. But that's oversimplifying it a great deal. It doesn't help that the newer generations don't really know what it's about. They call them spooky kids; they buy a leather dog collar and steal their daddy's trench coat and go out on the town, looking for shock value. A lot of it, though, the real gothic culture, stems from a fascination with the Victorian era and a love of gothic literature and art. That's actually what people have begun to call gaslight now, to separate the real from the trendy. That's Caleb. He's about the history. That's one of the reasons I thought he and Noah would hit it off."

"So you're saying it's more a state of mind than an appearance?"

"The attire is simply a fringe benefit." Ash grinned. "I bet you wear patches on the elbows of your corduroy jackets just because you can."

Wyatt laughed. "Point made."

"You've never seen Caleb in full-on ensemble, but he's genuine. He will occasionally break out a suit coat with tails, a top hat, and a cane."

"I can't picture that. And you don't go all out like I've seen some do."

"Well, I told you. It's a fringe benefit. I like most of the clothes, but every once in a while I just want to wear sweatpants and a T-shirt. Ryan wears a Redskins jersey and jeans when he barbeques on the weekends. The tone of the bar requires that we play it up some, and I've accumulated a good deal of favorite things. I've absorbed some of the culture, I guess. I like elements of it, and it kind of reminds me of home. New Orleans was gaslight before it was cool. But I also like to go to the grocery store in a pair of Rainbows and a polo shirt. It's like going in disguise," he said with a grin.

"Fascinating."

"It can be." Ash leaned back in the chair and propped his feet up in Wyatt's lap. Wyatt slid his hands around Ash's foot, running his fingers up his leg, and Ash smiled as the warmth of Wyatt's hands soaked into him. But then his smile fell and he looked down at the table. "Were you serious about me seeing the exhibit?"

"What?"

"You said I should come see it. But would I embarrass you?"

Wyatt's hands stopped and he furrowed his brow. "What do you mean?"

"I mean, at the museum, around your colleagues."

"No," Wyatt said, sounding horrified by the suggestion. "If anything, I'd be embarrassing you with my loafers and patches. You can't take me anywhere."

"I could take you a lot of places," Ash said softly, enjoying the way Wyatt blushed. But it didn't seem fair to keep torturing him, so he veered the conversation into Wyatt's exhibition, and they began talking about some of the cases Wyatt had dug up.

"I'm looking into the Gravedigger's address, but I haven't found much yet. I have discovered the top layer of a whole lot of people going missing. It might be connected to what was found on that plot."

Ash shivered, remembering the face in the mirror. While he wasn't sure if he believed in ghosts, he sure as hell believed in head injuries. No wonder it was manifesting in scary shit.

The conversation veered off into the LaLauries again. He tried to remember what he knew of the story from his childhood.

"The LaLauries are big time in New Orleans; their house is the first stop on every ghost tour, and their names are still a curse on the tongues of locals. Back in their time, they threw parties, were well-respected because of their wealth. Seems like a relative of one of them was actually mayor of the city at one point. Anyway, the neighbors on Royal began complaining about the way they treated their slaves. This was in 1830 . . . something."

"Eighteen-thirty-four," Wyatt said.

"Right. Wait, do you know this? Did you go research it?"

Wyatt smiled crookedly. "A little. Go on."

"Imagine the atrocities going on in that house for someone to report them for abuse of their slaves at that time," Ash said, shaking his head.

Wyatt was silent.

"Delphine LaLaurie was said to be a gracious and attentive host. Beautiful, charming. The house was lavish and extravagant, made for entertaining rather than living."

"Sort of reminds you of the mothers who make their children sick for attention," Wyatt said. "Perfect on the outside, horrible on the inside."

Ash cocked his head, squinting. "I think she was just a straight sadist. And possibly insane. I never looked at the details. I get . . . easily weirded out by true stories of evil."

Wyatt nodded and stroked his thumbs over the sole of Ash's foot.

"Come to think of it, I'm easily spooked by a lot of things."

Wyatt snickered. "Noah's that way too. I thought he was going to crawl under my jacket and cry at one point during that ghost tour we took. And he swears the ghost of Pocahontas got after him and Caleb the other night on the parkway."

"Caleb was with him that night?"

Wyatt pursed his lips and shook his head. "No," he said, completely unconvincing.

Ash nodded, but couldn't quite manage a smile. He thought about telling Wyatt what he'd seen and heard over the last week or so, but decided against it. The more he pondered it, the more he was convinced that Gravedigger's was haunted. He felt very alone for a moment, wishing he could rattle on about it to Wyatt and not sound crazy.

Eventually, Wyatt had to leave and return to work. He complained about it, and Ash teased him as they said good-bye at the door of the building.

"Can I come back tonight?" Wyatt asked.

Ash leaned against the doorjamb. "I think we'd both enjoy that."

Wyatt grinned and he leaned forward to give Ash a chaste kiss good-bye. He was turning to go when he stopped and looked down at the sidewalk. He bent to pick something up, then showed it to Ash. "Is this yours?"

It was the small fleur-de-lis charm he kept on his keychain. Ash blinked and reached out for it. "Yeah. How'd it get down here?"

Wyatt shrugged. "Maybe it fell off when you left earlier."

Ash gave that a dubious grunt, but he nodded and kissed Wyatt one more time for good measure. "See you later."

Wyatt left grinning. Ash stood at the door until Wyatt got into his car, then turned and made his way back upstairs. He stared at the empty rooms and frowned, turning the fleur-de-lis over in his hand.

"Weekends off suck ass," he muttered, realizing that after a little bit of company, he was likely to become bored and lonely. He looked down at the charm. And maybe a little freaked out.

He glanced at his watch and huffed. He was feeling fine now, and he could still get to Gravedigger's in plenty of time to help out on what was sure to be a busy Saturday night.

He glanced back at the door guiltily, as if Wyatt might somehow know what he was thinking and come back to scold him. He would call Wyatt in an hour or so to tell him he'd be at the bar. His inherent restlessness just wouldn't let him sit idly by on a day when he knew he should be doing something else. His head felt fine now, despite the slight ache and occasional lightheadedness when he stood too quickly.

He took his time getting ready, changing into his black pinstriped trousers and a white dress shirt with just a hint of ruffled, shabby details around the seams. He hunted down his black suspenders and struggled with them while trying to run gelled hands through his hair. It was too clean to cooperate and he ended up having to wet it and then slide his fingers through it to make it slick back and curl on the ends like it usually did. He then applied the kohl and changed to a tongue ring that glowed blue in his mouth.

As he examined his reflection in the mirror, he glanced over his right shoulder and stared, picturing where the face of the man in the mirror at Gravedigger's had been. He turned to look at the floor and see just how close someone would have to be standing in order to be in that spot. Really damn close.

He shivered violently and closed his eyes.

It would be okay. There was nothing to be afraid of. Even if it had been something paranormal, ghosts couldn't harm you. Could they?

And if it wasn't a ghost, then it was just some weird result of his knock to the head. When he started seeing pink elephants, he would go to a doctor.

He argued with himself during the entirety of his walk to the bar, contemplating the supernatural and wondering if he should maybe do some research into it. The likelihood that a house built in 1909 on top of an older structure full of dead bodies was occupied by some spirits was pretty high, after all. And they were always getting reports from customers about hauntings. Some of the reports even came from people who were moderately sober.

Caleb had been saying the place was haunted for years, and Delilah patently believed there was something there. Sometimes she refused to go into rooms because she said they felt funny. It shouldn't surprise Ash now to start seeing them. Unless they were the result of a concussion, in which case his brain was probably going to explode soon.

When he stepped into the bar, it was still quiet for a Saturday afternoon. He had missed the lunch crowd rush and hit the lull that always graced Gravedigger's before the dedicated drinkers started coming in.

When the cowbell on the door rang, Ryan glanced up and did a double take as he saw Ash shrugging out of his coat. "Caleb!" he called immediately, like a small child enjoying tattling on his sibling.

Ash rolled his eyes and stretched his hands over his head as he walked toward the bar. Several regulars greeted him and asked how he was feeling. A moment later, Caleb poked his head out of the kitchen door and looked around with a scowl. Ryan pointed at Ash and raised an eyebrow.

"I thought I told you to stay home!" Caleb bellowed as he came into the room.

"Did you?" Ash asked in feigned confusion. "I didn't remember . . ."

The look of alarm in Caleb's eyes was amusing enough that Ash cracked a smile and ruined it.

Caleb growled and crossed his arms over his chest. "Well you're not flairing tonight."

"That's fine. I just . . . got bored," Ash said with a shrug. "And lonely. Let me take the bar now and give Ryan a breather. Then I promise I'll just wait tables and sit on your crate for you."

Caleb narrowed his eyes and Ryan chuckled. "Fine," Caleb said. "First hint of dizziness or seeing strange men in empty rooms . . ." He pointed a warning finger in Ash's face.

"I know."

Ryan leaned over the bar and looked at him with narrowed eyes. "He's being *agreeable*," he said, sotto voce, to Caleb.

Caleb nodded without looking away from Ash. "Must have hit his head harder than we thought." Then he eyed Ash up and down and turned to go.

"Or he got laid," Delilah said as she swept past with a tray full of dirty dishes. Several of the patrons at the bar turned and looked Ash over, smirking as they turned back to their drinks.

Ash grinned at Ryan and strutted off to the kitchen to stow his gear.

Wyatt was disappointed almost to the point moroseness after getting off the phone with Ash. He had tried to convince Ash to go back home and rest, but his argument was pretty weak considering he had put Ash's body through quite a lot of stress himself just a few hours ago.

He told Ash he'd come to the bar after work, and he promised to bring Noah, who would improve Caleb's mood and keep him from yelling at Ash.

He waited impatiently for the time to come when he could leave. It was an odd feeling. He'd so rarely ever looked forward to leaving the museum, even when he was alone and walking the dark, echoing halls by himself. Unfortunately, this particular Saturday had piled work on them, mostly because they had neglected much of their duties the last week in favor of preparing the exhibition. It was nearing five when Wyatt glanced at his watch.

"You're in *lurve*," Noah said as they sat alone in the lecture hall, clicking through photos that popped up on the big screen. It was the usual Saturday fare. They purged the archives, went through a series of articles that were being moved from microfiche to digital, and categorized them as Wyatt did administrative paperwork. Sometimes, instead of working on a laptop, Noah would use the lecture hall for the better equipment.

"Don't sound so gleeful," Wyatt said. They were both fighting to stay awake. Even historians had their limits of boredom.

Noah clicked to the next picture and they both tilted their head to the side and looked at it with identical frowns. "What's that?" Noah asked.

"Crime scene photo." Wyatt scrunched his nose and tilted his head the other way. It looked almost like art, but not quite. The film was black and white, grainy and aged. The aging made it somehow more eerie, rather than less so, because it didn't seem to change the haunted, faraway look in the figure's eyes. A drop cloth had been laid out on the floor and crumpled, as if someone had struggled on it. A man lay splayed, staring sightlessly upward. A pool of black blood spread over the cloth below him.

"Crime scene photo from what?" Noah studied the file that listed all the pictures they were viewing and their provenance. "Whoa," he said as he lifted one of the sheets. "Look at the address where that was taken." He pushed the papers at Wyatt.

Wyatt glanced at it and did a double take. The address now occupied by Gravedigger's Tavern. "Let me see that." He snatched the paper and held it closer. It listed the date as 1924.

"Yeah, use the X-ray vision," Noah said. "That'll make it less weird."

"What's this from?"

Noah leaned forward. "He looks kind of like Ash."

"No, he doesn't."

"He kind of does."

Wyatt looked where Noah was pointing. The man was by no means the spitting image of Ash Lucroix, but he was lithe and wiry, with dark hair that seemed too long for the period. It was the suspenders that did it, though.

"Keep going," Wyatt said as he shoved the papers back at Noah and jabbed at the keys on his laptop to enter the description.

Noah clicked to the next picture. It was almost identical to the first, including the suspenders, but it was in grainy color and the body was well-lit. It was a young man, thin and dark-haired, staring sightlessly upward.

"What the hell," Wyatt said in growing irritation.

"This is from a copycat case of that first one, in 1976." Noah frowned down at the papers he was reading. "The next slide is an article about them. This one was taken at Gravedigger's too."

"I'm done," Wyatt said. He stood abruptly, and Noah stood with him, turning off the projector.

"You okay?"

"I'm just starting to get sort of freaked out about that damn place, you know? Ash and I were talking about those people today, the LaLauries? And I did some research. They were . . . *evil*. The things they did, they weren't human. I've never really believed in . . . supernatural stuff or . . . but those people? If anything's going to leave an evil imprint, it was them."

"They were in New Orleans, though," Noah said slowly. "Nothing to do with here."

"But that house is full of dead people," Wyatt said, pointing at the blank screen. "Something like the LaLauries happened there. Something just as evil."

Noah frowned at him. "You know how easily I spaz out, right?"

Wyatt barked a laugh and shook his head. He was trying not to spaz out himself, and the only way to do that was to poke fun at Noah.

"Are you trying to make me spaz?" Noah asked.

"No," Wyatt promised with another laugh. "Come on. I'll buy you a drink."

"At the evil bar? Are you kidding me with this shit?"

Wyatt laughed harder. Noah watched after him as he climbed the stairs, then began muttering as he followed along.

When they got to Gravedigger's, Wyatt was shocked to see Ash and Ryan climbing up onto the bar. The music began with a train whistle, and they raised their hands in unison along with it like orchestra conductors. People turned their attention and began clapping and whistling. Much like the first time Wyatt had seen them flair, it reminded him of a carnival. He supposed that was the point, though.

Ash and Ryan began their performance as Wyatt and Noah crowded into the back of the audience. The bar was packed already, and the patio was no different. Wyatt assumed word had gotten out of the incident Thursday night and had attracted some of the crazies. He turned his attention back to Ryan and Ash, half annoyed because Ash was up there, and half impressed and pleased with the performance. It purged the crime scene photos from his mind.

The routine wasn't as complicated or involved as the last one Wyatt had witnessed, and for that at least he was thankful. But he still worried that Ash would get dizzy and just step off the bar top. Both men moved identically, spinning and juggling the bottles in their hands and doing a simple little dance as they did so. They weren't mixing.

"They're like gypsies," Noah commented. He stood at Wyatt's shoulder and watched the bottles flip and spin.

Wyatt nodded and grinned.

"You've got it so bad," Noah said with a snicker.

"And I am not ashamed of that."

"There's Caleb," Noah said, pointing his finger toward the end of the bar. The man stood leaning against the wall, watching Ash and Ryan like a hawk. He didn't look happy. "God, I love it when he's huffy."

"And *I'm* the one who has it bad?" Wyatt asked as they made their way through the packed crowd.

When they approached Caleb, the man growled at them.

"How's his head?" Noah asked, regardless of the grumbling. In fact, he seemed to like it.

"He took some Advil and said he felt fine. I told him if he fell off the bar I wasn't going to call an ambulance."

"Too bad he knows you better than to believe it," Noah said. He slid his arm around Caleb and glanced back up at the bar.

Wyatt watched for a moment as Caleb turned his head and closed his eyes, just resting his chin on Noah's shoulder and appearing to soak in his presence. He might have even been breathing in Noah's scent. They really were quite the cute little odd couple. Wyatt could practically feel the attraction and contentment between them.

Ryan and Ash finished their short performance with a flurry as the song wound down. They held up their bottles and bowed amidst applause and catcalls, and then Ash sauntered to the end of the bar and knelt down to greet them.

"Liar," Wyatt said as the next song filtered through the crowd, slow and mellow to calm them.

"Ouch," Ash said with a laugh. He set the bottles down and reached out his hand. "Help me down, huh?"

Wyatt steadied him as he hopped off the bar. "You feeling okay?"

"Eh. A little dizzy, but whatever you do, don't tell Caleb." Ash glanced over Wyatt's shoulder. "Aw, they're all cuddly. It's like watching grizzlies mate."

Wyatt groaned, trying to purge that image from his mind before it could settle. "You should really go home."

Ash looked hurt. He waved his hand at the room behind him. "Do you see this crowd?" he asked. He made a gesture at Ryan and Delilah. "I can't leave them alone."

Wyatt gritted his teeth. The bar was busier than he'd ever seen it. It was very nearly standing room only. "Noah and I can help."

"What? No, we can't ask you—"

"It's not asking if we volunteer." Wyatt turned and found Caleb and Noah talking in low voices. "Noah."

Noah stopped mid-sentence and glared at him.

"We could help out here, right?" Wyatt said.

Noah's expression changed to one of amused surprise. "That's what I was just telling Caleb," he said, jabbing his finger at the man.

Caleb looked dubiously at Ash. "If they stay here to take your place, will you go home and get some sleep?"

Ash glared at Caleb, then at Noah, then at Wyatt, the rest of his body not even twitching with the movement. For some reason, Wyatt found Ash's annoyed look incredibly sexy.

Noah was right; he had it bad.

"Fine," Ash said. Wyatt began digging in his pockets to find his keys, but Ash stopped him. "I'd rather me walk home now than you walk to my place at two in the morning."

"But—"

"I've got my phone and there are people around. I'll be okay. I'm not weak and infirm." Ash grabbed his bottles and slid past Wyatt behind the bar to put them up, then walked over to Ryan to let him know he was leaving.

"He'll be fun when you get home," Caleb said to Wyatt almost sympathetically.

Wyatt just grinned at the thought. "Going home to him sounds pretty good regardless."

Ash started getting edgy as he walked home alone. He sought out the source of every rustle. Jerked his head at every movement in his peripheral vision. He was so twitchy by the time he got a few blocks away from the bar that he was afraid he'd be mistaken for a drug addict and get picked up by the cops.

He closed his eyes as he walked, rolling his head back and forth and exhaling to release the nerves. His foot hit a bit of uneven concrete and he pitched forward, barely catching his balance before he fell. His house keys went flying off into the dark.

He stopped short and hung his head, cursing under his breath. Finally, he looked up at the night sky and shook his head. "Did I fuck karma in the ass without lube or something?"

A pair of women walking down the other side of the street giggled, glancing over their shoulders at him.

"I'm sorry," he called.

One of them waved him off and smiled.

"Do you need help?" the other asked with a laugh.

"I'm good," he said dejectedly. "Thanks."

"Hope your night gets better," she said, and they went on their way.

Ash watched them until they reached the well-lit crossing, then turned back to look for his keys. A man was standing at the other end of the street, maybe ten yards away, watching impassively. Ash managed not to jerk in surprise. The guy was wearing a long coat and, if Ash's eyes weren't mistaken, a black top hat. Ash had seen too many strange outfits over the years to think twice about the fashion choice, though.

"You look lost," the man said in an oddly scratchy voice. It had a faraway quality to it that made Ash's spine tingle.

He swallowed hard and shook his head, his pride not letting him back away. Not yet. "No," he said curtly. "No, not lost."

"I think you're lost," the man said, his voice getting deeper but still hoarse and eerily distant.

Ash retreated a step, frowning as he risked a glance over his shoulder to see if anyone was around. When he looked back, he found that the man had covered half the distance between them. He gasped and took another quick step away.

Though the street was reasonably well-lit, the stranger's face remained shadowed.

"What do you want?" Ash asked breathlessly.

"I seek the lost." He moved toward Ash with measured steps. He inclined his head, revealing his face. The light struck his eyes, making them appear a milky, luminescent blue.

Ash's breath left him as if he had been punched in the gut. It was the same face he'd seen in the mirror behind him at the bar. He backed away another step as cold terror flooded him, putting his back to the nearby building.

The man darted faster than Ash had ever seen a person move, and a gust of wind seemed to slam Ash against the building. He squeezed his eyes shut as his head banged against the brick. When he opened them, the man was in front of him. His cold fingers curled around Ash's biceps, lifting and pinning him, his toes barely touching the ground.

A horn honked on one of the main roads and the cold fingers released him. Ash dropped to the ground and took off at a dead run toward the corner. He didn't look back until he'd run out into the road itself.

The side street behind him was empty.

He stood in the middle of the road, panting and shaking all over. Cars moved on either side of him.

"Are you okay?" someone called from one of the cars.

"Get out of the road!" another voice shouted as a car honked.

Ash spun around, stunned. How had he not been hit by a car? He could have been killed.

"Christ." He picked his way through traffic to the other side of the street, where he fumbled for his phone and called the bar. His keys were somewhere in that alley and he had no intention of finding them until morning. If ever.

When Caleb answered the phone, Ash shakily requested that someone come get him and bring along their keys to his place. He hung up as Caleb was still demanding to know what had happened.

Ash put his back to the wall of the building behind him and slid to the ground, his eyes on the alley and his entire body still trembling.

Just minutes later, Wyatt's blue Civic passed by him and then screeched to a halt. It backed up, and Wyatt jumped out of the car, leaving it running in the middle of the road.

"Are you okay? What happened?" He knelt in front of Ash and began pawing at him as if checking for injuries.

"Do you believe in ghosts?" Ash whispered.

Wyatt frowned and then shook his head as he helped Ash to stand. "Let's get you home."

Hours later, after the others had shut down the bar, Ash was curled on his couch with Delilah beside him, her arm around his shoulders and her fingers smoothing over his hair. He had a blanket draped around him and a cup of tea cooling in his hands. Wyatt, Caleb, Noah, and Ryan were sitting around his little dining room table talking.

They were treating him like a child scared by the bogeyman, but did he give a fuck? Hell no.

Ryan and Caleb filled Wyatt and Noah in on the incident with the man in the mirror. Ryan also discussed the banging and the music they'd heard, but then explained it away by saying that the batteries in the radio had been ruined and so was the refrigerator.

"So he's seeing things," Wyatt said grimly. "We should take him to the hospital."

"You don't believe in ghosts?" Caleb asked.

"No. Especially when the person seeing them might have brain damage."

"Hey, we saw some of those things too," Delilah said. "The night the music was playing, it did not feel right in there."

Ash shook his head as a shiver ran through him. If it had been just one instance, he'd be willing to chalk it up to the head injury too. Give him bleeding on the brain. Give him hallucinations. Anything but ghosts. But it hadn't been just one fleeting shadow or strange sound. Concussions did not slam people into walls.

They continued their discussion as Ash stood and flopped the blanket onto Delilah's lap. He walked into the dining room, and everyone fell silent.

"I'm okay. I don't have a concussion, and I don't want to go to the hospital," he said. They all continued to study him and Ash rolled his eyes, raised his glass, and then headed for the kitchen.

He stood at the sink, rinsing the glass out. He could feel one of them standing at the entryway watching him, but he didn't turn around. He didn't want to see that doubtful, ready-to-pounce-and-call-an-ambulance look in their eyes. Instead he grabbed a paper towel and looked out the window above the sink.

His fingers went numb. His glass clattered to the sink. The man from the mirror was in the alley behind his building.

He was still in the long black coat and a top hat, leaning against the corner of the building, hidden in shadow.

Wyatt hurried over. "Ash?"

The figure outside raised his head, looking up into the window. His eyes seemed to flash as the light hit them, and he held up a set of keys.

Ash backed away from the sink, heart racing, lungs frozen. Wyatt reached him and grabbed his elbow.

"Do you see him?" Ash asked, unable to tear his eyes from the window.

Wyatt turned to look out the window and shook his head. "There's no one down there." He sounded frustrated.

The others crowded into the galley kitchen. Ash pressed himself against the wall and tried to catch his breath as they all looked out the window in turn.

"He was there. He had my keys." Ash put his hand to his chest and tried to gulp in air. His entire body was shaking. His head began to swim.

"Calm down." Delilah's hands were cold when she put them against Ash's cheeks, and he flinched away from her touch.

"He's having another panic attack," Caleb said, voice remarkably calm as he grabbed his keys off the kitchen counter and left.

"Fuck, we have to get him to a hospital," Ryan said.

Wyatt and Noah both nodded. Ash shook his head in protest even as he was overcome with wooziness.

"He hates hospitals," Delilah said, sympathy and worry clear in her voice.

"It's not . . . he was there," Ash said desperately, looking at Wyatt, begging him to believe him.

"I know," Wyatt said, but he was speaking in that condescending manner people used with children, animals, and the mentally unstable. He slid his arm around Ash's shoulders.

Ash opened his mouth to respond, but nothing came out. He couldn't catch his breath and the dark around the edges of his vision was closing in.

"Breathe, Ash, breathe," Wyatt said somewhere in the distance. Ash's world went bright, and then even Wyatt's soothing voice was gone.

"You did the right thing, bringing him in," the doctor told Wyatt and Caleb as the others sat in the waiting room out front. They'd given Ash a CT scan and had him on twenty-four hour watch. He was curled on his side in an ER bed behind a curtain, finally calm enough to sleep, and the doctor kept his voice low as he spoke. "He has some minor swelling."

"Could it be causing these visual disturbances?" Wyatt asked.

"I don't believe so."

"He's very sure that he's seeing these things," Caleb said.

"Typically, hallucinations are not associated with a head injury," the doctor said. "But everyone reacts differently to trauma. It could even be a post-traumatic stress reaction to the original attack."

Caleb ran his hands through his hair and shook his head, and Wyatt frowned as he looked at the curtain.

"He's not that type, doctor," Caleb said. "He's not . . ."

"Weak?" the doctor supplied with a knowing smile. "PTSD doesn't mean you're weak, physically or mentally. It's your brain's way of coping."

Caleb closed his eyes and nodded.

"You said he was seeing things at his place of work?" the doctor said as he flipped up the chart and scowled at it.

"Yeah. Until tonight, and then it followed him home," Caleb said.

"Is he happy with his work?"

"He loves it," Caleb and Wyatt answered in unison. They glanced at each other, and the doctor raised an eyebrow.

"Well. Hallucinations are typically associated with something deeper."

"We've been talking about hauntings for an exhibit at the museum," Wyatt said. "And about the history of the bar where he works. It's . . . sordid, to say the least."

"Well, perhaps that explains why his mind has gone there," the doctor concluded.

"And the bar's haunted," Caleb added.

The doctor wrinkled his nose. "His mind may be creating something out of these recent conversations. The biggest worry, then, is why these stories are suddenly moving out of their origin and following him around."

"Look, I'm not really concerned with the why," Caleb said. "Will he get better?"

"As soon as the swelling goes down, the hallucinations should stop if that is the cause," the doctor said with a shrug. "If it's not . . ."

"Well, can you . . . drain the swelling or something?" Caleb asked.

The doctor shook his head. "You're talking brain surgery for a problem that could be easily solved with patience. A few days, he could be back to normal. Unless it's a psychological issue, of course. But I don't recommend taking steps until his head has had a chance to heal, and that includes medication. Until then, stay with him, make him feel safe."

Wyatt sighed and thanked the doctor as Caleb turned away, muttering.

"Caleb," Wyatt whispered.

"Ash is not going to accept that," Caleb said. "Hell, I'm not sure *I* accept that."

Wyatt frowned and pressed his lips together, then looked at the curtain and back to Caleb again. "What if we do a . . . an exorcism or something?"

"What?"

"I could research the property some more, bring him more information—"

Caleb shook his head. "That can't end well."

"We've got one of those paranormal investigator teams working with our exhibit. We can tell them what's going on, ask them to come help."

Caleb stared at him for a few moments, then glanced at the curtain. "If he's seeing things, it won't do any good," he whispered. "But if it really is a ghost after him, it can't hurt." Wyatt nodded. "Okay. You and Noah go and contact these people. Ryan and I will watch over him."

Wyatt hesitated. Caleb snorted. "He's a big boy, Wyatt. He'll be okay."

Wyatt felt himself blushing, and nodded. "I'll be at his place tonight to help out." He stepped into the little curtained room and peered at Ash's peaceful face. He appeared to be sleeping. Wyatt bent closer and kissed his cheek.

"Can we go now?" Ash asked.

"Soon. They're going to keep you for a little bit longer, then Caleb's going to take you home."

Ash opened his eyes and met Wyatt's without moving. "You leaving?"

Wyatt smiled down at him. "I'm going to get my laptop so I can do some work while I'm at your place."

"Work?"

After a moment's thought, Wyatt said, "I want to see just who this guy is that's following you."

Ash looked away before meeting Wyatt's eyes again. "You don't believe me, do you?"

Wyatt just smiled, unable to bring himself to lie. "I . . . I just need some more research before I can believe anything."

Ash snorted. "Museum set."

Wyatt's heart twisted at the relieved expression on Ash's face, and he bent and kissed him. He did believe Ash was seeing something. He just didn't believe in ghosts.

He left the room, nodding to Caleb as he made his way to the outer waiting room. When he got there, Noah and Ryan both stood expectantly.

Wyatt nodded at Ryan. "You can go back there."

"Ha! Seniority, bitch," Ryan said to Noah as he sauntered toward the door.

"Asshole," Noah grumbled.

"Come on," Wyatt said. "We have some work to do."

CHAPTER SEVEN

Noah crossed his arms and said for the third time, "I don't like this, not one bit. I don't have many morals, but the ones I do have are not happy."

"Spare me the lecture, okay?" Wyatt sighed as he flipped through the ancient microfiche.

"You should be back there with Ash trying to convince him he can't see dead people, not here searching stuff to feed his delusions," Noah said. "Christ, that sounded weird. And what if they're not delusions? What if he's really seeing ghosts?"

"Noah!"

"What?"

"I don't really believe in ghosts, but I believe he's seeing *something*, okay?"

"There's no scientific evidence that disproves paranormal—"

"Oh God, stop."

Noah narrowed his eyes at Wyatt. "Weird. I'm getting the 'I'm going to kick your ass' vibe off you now."

Wyatt laughed and ran his hands through his hair. "I don't know what I believe. I do know that I'm more open to accepting something paranormal than I was a week ago. I know he's really seeing this stuff. I just don't know if it's really *happening*."

"Fair enough. We also need to consider that it's a real-life dude just stalking Ash's pretty ass."

"I'd rather it be a ghost."

"Me too."

"All I know is, he was terrified when I picked him up," Wyatt said. "He can't go on like that for days while the swelling goes down; we've got to do something to help him sooner. Even if it does involve ghosts and Wiccan witch doctors or— whoa."

"What?"

"Look, it's another one." Wyatt pointed at the screen, and Noah came closer as Wyatt found the larger picture of the article he'd stumbled over. He rolled it up on the screen and they both read it. The picture of the dead man was eerily similar to the other two, even down to the sheet spread under the body.

"Nineteen-forty-nine," Noah said. "The others were, what, '23 and '76?"

"Nineteen-twenty-four, I think, yeah." Wyatt frowned, disturbed. He knew Noah was running through calculations in his head.

"No discernible pattern on the surface of it," Noah finally said. "Just guys that look alike."

"We need to find the Fossors. They built the house. And we need to find out what the hell was there before they were."

"Are you enjoying this?" Noah asked.

"What?"

"You are, aren't you?" Noah stood back up and looked down at Wyatt. "You've found something that *interests* you and you're really sinking your fangs in."

"Ash is what *interests* me," Wyatt said as he stood to face him. "And I resent the fact that—"

Noah laughed. "No, you don't."

Wyatt glared at him for a moment, and then looked away with a sigh. "I really hate you sometimes."

"Yes, I know," Noah said as he put his arm around his shoulders. "But listen, if I'm going to be helping you do this shit, I'm going to need some assurances."

Wyatt looked at the hand Noah had put on his shoulder. "What sort of assurances?"

"First, that if this goes tits up, you take all the blame."

"Oh hell, no. If I go down, you're going with me."

Noah removed his hand. "I'm serious, Wyatt. I won't lose a friend over this. You think about that before you go pretending that you're buying into all this ghost stuff."

"I'm not pretending," Wyatt insisted. "I . . . I'm skeptical. But I'm willing to keep an open mind, because—"

"Because Ash is an incredible lay."

Wyatt frowned at him.

"I say we nix the ghost thing and just don't leave him alone for a while," Noah said. "I'm serious, I don't like messing with this shit."

"Are you scared?"

"Yes! It freaks me out, okay?"

Wyatt laughed. "Noah! You have a black belt!"

"What good does that do against ghosts and hobgoblins? Just because I can kick your ass doesn't mean I'm not tender."

"Please." Wyatt's eyes fell on the grainy news photo, and he sighed. "You've got to admit there's something weird there."

Noah nodded. "I do. What I don't understand is why you do. You're obsessing about this."

"It's just so odd. Call it academic curiosity."

"Whatever you say, boss, but I want to go soon." Noah glanced around the archives. "I'm allergic to spooky basement-type places at night."

"Yeah, yeah. What do they call a collective of ghosts?"

"I don't know. What?"

"A fraid."

Noah barked a laugh and slapped a hand over his mouth like he thought he should be ashamed for laughing. "Touché," he said as they settled back down to dig into the archives.

Ryan was stretched out beside Ash on his own bed, reading a motorcycle magazine as Ash stared at him listlessly. Caleb was in the other room, cooking something that smelled wonderful but made Ash's stomach protest.

"I hate you a little bit right now," Ash said to Ryan, who nodded and flipped a page without looking up.

Neither of them moved when Wyatt and Noah arrived at his condo. Both men had their arms full of documents and books. Ryan stayed in the bedroom as the other three settled in the kitchen. Ash could hear them discussing something. He suspected he should care what they were saying, but right now, nothing mattered.

Wyatt stuck his head in the bedroom and smiled when he saw Ash lying there awake. "Hey."

Ryan closed his magazine and gently bopped Ash on the shoulder with it as he got out of bed. Ash didn't even have the reflexes to shut his eyes when the magazine touched him. He blinked at Wyatt and then focused his attention back on the sheets in front of him.

"Gave you a little medication, huh?" Wyatt asked as he walked over to the bed.

"Ghostbusting pills," Ash murmured. "That's what the doctor said. Like I was an idiot and didn't know he didn't believe me."

Wyatt's brow furrowed and he sat on the edge of the bed. He reached out and ran his fingers through Ash's spiked hair. "You need a shower. Make you feel better. And smell better."

"Am I crazy?" Ash asked. "Am I delusional or . . . is this really just in my head?"

Wyatt licked his lips and hesitated.

"I felt that man grab me," Ash said. He reached for his arm and rolled up the sleeve of his T-shirt. Wyatt peered closer at a set of bruises on Ash's bicep. "There's more on the other arm."

Wyatt swallowed and reached out to place his fingers over the shallow bruises. "I grabbed you there," he said, his voice low and intimate. "Remember?"

Ash let his eyes travel down to Wyatt's hand where it still lay on his arm. "Yeah," he said, his brow furrowing. It was confusing, all the facts and memories jumbled in his mind. Like trying to put together a puzzle through a blindfold of gauze.

For the first time since he'd seen that face in the mirror, he began to doubt what he had witnessed with his own eyes. Could he have just imagined everything? He'd never been hit in the head so hard before, and it wasn't the only knock to the head he'd had in the last two weeks. Was it possible that he was just suffering from some weird concussion symptoms?

He closed his eyes and sighed. Wyatt bent over him and pressed his lips to Ash's temple as his arms slid around him.

"I feel so lost," Ash whispered. He stopped short as he realized what he'd just said. *I seek the lost.* A shiver of panic ran through him, halted by Wyatt's arms around him. "That's what he told me, Wyatt."

"Who?"

"The top hat. He said he sought the lost. Is that why he's after me?"

"No, Ash. No," Wyatt murmured against his temple as he tightened his hold. "You're not alone. You're not lost. We're all here with you. I'm here with you."

Ash nodded and met Wyatt's clear blue eyes. They were so very different from the luminescent blue that haunted his dreams.

Wyatt ran a hand through his hair as he looked down at him. Ash caught his breath just before Wyatt bent to press a kiss to his lips. It wasn't heated or lustful like the others had been. There was something sweet and comforting about it, something that felt safe and familiar. Warmth stole through Ash's body, and he hugged Wyatt's neck and tugged him down to lay with him.

"I'm here," Wyatt whispered against his lips.

"Thank you, Wyatt," Ash said. He closed his eyes and let Wyatt's presence chase away the doubts.

Caleb came to check on them a short time later. He cleared his throat from the doorway. Wyatt raised his head and Ash forced his eyes open to look.

"Need anything?" Caleb asked.

"Is everyone still here?" Ash asked, a mixture of shame and guilt filtering through the fog.

Caleb nodded. Ash sat up. "I should get up."

Wyatt sat with him, swinging his legs off the bed. "You want to see what we've found?"

Ash nodded. He managed to roll himself out of bed and trudge to the outer rooms. Noah had deposited their finds on any hard surface he could manage. There weren't enough places for all five of them to sit in the living room, so they gathered around the dining room table instead.

"Turns out a little hard research on the LaLauries was all it took to find them," Wyatt started as he settled down and frowned at all of the crap on the table. Ash propped his feet in Wyatt's lap and stared at him blankly. "They fled New Orleans and went to Mobile, Alabama, where they took a ship headed for New York. The ship made two stops, one in Charleston, South Carolina, and one near Richmond because of some sort of mechanical difficulty. They were here overnight."

"That's where the rumors started, then," Ryan said, then bit into an apple. They all stared at him as it crunched, obscenely loud in the otherwise heavy silence. He looked around. "What?"

"Calm yourself," Caleb said gruffly. He looked back to Wyatt. "So. Richmond?"

"Yeah. They went on to New York after the ship was fixed, stayed in a luxury hotel, went to the opera a few times," Wyatt said in what Ash thought might be his lecturing voice. It was slower than his speaking voice, and deeper. It sent a thrill through Ash's body despite how freaked out he was. "Then they sailed for France and lived out their lives just outside of Paris. Dr. Louis LaLaurie actually published his memoirs, the notes that he kept during his experimentation on his New Orleans slaves." Wyatt's lip curled. "It was used as a teaching manual for about fifty years."

"So much for justice," Ash whispered.

"He's burning in Hell now, at least," Caleb growled.

"The doctor died in the 1850s, a wealthy and revered man," Noah said with distaste. "Delphine LaLaurie died in the 1870s. When news of her death reached New Orleans, there was a celebration."

Caleb crossed his arms and frowned. "So, what's this got to do with us?"

"Not a damn thing," Wyatt said, frustrated.

Ryan groaned. "What the hell, man?"

Noah looked to Ash. "We just wanted you to know what it's not."

Ash nodded and gave him a weak smile. He knew Noah was terrified of the supernatural because he believed, and he knew Wyatt didn't. The fact that they'd both spent most of the day doing this for him was enough.

"But," Wyatt said with a little more enthusiasm, "we did find some history that does pertain to you."

"Let's have it," Caleb said.

"The original plot of land that Gravedigger's sits on was used as a tavern, inn, and medical practice all rolled into one," Wyatt said, going into his lecturing voice again. "It was built on the land of the French doctor I told you about, and he leased some of the space out for extra cash."

Ash stared sightlessly for a long moment and then nodded as he tried to refocus. "And the Fossors?" he asked with a frown. "What have they got to do with it?"

Wyatt shrugged. "There's no record of any family named Fossor in the early twentieth century until they showed up in Richmond and bought the land. It's possible they were immigrants who changed their surname, but there's nothing on them. Don't know where they came from or why. But I'll get to that in a minute."

Noah broke in; it seemed the two of them were used to tag-team lecturing. "So far, we have a tentative timeline for the Gravedigger's land. The original farmland was parceled up and sold to a Virginia newcomer, a doctor who was said to be from France. His name was DuBois."

Ash sat forward, eyes wide. "DuBois. So the legend got it partially right."

"It seems," Noah said. "He opened up a practice from his home, and when that began to grow and prosper, he turned the original house into the tavern/inn/doctor's office and moved his family to a larger home built further back on the land. By all accounts, the doctor and his wife were good people, well-respected, blah blah blah. They were here for roughly thirty years."

Wyatt flipped through one of the folders they'd brought. "When rumors of war started brewing, the doctor picked up his family and moved them back to France."

"Right. All but one son," Noah stated as he pointed to a particular document. "This deeded the land from a Dr. Francois DuBois—"

"Rhymey," Ryan said.

"Shut up, crab cake. From the doctor, to his son, Vincent." Wyatt held up an old tintype of the son to show them.

"Tall, thin, dark hair," Ryan said as he peered at it. He looked at Ash critically. "Kind of like you."

"I hate you. Shut up," Ash grunted, earning a chuckle from Ryan as he took another bite of his apple. "Why'd the son stay?" he asked Wyatt. "Watch over the land?"

"Possibly. My feeling, though, from all these accounts and reading between the lines, is that the son was a bit of an outcast. His family was glad to leave him behind. As a young boy he hung around his father's office and spied on the procedures he did. The records describe him as 'touched.' That's pretty much—"

"Polite way of saying batshit crazy," Noah said.

"Right," Wyatt said. "He was intelligent, though, and charismatic, although he never courted any of the local daughters. General feeling seems to be that he may have been a repressed homosexual who turned violent in his youth because of his 'confusion.'"

"Why are you queers all so violent?" Ryan asked with mock sincerity.

Ash snorted and kicked him under the table.

"See!" Ryan cried, pointing at Ash.

Wyatt huffed at them and shifted in his seat. "Anyway! By the time Vincent DuBois turned twenty-five, strangers, drifters, and the occasional visitor to town were known to be disappearing with frightening regularity. Rumors started about his involvement, but nothing was ever proven."

Ash swallowed hard. "Was he killing these people and then hiding them in that storeroom under the tavern?"

Wyatt held his breath for a moment, then nodded. "From what I can tell, he killed them there, too. It was his own little doctor's office, complete with all the tools his father had left behind."

"Sort of like LaLaurie after all," Ryan said.

"That's just great," Caleb said.

"When the Civil War came along, it gave him a new outlet," Wyatt continued. "Vincent DuBois rose all the way up to lieutenant colonel in the Confederate army before being demoted due to 'cruel and unusual' acts against both prisoners of war *and* his own men. I couldn't find anything detailing what he'd done, specifically, except this reference in one infantryman's diary that talks about an unnamed officer who he saw 'engaged in unnatural acts' with the dead bodies of enemy soldiers."

Noah grunted. "Ew."

"Oh, gross."

"Agreed," Caleb said.

Ash glanced at him and nodded, his lip curling in disgust.

"Yeah," Wyatt said. "After the war, his land was confiscated and he was sent to jail for a very long time. The court records of what exactly it was he did or was accused of have been lost or destroyed. I couldn't find them anywhere."

"Damn," Ryan said. "And I was so hoping to have more detailed nightmares tonight."

Noah held up his hand. "Word."

"The records go on to say that Vincent DuBois was released from prison ten years later for his 'exemplary behavior and gentlemanly conduct while incarcerated.' He immediately went back to his family's land, which was no longer his, remember, and set fire to every building on the property, save for one. Five people were killed, either caught in the fires or trying to put them out. Vincent was found in the one building he didn't destroy, the old tavern. He was rumored to have been found on a rumpled sheet, bleeding from a self-inflicted wound in his neck."

"The tavern was his sanctuary," Ash said distantly. "He didn't want to sully it."

Wyatt stared at him for a moment, then nodded. "The tavern was condemned and then destroyed within the year. The town promptly forgot about the embarrassment and swept the story under the rug. Over thirty years later, the land was parceled up, the lot was bought by the Fossors, and the house was built."

Ash frowned at Wyatt. "Is that the end of it?"

"Not really," Wyatt said. "There have been three deaths on the property that mirror the death of Vincent DuBois almost exactly."

"Murders?" Ash asked.

"Suicides."

"Oh."

"Yeah. Three that we've found. 1924, 1949, and 1976. All the victims were young men in their late twenties to early thirties, dark hair, around six foot, and slight of build."

"Like me."

Wyatt nodded. "I've got the pictures of the—"

"I don't want to see those," Ash whispered. "I don't get the connection."

Wyatt blinked at him and then glanced at his copied articles as if they should be self-explanatory. "If you'd look at the photos, you'd be able to see how similar they are."

"Then explain it, 'cause I'm not looking at pictures of dead guys who look like me."

Wyatt nodded. "Right. Sorry."

With a sigh, Ash looked down at the papers spread across the table. "Who were they?"

Wyatt looked less sure of himself after Ash had snapped at him. He'd come a long way from the shy curator who'd stepped through the door of Gravedigger's a week and a half ago, but Ash wasn't the only one who needed a little coddling right now. He reached out and patted Wyatt's knee.

Wyatt took a deep breath and shuffled his papers. "The first victim was the Fossors' youngest grandson. By all reports he was a stand-up guy, well liked. Battled with what appears to be depression. The most popular rumors of the day involved him and a boarding school classmate."

"Sounds like he was a queer who managed *not* to turn into a sadist," Caleb said, glaring at Ryan almost playfully.

"Right." Wyatt looked between them, probably still not used to the antagonistic way they played off each other. "His death was ruled a murder, and the case was never solved despite all the money the Fossors threw around trying to find the killer. The Fossors lost everything shortly after that when the Great Depression hit. Their house was sold, and then sold again less than a year later halfway through a restoration because the family who'd bought it swore it was haunted and wanted nothing to do with it. By the time of the second death in the late forties, the house had been cut up into apartments."

"Like every other house in the area during the Depression and after the War," Ryan offered.

"The 1949 death was ruled a suicide," Wyatt said. "He was a soldier. He came home from the war traumatized, having lost his best friend to a sniper round. The rumors, again, said that he and the other young man had actually been lovers. People thought it was just the last straw for him after what he'd seen in the European theater. No one knew about or remembered the earlier death in the same house, so they didn't connect it."

"So what do you propose is the soldier's connection?" Ash asked.

"The way he died, his appearance, his location, and his rumored sexual orientation."

"Well that's not shaky at all," Ryan said.

Wyatt shrugged, unapologetic. "I'm stretching my mind here to ponder the fact that a vengeful ghost is popping up every few decades and killing people, okay? Work with me."

Ash stood up and paced away a few steps, a frown furrowing his brow. "Ghosts don't kill people," he said, trying to convince himself.

"Then why are you afraid of him?" Wyatt asked. Ash turned around and glared at him. Wyatt just shrugged.

"So, what, you propose that these men were all killed by a ghost?" Noah demanded.

"No. Okay? No. I'm just saying, here are the facts. Make of them what you will."

"Lay it out for me," Ash said, watching Wyatt and Noah with a frown. They were fighting, he could tell that much. He wasn't sure why, though. Wyatt peered up at him.

"At the time of the third death, the press thought it was a copycat of the first, which someone managed to unearth for the sensationalism of it. But later, forensics proved that the man killed himself." They all stared at Wyatt with blank expressions. He continued. "There were no ligature marks, no signs of struggle. He just set the sheet up, laid down, and stabbed himself in the neck. It took him a long time to bleed out and he never even tried to get help. The press got a hold of it and someone investigated the initial murder and found the same things. In most suicides, there are signs that the person hesitated, had second thoughts or shied away from inflicting the killing blow. Not the case with any of these. All three cases are nearly identical: an otherwise healthy, sane, intelligent young man just up and offs himself for no apparent reason."

"With the exception of the soldier," Ryan said.

Wyatt shrugged. "His motive was just rumor and conjecture."

"You're implying the ghost of Vincent DuBois drove them to it." Ash could hardly force the question from his locked throat.

Wyatt shrugged again. "You said he told you he was seeking the lost. Maybe he considered himself lost, and he saw himself in these men." He bit his lip. "Maybe he sees himself in you."

"Wyatt!" Noah shouted. "What the hell, man?"

"I see myself in you. Worst pickup line ever," Ryan grumbled.

Ash looked between them uncertainly and licked his lips. "Are you saying this to humor me? Because you think it's what I want to hear?"

"Is it?" Wyatt asked.

Ash breathed in deeply. "Maybe."

Noah leaned closer. "You want to hear that a homicidal ghost is after you?"

Ash frowned. "Not when you put it that way." He turned to Wyatt. "You're not making it up?"

Wyatt gestured to the array of historical documents laid out as proof and shook his head. He met Ash's eyes, looking a little scared, but not breaking eye contact.

"I guess . . . I appreciate the thought?" Ash finally said. "But now I'm even more freaked out, okay? What do you propose we do?"

"You can't go on like this," Caleb said.

Ash glared at him and crossed his arms, but he knew Caleb was right.

Wyatt reached for Ash's hand. "Let me call the people who worked with us to set up the exhibition."

"What people?"

"We did a lot of consulting with local ghost hunting societies," Noah said. "Exorcists, ghost . . . purgers, whatever they're called.

Wyatt nodded and smiled at Ash. Ash remembered him talking about the several groups he'd contacted, including an affiliate of the Atlantic Paranormal Society and a Wiccan spiritualist.

Ash hung his head and tried to come to terms with whether he should be embarrassed or relieved. Even if it was all bullshit and Wyatt was just humoring him, it wouldn't hurt anything. If it was real, though, if there really was some homicidal ghost after him because he had curly dark hair and liked men, he wanted help. But this was too much. It was ridiculous. "No."

"Ash."

"I said no, okay? I'm not a fucking sideshow."

"That's not what we're saying. We're just looking out for your peace of mind."

Ash closed his eyes and took a deep breath. He could still see the milky blue of the apparition's eyes, and it sent shivers down his spine. "Fine," he said after taking a minute or two to simply breathe.

Wyatt stood to retrieve his phone from his satchel. As he dialed, Noah looked around at the others and smirked. "Is this an appropriate time for a 'who you gonna call' joke?"

Caleb rolled his eyes and tossed a napkin at Noah's face. "It's a good thing you're pretty, lad, or I'd have to kick you out of bed."

"I'm bendy too."

"Aye, you are that," Caleb said with a laugh.

Ash covered his face and retreated to his bedroom before any further mental images could embed in his mind.

Wyatt wasn't sure what to expect from the people he called to come to the bar. They were a Wiccan group of spiritualists who helped people with possible hauntings and houses that needed spiritual cleansing.

The members he'd spoken to had seemed nice enough, and surprisingly normal and reasonable when Wyatt expressed his doubts about the whole thing. They arrived at Gravedigger's the next Sunday, the first day the bar had been closed down and empty since they'd made their plans. Four of them showed up and greeted Wyatt and the others, requesting they not be given any information about what had been happening until after they had completed their tour of the tavern.

Ash sat on the bar and bounced his knee on a stool as they walked around the tavern. They reminded Wyatt of people in a trance. They were silent and peaceful as they moved, cocking their heads back and forth as if they saw and felt things Wyatt couldn't.

One of the women—Gwynn, Wyatt thought—came up to Ash and studied him until Ash shifted. "Your gift is stronger than most," Gwynn said to him. "Are you the one having these experiences?"

Ash nodded.

"Some people are more sensitive than others. I believe that's why you've been targeted. We don't encounter many evil beings," she said, as if it were an everyday statement. "But I fear you have one here. It is very strong. Don't worry."

Ash glanced at Wyatt in silent accusation, but Wyatt smiled back. It was unsettling, and he wasn't even sure if he believed in any of it.

The lone man who had come with the team stood at the bottom of the stairwell that led upstairs and retrieved a sketchbook from his bag. "Is there a downstairs?" he asked without turning around. He was peering up the steps.

"There's a root cellar," Caleb said. "You can only get to it from outside now."

"But the entrance used to be inside?"

"Yes. Where the bathroom is now."

The man nodded and started up the stairs.

"The house has been renovated?" one of the women asked Caleb.

"Several times, yes."

"You've been doing renovations recently, though?"

"Little by little, over the last decade or so."

"And in the last few months?" the woman asked. "Anything large?"

"We completely redid the kitchen. There was a fire, it had to be gutted."

The woman was nodding. "Renovations can disturb the spirits. To them, this is still their home. They want to know what you're changing and why. Fire is especially troubling to them, though. It can cleanse them. The fastest and easiest way to rid yourself of a ghost is to burn the house down." She laughed, as if anything about what she'd just said had been funny.

"I see." Caleb scowled at Wyatt with the same accusing kind of look Ash had given him. Wyatt was hard-pressed not to laugh.

The team moved around for roughly an hour before congregating once more in the bar room. The man turned his sketchbook around and tapped it to get Ash's attention. "This man is not happy."

Ash lost all color as he stared at the drawing—an uncanny likeness of the tintype of Vincent DuBois Wyatt had produced from the museum.

Instead of a Confederate uniform, though, the man in the drawing was wearing a long black coat and a top hat. His eyes, even in the charcoal drawing, were intensely disturbing. They seemed luminescent somehow.

Wyatt shivered and looked away.

"There has been much pain here," Gwynn told them. "There are spirits that need to be freed and we can guide them by doing a cleansing of the structure and showing them the light. Most ghosts are merely the spirit of a person who has died, left in this plane of existence for one reason or another. They cannot see the light when they die for various reasons, whether because of unfinished business, addiction, or a sudden, confusing, painful death."

"Addiction?" Caleb asked.

"Oh, yes. That's one not many people know of, but addicts quite often cling to this world. Even in death, they are plagued by their cravings. Bars and taverns, crack houses, and rehab centers are especially haunted places."

"Huh."

"Most spirits are harmless, merely confused or lost. This one, however, he doesn't want to leave," she said as she pointed to the charcoal drawing the man still held. "A simple cleansing may not be enough."

"He's malicious. Very much so," one of the other women said.

"And he's fixated on the young man," Gwynn told Wyatt with a concerned glance at Ash.

"Why?" Ash asked.

"I can only guess. You do look quite like him. You're a fixture here, a place he still considers his. You're more sensitive to his presence than others. And I understand you were attacked? He may even see you as an easy target or lost due to your injury."

"Lost?"

"Yes."

"That's the word he used. He said he seeks the lost."

She nodded, unperturbed. "Don't worry." She began taking out twined rolls of what smelled like sage and setting them on the bar. Wyatt knew from his research that they were called smudge sticks.

"It can be risky," the man said as he set the charcoal drawing down on the table. "There's the possibility that it won't work and will provoke him further."

Gwynn nodded. "And especially strong spirits have been known to insinuate themselves into anyone who is not sober, is unsettled, or is overly emotional."

Wyatt looked at Ash, thinking that he sort of qualified as all three at the moment.

"It may be best if you leave while we do this," Gwyn told them.

"I'm sorry, leave?" Caleb said. He bent an ear toward Gwynn like he might have misheard her.

She nodded.

"I'm not comfortable with that," Caleb said. Wyatt was surprised he was that polite about it, from everything Noah and Ash had said about him.

Gwynn looked at a loss for a moment, but then she brought her hands together and rounded her shoulders. "Well then, perhaps it's best if you join us in the cleansing. I'll instruct you and we can each take a room."

Wyatt and the others looked from her to Caleb. No one in the room seemed to want to do that.

Caleb rolled his eyes. "All right. Let's get this over with then."

Wyatt groaned inwardly, but he tried not to let it show. He was there to support Ash, no matter how freaking strange he found this whole thing.

Gwynn gave them each a smudge stick and a plastic bowl, then instructed them to stand in a circle in the middle of the room. Wyatt had to fight not to be cynical about this hippy dippy stuff. While he might believe in ghosts, the rest of it just didn't wash with him, but he didn't want Ash to see any trace of that.

Gwynn walked around and lit each of their bundles of sage, and told them to make certain the ashes fell into the bowls. Then she took up her spot in the circle.

"Now. We're going to stand still and close our eyes," she said, affecting a calm, almost hypnotic voice. "Focus internally, and imagine a bubble of white light inside of you."

"Wait, what?" Noah asked.

"Imagine the bubble deep in the center of your body and let it grow."

Wyatt bit his lip to keep from laughing when he glanced at Noah, who was looking at the woman incredulously.

Delilah shoved her elbow into Noah's ribs and glared at him. "Would you just try it?"

"I don't even know how to make my brain do that."

Ash snorted, but his eyes were closed.

As the woman continued talking, valiantly ignoring the peanut gallery, Wyatt closed his eyes as well, trying to do as she instructed.

"Imagine this bubble expanding, filling your body and moving past it, pushing negative energy away from you. Let the bubble grow until it is filling the room, and all the negative energy has been pushed out through the doors. In your mind, command the white light to stay and fill the room, right up to the walls, and tell it to stay in this room and protect it."

The scent of sage wafted around them, and while Wyatt could feel it growing warmer, he was pretty sure it was because he was embarrassed to even be standing there listening to this, much less attempting to do it. He didn't have a bubble in him.

He cracked one eye open to peer sideways. Ash was biting his lip, his head lowered and his eyes squeezed shut. He was either taking it very seriously, or he was trying not to laugh, and Wyatt didn't think it was the latter. A shiver ran through Ash as Wyatt watched him, and Wyatt felt a sympathetic chill slide over his skin. The room was growing colder. Wyatt opened both eyes to look up, not sure why his gaze was drawn that way. There was nothing out of the ordinary, and certainly no giant white bubble chasing evil out of the building.

"This is ridiculous," Ash muttered.

There was a fine line between believing that the bar was haunted and standing here trying to form a thought bubble to chase away evil beings. Wyatt also had a feeling that the others were all just as nervous as he was. The only outlet seemed to be laughter. Caleb cleared his throat as they all began to snicker. "You know, maybe it's better if the professionals take care of this."

"I believe that's best," Gwynn agreed.

They filed out onto the patio to wait. Wyatt sat next to Ash, whose knee bounced so rapidly that Wyatt thought he might get seasick just watching. His nerves were starting to spill over, and Wyatt felt like they were spreading to the rest of the group too, making everyone tense and edgy. Delilah paced, her arms wrapped around herself. Ryan was going from table to table, straightening chairs, the grating sound of metal on the concrete adding to the edgy heft in the air.

"Ryan," Caleb finally said through gritted teeth. "Sit down."

"Please," Noah prompted. He put a calming hand on Caleb's shoulder.

"Sit down, please. Now."

Ash snorted and shook his head as Ryan found a chair and slid into it. Ash leaned closer to Wyatt's ear. "Noah and Caleb need to reproduce and make little Buddhist ninja babies."

Wyatt laughed before he could stop himself.

It took another twenty minutes before Gwynn appeared in the doorway. She was still holding a smudge stick in one hand and an abalone shell bowl in the other. She snuffed out the smudge stick in the convex shell and held it there until she had smothered out the embers and it was no longer smoking. Then she took the ashes and sprinkled a line across the doorway.

"Health code violation," Caleb grumbled under his breath.

Wyatt glanced at him, but his attention was drawn back to the woman when she spoke. "I went through each room on both levels, and Frederick addressed the root cellar. It's hard to tell if there is still a presence here now. Give it perhaps a week or two, and if you're still experiencing things, we can return and try something more aggressive."

"Like burning down the house?" Wyatt asked, smiling gently.

"Sometimes, Dr. Case, that's all you can do," Gwynn said, and again it was difficult to tell if she was joking. "Blessed be," she said with a bow of her head, and she and her three companions gathered the bags they had brought and departed.

Ash rubbed his hand over his face. "That was weird. This is weird."

"You're weird," Noah said.

"Stop," Caleb said before the discussion could degenerate further. "What now?"

Wyatt shrugged, and no one attempted to answer for a long time. The wind picked up and pushed leaves and bits of paper around their feet. The ash along the doorway began to scatter. Wyatt looked up at the house, for the first time feeling uneasy about the whole business. It felt so anticlimactic.

"I guess . . . we wait?" Ryan finally said.

Wyatt met Ash's eyes, seeing the same uncertainty there. They all seemed to feel as if something still hung over them, waiting to be untethered and fall.

"Great." Caleb grunted as he stood. "I'm going home to get laid."

Noah raised his hand like a child in school and pushed himself out of his chair to follow. "That's me."

Ash smacked his forehead and Ryan groaned. He offered his hand to Delilah, and just like that, the group dispersed, leaving Wyatt and Ash sitting there alone.

Wyatt reached out to take his hand. "Feel better?"

"No."

Wyatt snorted. "Hey. How would you like a private tour of the Virginia Historical Society?"

Ash smiled gamely and raised a sardonic eyebrow. "You think a creepy old deserted museum will make me feel less haunted?"

Wyatt winced. "Not when you put it that way."

The wind picked up again, plucking at Wyatt's pants legs and ruffling his hair.

Ash squeezed his hand and gave him a more genuine smile. "If you're the one giving it, Dr. Case, I'd love a creepy tour."

The museum was dark and quiet, heavy with the sense of time and history that inundated every corner and crevice of the buildings. Wyatt loved the museum at night. He loved the fluttering feeling in his belly that came from knowing he was the only one there, that he had the entire sprawling sanctuary to himself.

Only this time it was ten times better, because he wasn't alone.

Ash looked around in the dim illumination that came from the few lights still on. "I have to tell you, Wyatt, this is one of the more impressive dates I've ever been on."

Wyatt grinned and wrapped an arm around him. "I've never brought anyone here like this."

A fond smile curled Ash's lips. "You can be quite charming, you know that?"

Wyatt turned to face him, letting his hands settle on Ash's hips. "Thank you. I didn't deserve a second chance, but you gave it to me anyway. I promise you won't regret it."

Ash smiled, eyes warming, biting his lip as he stepped closer. "I don't regret it yet." He kissed Wyatt briefly, then gave him a tap on the chest. "Okay, show me the creepy parts so we can go find your office and do unseemly things that will make it smell like sex."

Wyatt burst out laughing even as his body responded to the suggestion. "Come on."

He led Ash toward the hall where the new exhibit had been set up, holding his hand and letting his fingers play over Ash's. Ash had surprisingly strong, callused hands. But then, Wyatt assumed he had to, considering some of the things he'd seen Ash do with a flair bottle.

Wyatt skimmed over most of the exhibits, realizing that the displays were inordinately creepy at night while the museum sat in otherworldly silence. Ash seemed grateful to be able to hurry past most of them.

Wyatt stopped him at his favorite display, though, turning to Ash with a proud smile. "This was all your idea."

Ash looked over the case, taking in the various and sundry tools of the ghostbusting trade. Just as Ash had suggested to him, Wyatt had implemented a display that went over the ways to rid a house of ghosts and to repel spirits, both good and bad.

There were smudge sticks and a plaque describing what they were and how to use them. There was a vial of salt and another plaque that outlined why it was effective: supposedly, a ghost couldn't cross a line of salt. There was a clove of garlic, a jagged spike of pure iron, a large door painted red, sticks of incense, and a bowl of holy water on a shelf.

Ash looked over all of it, nodding and sighing heavily. "Where's the white mind bubble?"

Wyatt laughed and slid an arm around his shoulders. "I'll have to add one." He turned his head to nudge his nose against Ash's cheek. "Are you okay?"

"I'm not sure. I'm uneasy. I feel like nothing's settled yet." He met Wyatt's gaze, his eyes weary and imploring. "Will you take me home with you?"

"Of course."

"I'm sorry, Wyatt, I thought I'd be okay. But it really is freaking creepy in here. Makes me feel like there's someone looking over my shoulder."

Wyatt laughed and nodded as he turned Ash toward the exit and started walking. "It is. It's better during the day."

"I'd like to come back and see it. I know how much work you put into this."

"We'll do that. But for tonight . . ."

"Tonight, I'll let you take me home and do peculiar museum-type things to me."

Wyatt laughed, and the happy sound echoed through the lofty halls, reverberating back to them as a more sinister noise. Wyatt waved to the poster of Thurston he had hung near the entrance to the hall as they passed it, and they headed out of the museum into the chilly October night.

"I'm closing down the bar for the week."

Ash looked to Ryan before turning his attention back to Caleb, who stood behind the bar with boxes of liquor and other supplies.

"Why?" Delilah asked.

All three of them were sitting on barstools, looking at Caleb with their mouths hanging open. It was the third week of October. They were through Oktoberfest, but they still had Halloween. The Gravedigger's Brawl. Even the World Series. It was the month that paid a year's wages.

"Well for one, Ash is fucking losing his mind."

"I am offended by that statement," Ash said. He could still smell the sage from yesterday's cleansing.

"I don't bloody care. And you're high, you can't flair anyway."

"Can't, my ass."

"Ash is losing his mind, the fucking appliances are breaking down one by one—even the new ones—and has anyone noticed that the electricity has been doing odd things?"

Delilah shook her head and Ryan grunted a negative.

Caleb walked over to the electrical box hidden behind a wooden panel at the end of the bar. He opened it and flicked one of the switches. Sparks flew out of it and Ash jumped as he watched them sputter through the air.

"That can't be safe," Ryan said, standing to peer down at the floor where the sparks had arced and landed.

"Really?" Caleb said. "You think? You think that's not safe?"

"So what do you want to do?"

Caleb ran his hand up along his neck, wincing. "We'll close for a week, rip the place to shreds, and redo all the wiring."

"Are you serious?" Ash said before he could stop himself.

"It's a better option than having the place go up in flames."

"You really think faulty wiring is doing all this?" Delilah asked.

"All what, Lilah? Making Ash lose his fucking mind?"

"Again," Ash said, "I am offended by that."

"A week won't hurt us. You two will be gone three days as it is to that Flair Vegas competition, so it's not much longer."

"Caleb, we're right in the middle of our biggest month of the year," Ryan said as he drew circles on the bar with his finger.

Caleb growled under his breath.

Ash cleared his throat. "Look, let's get through October, close it down after the Brawl, and do everything you want to do during November. We'll be back up and running by Thanksgiving and cash in on all the family drinking angst."

Caleb snorted and pursed his lips, looking between the three of them.

"Please, Caleb," Delilah finally said, batting her purple false eyelashes.

Caleb rolled his eyes and slammed the electrical panel shut. "Fine. But if I hear one more word about ghosts, electrical fires, or watered down beer, I'm burying all three of you in the basement too."

Ash pressed his lips together and nodded. Above them, a rumbling noise started in the attic. They all looked up with the sense of impending doom that had hung over their heads for the last few weeks, and Ash half expected to see a string of ghosts doing the rumba on the ceiling.

The rumbling became a growl, and the cord of lights hanging from the ceiling began to vibrate.

"Okay," Ryan said, sounding defeated. "I am not going up there this time."

"What the hell is that?" Delilah asked. Her hand landed on Ash's forearm.

A dark stain began to spread on the ceiling, barely discernible from the shadows and ambient light of the room, but Ash could see it getting bigger as they stared. To his horror, a drip of blood red liquid formed out of the center of the stain, and it took its sweet time as it bulged out of the ceiling and finally plunged to the floor. When it spattered on the worn hardwood, it was the color of a bruised tomato.

"Oh my God," Delilah whispered. Her fingers dug into Ash's arm.

"Good call on closing the bar," Ryan told Caleb as another drop joined the first. "I'm down with that."

Ash nodded as he watched, almost numb to the spectacle. The pool spread until it was a literal stream from the ceiling.

"I'll write up an announcement," Caleb said.

CHAPTER EIGHT

"I have to tell you, Dr. Case, I wasn't sure you would be able to pull this off," Emelda said as she and Wyatt stood at the entrance to what the interns had been calling the Haunted Hall.

"I'm still not sure we have." Wyatt glanced around uneasily. The exhibit was done, and it looked good on the surface. Things like this should take months of preparation, and Wyatt wouldn't exactly say he was proud of what had been done here. But there were droves of people here on a weekday for the invite-only preview, and they weren't just filling up the Haunted Hall, but filtering out into the rest of the museum. That alone made the hit to his professional integrity worth it.

They had yet to discern whether the exhibit was enough of a success to save Wyatt's job, but it was out of his hands now.

Emelda put a hand on his shoulder. "I can tell there's somewhere else you'd rather be."

Wyatt turned to look at her, surprised by the words and wondering if they were true. It seemed like his entire life had been about the museum for so long, he'd never wanted to be anywhere else. But now, his thoughts drifted more and more often, ambling down the road to the tavern and to Ash. They had spent last night and the night before tangled together in Wyatt's bed, their first night together in which neither of them had to get up and go right after sex. Waking up to find Ash next to him, all warm and sleepy and oddly sweet, had been enough to whet Wyatt's appetite for a lifetime of more.

"I wouldn't say I'd rather be there," he said, eyes taking in the exhibit. "But it has become an intriguing alternative."

"I daresay that's a good thing, Dr. Case. Whoever he is, he is a lucky young man. I must be going," Emelda said with true regret. "Once again, this is a remarkable example of pulling something out of your ass and calling it gold. I applaud you," she said, a smirk pulling at her lips as she turned away.

Wyatt laughed as he watched her go. She was right, of course, but only Emelda Ramsay could call it that and not offend anyone.

A shout from the far end of the exhibit ripped his attention away from her retreating form, and Wyatt hurried into the crowd of people, following the commotion. He weaved his way through them and finally found the source of the problem near the barely completed witchcraft display. Noah stood with one of the interns, holding a mannequin's head under his arm and waving a crooked broomstick in the other.

"I'm telling you, Dr. Drake, it moved," the kid was saying as Wyatt came up on them.

"Of course it moved," Noah said. He shoved the broom into Wyatt's hands without otherwise acknowledging his appearance and held up the mannequin to show the intern. "It's a creepy mannequin, they always come to life when you've been awake for thirty straight hours. Go home and sleep. Lay off the energy shots."

The intern nodded, giving Wyatt a sheepish glance as he retreated through the staff door at the side of the display.

Noah turned and flopped his hands. "Your damn exhibit is wigging out all my interns."

Wyatt tried not to laugh, but only half succeeded as he took the mannequin's head from Noah and stepped into the display to replace it.

"He said the head turned as he walked past so he took it upon himself to jump into the display and swat it off its shoulders with its own broom."

Wyatt reattached the broom. "Other than that, how's it going?"

"So far, so good."

"Nothing unusual or spooky?"

"The whole exhibit is unusual and spooky, Wy."

Wyatt snorted. He stepped out of the display case and Noah closed the glass door and locked it up. They turned together to survey the hall, which held everything from ghost stories and local myths to witches, magicians, and the art of ghost hunting. He'd given Thurston and his fellow masters of magic a section of the exhibit, just because he could. The colorful posters were a splash of vibrant, vintage color amidst a sea of otherwise drab and dreary displays.

"What did Ash think of it?" Noah asked as they walked through the exhibit together.

Wyatt winced. "He was more impressed with the, uh . . . legit exhibits."

"Uh-huh. Which one did you screw him in?"

Wyatt couldn't help the shocked look he gave Noah.

"Oh come on! New relationship, deserted museum, tongue ring. You do the math."

"We did not screw in any of them, thank you. Mind your own business."

"Not even in your office?"

"We went home and did that."

"Ha!"

Wyatt grinned, but it fell quickly. "Ash called and told me they're closing down the tavern for the week. But I didn't have time for him to tell me why."

"Caleb said he was thinking about closing up shop," Noah said. They made their way through the main lobby and headed for the break room downstairs. "He called me an hour ago all pissed off. They had talked him into waiting until after Halloween, and then as they were sitting there, the ceiling started dripping blood."

Wyatt stopped mid-step and grabbed Noah's arm. "What?"

Noah laughed. "That's what he said. Apparently the new fridge they got had an accident. They didn't set up the ice maker thingy right. It leaked all the hell over everything. Started dripping through the ceiling. It seeped through the floorboards, right? So it picked up all this wood stain and paint and ended up a nice bloody color by the time it started dripping on their heads."

Wyatt closed his eyes, snickering.

"He said they had a lot they needed to do. They're going to rewire a lot of stuff, repaint, and everything, so they closed down for a week. They're doing it all themselves instead of hiring. Caleb's a cheap bastard. He's lucky Ash and Ryan can do everything they can."

"Yeah," Wyatt said. "How did Ash take it?"

"Closing down?"

"No, the dripping blood."

"Oh. About as well as the others did, I think. Caleb said Delilah was ready to quit right then and there, but he convinced her to take a week's vacation instead. Even Ryan doesn't want to go upstairs now. It's getting spooky over there."

"That is their bread and butter."

Noah hummed and they continued to the break room. Wyatt couldn't help but worry about Ash, though. Despite the perfectly legitimate explanations for all the weird things happening at Gravedigger's and for the things Ash had seen after the knock to his head, Ash was probably seeing ghosts behind every odd sound and unfortunate accident now.

They had just sat down when Noah put his hand on Wyatt's arm. "Are you worried about him?"

"A little."

Noah grinned and shrugged. "Let's go check it out right now. Maybe they haven't cleaned up the blood yet." Before Wyatt could protest, Noah was out of his seat and dragging him up and out of the break room.

When they got to Gravedigger's, the windows and the glass in the door were covered over with paper grocery bags from Ukrop's, but they could hear music coming from inside. To Wyatt's surprise, Noah produced a key and unlocked the door.

"Wow, look at you."

"What?"

"All domesticated."

Noah gave him a goofy grin, then bit his lip. "I love him."

Wyatt patted his shoulder. "I'm glad."

Noah glanced at him, still grinning. He pushed the door open, taking care to make certain there was nothing like a ladder standing in the way.

Wyatt followed him into the darkened bar, and the sight that met them seemed to freeze his blood. Ash was on the floor, spreading out a white sheet across the wooden floorboards. He held an old screwdriver in his hand as he smoothed his fingers over the white material. Red paint had seeped through a corner of it. It was a scene from one of the old photos they'd found, brought to life.

The door opened wider and the cowbell dinged. Ash looked over his shoulder and straightened up onto his knees as he looked at them. "Hey," he said in surprise.

"What are you doing?" Wyatt asked, voice muted as he tried to get over the moment of stunned horror.

Ash looked down at the screwdriver in his hand and then pointed to a can of paint near the edge of the canvas by a large ladder. "We almost got the ceiling done before we overdosed on paint fumes and broke for lunch. What are you doing here? Isn't it the exhibit preview or something?"

Wyatt stared at him. He couldn't shake the shock of seeing what had been haunting his dreams. He wondered if Noah and Ash had noted it and chosen to ignore it, or if it was so far removed from them now that they'd put it past them.

"We heard about what happened this morning. We came to see how you're doing."

"Oh." Ash looked back down at the screwdriver and then placed it on top of the paint can before standing up. He brushed the dust off his knees and nodded at Wyatt. "I'm fine."

"Interesting color," Noah said as he peered up at the mostly black ceiling.

Ash shrugged. "Matches the wallpaper. Shut up."

Noah began to laugh. "Is Caleb here?"

"He's taking the air out back," Ash said, making a sign with his fingers that Caleb was smoking. Noah sauntered off to the kitchen and left them alone.

Ash pursed his lips and narrowed his eyes at Wyatt. "You came to see if the blood dripping from the ceiling sent me back on the crazy train, didn't you?"

Wyatt thought over his answer for a moment, then said, "A little, yeah."

"I'm fine."

Wyatt nodded and took a step closer. He studied the canvas warily, but there was nothing unusual about the scene now. They were painting the ceiling, after all. "There's another reason I came."

"Oh yeah?"

"The gala opening of the exhibit."

"Gala? That sounds all fancy, congratulations."

Wyatt smiled. "Thanks. I was wondering if you'd be my date."

Ash raised one eyebrow and smiled, giving him that same air of innocent mischief Wyatt had been intrigued by when they'd first met. If Ash ever thought about getting that chip in his tooth fixed, Wyatt would have to protest.

"It's a costume party," Wyatt said, trying to entice him.

"Sounds fun." Ash grinned wide, then looked down at his feet as he licked his lips. "But I can't. We've got so much to do before we can get up and running, and we lose money every day we're closed."

Wyatt smiled to hide the disappointment. "I understand."

"I'm sorry I'm missing your gala."

Wyatt laughed suddenly. "It's okay. Hopefully there will be others."

Ash nodded. "You think you'll keep your job?"

"Only time will tell."

"Well, if not, we can always use an extra busboy here."

"Ha."

They stood in a silence that bordered on awkward until Wyatt straightened suddenly. "What if I came to help? Could you take a few hours away then?"

Ash narrowed his eyes. "You want to help?"

"Yeah."

"You want to help us tear down stuff and rewire stuff and build stuff and paint?"

"Yeah? Why, what's wrong with that?"

Ash smiled crookedly. "I don't know. It's weird."

"Well. I don't really want to help do any of that," Wyatt admitted. "What I really want is to spend more time with you. If I have to paint to do it, then so be it."

"Wyatt. That's kind of sweet."

"Is it working?"

"Yeah." He bit his lip, but continued to smile. "Oh yeah, it's working."

Wyatt wasn't accustomed to hard labor, that much was obvious to Ash as they worked into the wee hours every night, trying to get Gravedigger's Tavern back into shape. The only time they took a break was to attend the grand opening of Wyatt's exhibit.

It was a basically just an excuse to throw a huge costume party. Ash was delighted when Wyatt told him to come however he wanted, and he got quite a few compliments on the steampunk-inspired outfit he pulled together.

Wyatt kept him by his side, his fingers brushing the small of Ash's back or lingering on his palm whenever someone approached to speak to them. And when Wyatt introduced Ash to someone, he never flinched when he added the title of boyfriend.

Ash found himself oddly at home amidst the tweed and tails of the museum set. He was just as comfortable amidst Wyatt's peers as Wyatt seemed around his. Wyatt pointed out the trustees, making certain to note the evil little toad who wanted Wyatt's blood.

By the end of the night, Ash was ready to drag Wyatt into a storage room and do horrible, wicked things to him.

The exhibit went off without a hitch. At least, as far as Ash could tell. There was music and laughter. Wealthy patrons writing checks at a table in the lobby. Exceptionally creepy mannequins in the display cases.

When it was over and they'd come back to Gravedigger's, Wyatt was still obviously worried, even though the exhibit had seemed successful. Ash assumed that was why Wyatt was here now, painting in the middle of the night. He needed the distraction.

They were tired and sore by the time they halted work a little after midnight. They sat drinking beer with the others and discussing what had been done and what needed to be done. They'd gotten an amazing amount of work accomplished in the three days since they'd shut the place down, but there was still a ways to go.

The entire building had been rewired by a customer with a license, and they had just finished repairing the drywall where needed. It had been long, tedious work, but now they had to let the patching on the walls dry before they could begin painting them.

They had torn down the wallboard that had once enclosed the stairs, and Ash was surprised by how much it changed the look of the barroom. The old stairs really were beautiful, and once they got the upstairs in working order, it would create whole new possibilities for the bar and the business.

Despite a lingering sense of unease, Ash was excited about the prospects.

He knocked a knee against Wyatt's as they sat together, and Wyatt rewarded him with a game smile.

"You can go home, you know. You don't have to stick around."

"No, I'm good. You stuck through my stuffy exhibit opening last night, I can do this."

"Wyatt. You actually have a job to go to in the morning." Ash leaned closer. "Your effort is noted and you will be laid for it."

Wyatt snorted and looked sideways at Ash again. His blue eyes darted to look past Ash, above and over his shoulder.

Wyatt's eyes widened and he lurched to his feet.

Ash froze, panic burgeoning. "What?" he managed to ask, his voice a harsh whisper. A chill crept over his bones, but he couldn't move or even turn to look behind him.

"I thought I saw . . ." Wyatt exhaled slowly, his eyes darting back and forth. "I thought I saw something."

Ash clutched at his pants leg. He forced his head to turn, letting his peripheral vision take in the empty space behind him. "What did you see?"

Wyatt's eyes were still wide, and he'd gone completely pale.

"You saw him, didn't you?"

Wyatt was shaking his head before Ash had finished asking the question. "No. No, it was just a shadow or something. From a passing car or . . . I think I'm just tired and weird right now," he said quickly. He rubbed his eyes and turned away.

Ash stood, glancing over his shoulder again. "Could you do me a favor, Wyatt? Just . . . next time you see something weird, don't react, okay? What I don't know won't hurt me."

Wyatt cleared his throat and nodded.

The floor above them creaked and moaned, and they both looked up to follow the footsteps.

"It's just Caleb and Ryan. They went to hook the fridge back up," Ash said, telling himself just as much as Wyatt. Wyatt exhaled hard.

The door to the kitchen pushed open and Caleb stepped out, carrying an armload of stair railing. He raised an eyebrow at them. "Who walked over your graves?"

Ash looked back up at the ceiling. "Must have been Ryan," he answered with a grunt.

"What?" Ryan said as he followed Caleb through the door.

Ash looked at Ryan sharply as another chill crept over him.

"Who's upstairs?" Wyatt asked.

"No one." Caleb carried the railing pieces to the foot of the steps and laid them down carefully.

Ash watched him, but he didn't really register anything but the hammering of his heart and the chill in his veins.

"Okay," Wyatt said. Ash heard him exhale again, but he was watching Wyatt, and his chest didn't rise or fall with the sound. It wasn't Wyatt sighing.

He closed his eyes, trying not to panic. He could feel a presence, like a breath on his neck, like a person looking over his shoulder. When he opened his eyes, he half expected to see the face of the man in front of him.

It was just Wyatt, though, looking at him worriedly.

"Let's get you home," Wyatt said. "Let's just get out of here, go get some sleep, and finish this in daylight."

Ash ran a hand over his chin and glanced at Caleb and Ryan, who were both watching them with confused frowns.

"Wyatt and I are hearing ghosts again."

"Oh, Jesus," Ryan grumbled, throwing his hands up. "I officially hate my job now."

Caleb was nodding, though. "You've been up for too long, lad. Go home, sleep in. We'll start back up tomorrow after lunch."

Ash shivered again, but made a valiant effort at laughing it off as he thanked Caleb and quickly gathered his things. He and Wyatt headed out, both of them tense and quiet.

"It's an old house," Wyatt finally said as they drove toward Ash's condo.

Ash nodded curtly. "Right. It creaks."

"And we're both tired."

"Yeah. Exactly."

When they got to Ash's building, Wyatt began muttering to himself as he searched for somewhere to park on the street. Ash had to place a hand over his mouth to cover his fond smile. He was sure Wyatt didn't even know he talked to himself like that.

"Do you want me to stay with you?" Wyatt asked as he finally parked.

Ash winced. "Yes and no."

"Care to elaborate on that?" Wyatt asked with a self-conscious laugh.

Ash ran his tongue along his teeth, playing with his metal stud, brow furrowed. "I want you to stay, but mostly because I'm scared. And that isn't fair to you."

Wyatt reached out to pat Ash's knee. "It's okay. I'll stay if you need me to."

Ash shook his head. "Tomorrow."

"Okay."

Ash leaned over the console to give Wyatt a kiss, and they lingered over it until Ash was having second thoughts about letting him leave. He finally pulled away and gave Wyatt's cheek a pat. "I'll see you later."

Wyatt nodded. Ash got out of the car quickly, before he could change his mind, and waved as he headed for his building.

When he pushed his door open and flicked the light on, he stopped dead. His keys fell from his fingers.

Every piece of furniture in his house was tipped on its edge. The coffee table looked as if it were teetering on a precipice. The couch had tilted so far over that the edges of the cushions were touching the floor. Even the lamp that lit the living room was tilted, its shade askew, casting odd shadows on the ceiling and walls.

Ash began to panic, his breaths hard and heavy, a tingling sensation traveling from his fingers up his arms to his head. It felt like the hairs on his scalp were all standing on end.

He couldn't move.

Hands grabbed at his arms and spun him around. He gasped when he met Wyatt's eyes.

"Are you okay?" Wyatt asked, out of breath from his dash up the stairs.

Ash shook his head woodenly.

"You screamed."

"No," Ash managed to say. "No, I didn't."

"I heard you from my car. I heard you scream."

Ash shook his head again. It wasn't possible that he'd made a noise loud enough for Wyatt to hear on the street; he'd been paralyzed. He turned and looked into his condo again. Everything was normal.

"I..."

"Ash?"

He put his hand out and flicked his fingers at his furniture. "It was all..."

"Okay, come on," Wyatt said, his voice gentle and worried as he ushered Ash inside.

Ash sat on the couch, his movements feeling stilted and foreign. Wyatt headed for the bathroom, but when he tried the door, it was locked.

"You live alone, why do you lock your bathroom door?" Wyatt teased as he went to the other bedroom to try the other door to the bathroom.

"I don't," Ash answered, voice flat. He was sure Wyatt didn't hear him.

"This one's locked too," Wyatt called out.

Ash took a deep breath as a violent shiver ran down his body.

"How the hell did you lock both doors from the inside?"

"I didn't."

Wyatt came around the corner to look at him.

"I'm haunted."

"What?" Wyatt asked, laughing, though he looked uncomfortable. "I thought we got rid of all this."

Ash's eyes strayed to the lamp. He shook his head. There was nothing to say that didn't make him sound crazy.

"I can't get into your bathroom."

Ash nodded.

"Come home with me, Ash. Let's get out of here."

"Okay."

Wyatt looked relieved that Ash didn't fight him.

"Just let me grab some stuff."

"Want me to help?" Wyatt asked, still hovering over him.

Ash shook his head and glanced at the bathroom door. "I'll just be a second."

Wyatt looked doubtful, but he finally nodded. "If you're sure."

"I am. Go on. I'll be there in a second."

Wyatt bent to give him a kiss on the cheek, and then he was gone.

Ash got up, walking to the bathroom door with a growing sense of dread. He tried the glass doorknob, and the door swung open with ease.

He shivered as cold air flowed from the bathroom. "You don't like Wyatt?" he said to the empty room. "Well go fuck yourself. I'm keeping him."

"You're haunted?"

Ash nodded, morose.

"Are you sure about this?" Ryan asked as he wiped down the bar top.

"My apartment now, too."

"That place has always been drafty as hell, man."

"Drafts don't lock doors."

"Neither do ghosts," Ryan grunted

"You don't know that."

"You don't either, Ash. You're still coming off a concussion, you've been working hard, and you're falling in love. It's completely understandable that you think you're haunted."

"How is that understandable?" Ash turned and threw his own rag down on the table he'd been cleaning. "How does any of what you just said make sense?"

Ryan shrugged.

"You really think I'm falling in love?"

"Uh-huh."

Ash huffed, but he had to smile as he turned around and picked his rag up again. As if on cue, the bell rang, and Wyatt pushed through the door.

"Hey," Ash said with a smile.

Wyatt gave him one of his goofy, self-conscious grins that made Ash want to kiss him.

"I don't have much time," Wyatt said.

"Ooh, afternoon delight," Ryan crooned from behind the bar. "How you doing, Wyatt? Talk later." He headed for the kitchen.

Wyatt watched him go with a confused smile.

Ash laughed. "What are you doing?"

"I came to ask you on a date."

"Really? It's a little late for that, isn't it?"

Wyatt rolled his eyes. "What are you doing tonight?"

"I'm leaving on a jet plane, actually."

Wyatt grimaced and smacked his forehead. "Vegas!"

Ash laughed. "Yeah."

"I forgot."

"It's okay. It's just the biggest flair competition of the year."

"I'm sorry."

Ash leaned on the bar and grinned. "You get a pass 'cause you're cute."

"Are you up for that with . . . all that's been going on?"

Ash shrugged, uncomfortable again. "I don't know. I hope so. We'll be gone for three nights; if I'm not up to flairing, I'll just have to drink a lot."

"Just don't gamble and you'll be fine."

Ash tried to smile but failed. "I'm . . . I'm kind of looking forward to getting away for a few days."

"I understand."

"Can you do me a favor?" Wyatt nodded and reached out to slide his hand over Ash's hip and pull him closer. Ash smiled as warmth stole over him. "Can you walk Bullseye for me while I'm gone?"

Wyatt raised an eyebrow and leaned closer. "Bullseye?"

"The broken neighbor's dog."

"Oh. Yeah."

"It's a big sacrifice, I know. See, I'd have to give you a key to my place in order for you to do that," Ash said, narrowing his eyes and smirking.

"Yeah." Wyatt nodded. "Yeah, I think I can do that."

"Good. You'll have to pick me up at the airport, too, when I get back. And then let me into the condo cause I only have one set of keys left." He turned into Wyatt and kissed him.

Wyatt laughed. "I can do that." He kissed Ash again, unable to resist. It grew more heated, and Ash pulled him closer until Wyatt had him pressed against the bar.

Ash held Wyatt's face in both hands and kissed him harder. When he pulled back, he grinned and said, "If you want to know what color it is, all you have to do is ask, you know."

"I'd rather be surprised," Wyatt murmured. He kissed Ash again.

"Health code violation!" Caleb shouted from the door to the kitchen.

Wyatt broke the kiss to glance over, but Ash just laughed and slid his hand into Wyatt's pocket.

"We'll finish this later," Ash said to Wyatt before letting him go. "It'll have to be after Vegas, though."

Wyatt nodded, disappointed. Ash found it hard to let Wyatt go, and for the first time, he realized he wasn't looking forward to the competition. Maybe Ryan was right. Maybe he was falling in love.

Wyatt picked up Bullseye from the grateful young woman who lived across the hall from Ash, and they started on their walk. The dog was excitable, running full-speed at anything that moved until he hit the end of his leash and nearly yanked Wyatt's arm out of its socket.

The walk still started nicely. They made their way around Fountain Lake, where the paddleboats were in the summer. The fountain in the middle of the lake was lit from its center with colors of the season, and tonight the spouting water glowed an eerie red and orange. The day had been unusually warm, but the night was cold and the mist that had developed over the water was thick and swirling with the breeze.

Wyatt kept glancing at the lake, wondering why it made him so tense. Fog on the water was anything but unusual, and the lights weren't out of the ordinary either. Every special occasion had colored lights in Fountain Lake. Regardless, Wyatt pulled the dog off the sidewalk that led around the lake and started him across the street, back toward the Fan. When they reached the block that hosted Ash's building, they walked down the opposite side and turned the corner into the alley behind.

Bullseye found himself a patch of grass and continued to wag his little tail as he did his business. None of the grass at the lake had been appropriate. He was a ridiculously happy dog. Wyatt looked around the alley at the bones of the old buildings, not really interested in watching the mutt pee. There were parking spaces behind Ash's building, and a large dumpster. The entrances to the fire escapes were also back here, and it was interesting to see where old windows had been bricked up and new ones had been cut. There were several doors along the ground floor level that led to Wyatt knew not where.

Wyatt was still looking around when he caught a glint of metal on the ground. He frowned and took a step closer, and his heart leapt into his throat when he realized what he was looking at.

He bent down and fought off the dog's excited pawing and licks as he picked up the set of keys. They had a battered fleur-de-lis keychain attached to them, the same one Wyatt had seen on Ash's keys the first night he'd gone home with him. Wyatt dug the key to Ash's building out of his pocket and held it up to one of the three keys on the keychain. It didn't match. He pushed the dog away as it wrapped around him and tried the second key.

It was a perfect match, and Wyatt swallowed against a sudden tightness in his throat. How had Ash's lost keys gotten here?

"You look like you lost something," someone commented from behind him.

Wyatt whirled around, searching for the source of the voice in the dark crevices of the building. A man stepped away from the shadow of the dumpster and Wyatt's heart raced even as he tried to calm himself.

"No, I uh . . . I found them," he stuttered as he held up the keys and jangled them. The dog sat down behind him and whined, winding the leash around his ankles.

"Oh, that's good," the man drawled as he moved into the light. With a rush of relief, Wyatt recognized him as one of Ash's older neighbors. He turned and began strolling down the alley, using a cane to aid his progress. "You have a nice night, now," he said over his shoulder.

"And you," Wyatt managed to stutter. He watched the old man, realizing that he was nearly hyperventilating as he stood there. He ran his hand over his face and then opened his eyes again, half expecting the man to be standing right in front of him despite having recognized him. But the shadowed figure turned the corner and continued on into the night, leaving Wyatt alone and very nearly too scared to move.

He glanced down at the keys, found right where Ash had said he'd seen the man in the top hat holding them, and he began to shake. Suddenly all the nonsense about ghosts and hauntings didn't seem like such nonsense after all. Everything he'd been trying to tell himself, the explanations for the sounds, the shadows he'd seen in the corner of his eye, Ash's terrifying experiences.

They were all real.

When Wyatt picked Ash up Monday morning, he waited until after Ash had told him about the competition to mention the keys. Ash had placed tenth overall, which Wyatt found astounding considering his recent head injury and how many entries there were, and he had won almost $10,000 in prize money. Ryan had followed up with a twelfth place finish.

They really were studs of the flairing world.

"You have to make the overhead lights so they blind him, you know? Or he can't do anything," Ash said as he laid his seat back and closed his eyes. "He gets so easily distracted by low-cut shirts in the audience. Of course, hell, I'm the same way with anything shiny, so I shouldn't be saying anything."

Wyatt smiled fondly at him. Maybe now wasn't the best time to tell Ash he'd become a believer in the hauntings. Ash was exhausted. And happy. "Do you work tonight?" he asked instead.

"No, bar's still shut down." Ash sighed. "But we were going to go in and get some shit done since we left Caleb for three days."

"Caleb's done."

"What?"

"He got everything done. Noah and I helped a little. There's some finishing touches left and some things to be delivered, but the bar reopened today."

"You're kidding! That's incredible."

Wyatt grinned and glanced sideways at Ash. He saw a flash of a face in the window above Ash's head, a dark silhouette that seemed to be staring at him. When he turned his head to look at it more directly, it was gone.

His heart was beating harder and his body had gone cold. He looked again, trying to catch another glimpse, but all he saw were cars passing by and the city of Richmond growing larger as they neared downtown.

"You okay?" Ash asked when he noticed Wyatt looking back and forth between the road and the space over his head.

Wyatt gave the glass one last glance before turning his attention back to the road with a curt nod. "Yeah. Yeah, I'm good."

"You sure? You look a little . . . pale." Ash sat his seat up and leaned in close.

Wyatt nodded and tried to give a reassuring smile. He put his hand on Ash's knee. Ash's hand slid over Wyatt's, fingers threading through his. The tips of Ash's fingers were cold. Wyatt squeezed them, trying to warm them.

Maybe he wouldn't tell Ash about the keys just yet. He was obviously a little too close to all this ghost business if he was managing to spook himself now.

He gave that window one more glance. Yeah. Far too close.

The sound of a key in the lock and a door creaking open barely registered with Ash, and it wasn't until Caleb stepped in front of him and made eye contact that Ash forced himself to focus.

"What are you doing here, lad?"

Ash blinked and glanced around the bar. "I don't know."

Caleb raised an eyebrow and discreetly began to look him over.

"I woke up and I was here." He realized he was sitting on the bar, legs swinging free, staring listlessly at the newly refinished floor. Music played on the sound system, an odd mixture of hardcore rock and old-world sea shanty.

Caleb met his eyes again in alarm. "You don't know how you got here?"

Ash shook his head. "I don't have my keys," he whispered. "I don't know how I got in."

Caleb blinked at him for a moment before he seemed to shake it off. He nodded.

Ash remembered Wyatt driving him home last night. He remembered Wyatt staying the night. He remembered waking up after Wyatt had left for work, and going to take a shower. And then he was here.

"I'm going to call Ryan in. And then I'll call Wyatt and Noah, okay?"

"No," Ash begged. "Please. He thinks I'm half-crazy already."

"Ash. You like him, right? He likes you? Something is obviously wrong, so let him help you through this."

Ash shook his head, staring at the floor again. His eyes were losing focus. The world was beginning to blur into something that didn't matter again. All that mattered was the seductive draw of giving himself over, letting something stronger than him take control.

"I'm calling him."

Ash didn't protest. He continued to stare at that spot on the floor, unwilling and unable to look away.

The board was meeting to discuss a variety of things. Wyatt had seen everything on the agenda, from his position as curator to what to do about the mice in the attic that had been snacking on General Lee's dinner jacket. There was a news crew coming later that day to observe the unveiling of a one-hundred-year-old newspaper, and Wyatt and Noah were set to supervise that if Wyatt still had his job at that point. Some people had been complaining about strange noises in the Haunted Hall, but they were chalking that up to either overactive imaginations or pranks on the interns.

Wyatt shivered. He was so sick of ghosts, he almost wished he'd just taken his pink slip and walked away.

His phone began to vibrate just as the meeting was starting up. He moved around in his seat, plucking the phone out of his pocket and peering at it, trying to be discreet. Gravedigger's. That was odd, and though Wyatt was a little concerned, he didn't dare answer it while his neck was already on the chopping block.

"So, Dr. Case, what have you got to say for yourself?" Edgar Reth said to start the meeting.

Wyatt wished he had the power to make someone burst into flames with his mind.

Reth's gaze darted around uneasily, then settled back on Wyatt.

There was a knock on the door, loud in the tense silence. Noah poked his head into the room and hissed at Wyatt.

Wyatt turned wide, incredulous eyes on his friend. Noah pointed at the phone.

Wyatt gestured toward the table and the twelve board members who were watching them.

Noah pointed more emphatically, and Wyatt waved him away. Noah ducked out of the room again, and Wyatt turned his attention back to Reth, surprised to find that he was flustered now. What could be going on that would prompt Noah to interrupt this meeting?

"Dr. Case?" Reth demanded. "You're here to defend your job."

"This is completely out of line," Emelda said as she crossed one hand over the other on the table in front of her. "The troubles of the museum do not fall solely on Dr. Case's head."

"He *is* the curator," Stuart Lincoln said.

She was silent, and the little man sank into his chair as if he'd just realized what he'd done.

"He may be the curator, but the power of decision-making lies with the board, does it not? Therefore it would stand to reason that the responsibility for the museum's current troubles should lie with our director, who maintains the power of final decision-making, and not Dr. Case."

Wyatt and the other members of the board looked from her to Reth, who had just turned a ghastly shade of gray.

"We are not here to talk about me," Reth said.

"Perhaps we should be," one of the other members said, turning his chair toward Reth.

Wyatt sat back, surprised, and watched the ensuing attack like a man on safari watching a pride of lions take down a zebra.

When Wyatt finally got out of the meeting, his job momentarily secure and his faith in humanity partially restored, he was able to check his messages. It wasn't Ash who had called him, but Caleb. He'd left only the briefest of barely coherent messages before hanging up.

Wyatt tried to hunt Noah down, but he was nowhere to be found. Calls to Gravedigger's went unanswered for a full hour before Noah called him back to tell him what had been going on.

"Ash is having a full-on mental breakdown."

"That's what Ryan said last time," Wyatt said as he paced through the exhibition hall.

"Yeah, but I'm not trying to be funny."

"What happened?"

Noah gave him a brief synopsis, in typical Noah Drake fashion. "He was still staring at the floor when I got here."

"What's he doing now?"

"Wyatt. He's staring at the floor."

"No one can get him to move?"

"It's like he's not there. And we still can't figure out how he got in. He has nothing on him but his clothes, and none of the locks have been picked."

A sense of dread and terror stole over Wyatt. He thought of the keys he'd found in that alley, and the reflection of the man's face he'd glimpsed in the window.

"I'll be there in five minutes."

"No, Wyatt."

"What?"

"I just . . . Caleb said Ash asked us not to call you, and I think he was right. You shouldn't see him like this."

"Fuck that, I'll be there in five minutes."

Wyatt was already heading toward the parking lot when he ended the call.

"He was fine last night."

"I've never seen anything like this."

"Noah, I don't suppose you know anything about fugue states?"

"A valid question considering my extensive knowledge of odd things, but no."

"What is a fugue state?"

"Basically . . . what Ash is doing right now."

"Someone call those ghost people."

"Noah, come on."

"I'm serious, he's possessed or something. Call them."

"Can he hear us?"

A hand waved in front of his face and Ash closed his eyes, putting every ounce of his strength into trying to move his head. He was finally able to tear his eyes away from the floor and look up at his companions.

Wyatt, Ryan, Noah, Delilah, and Caleb were all staring at him.

"Ash?"

"I feel weird," Ash whispered.

"It's okay, we're going to get you some help," Wyatt said as he stepped closer and took Ash's hands in his.

"Wyatt, go away." Ash could barely force his voice out. But he didn't want Wyatt witnessing whatever was happening here.

"What?"

"Go away. Please."

Wyatt looked stricken, and he glanced at the others for help. Caleb was shaking his head, but Ryan and Noah were both nodding.

"We'll take care of him," Noah said as he pulled Wyatt away.

Ash closed his eyes so he didn't have to see Wyatt leave.

CHAPTER NINE

A week crawled by, and it was Halloween before Wyatt worked up the nerve to ask Noah about Ash.

"He's doing fine," Noah answered. "He still spits fire whenever someone mentions ghosts or stares vacantly at the floor where three men have previously taken their own lives, but . . . I mean, I'm sure that's normal after an exorcism."

Wyatt grunted, still terrified of the whole idea of ghosts or the supernatural or anything that might have been after Ash. He wished Ash had let him help, and he wished he hadn't left when Ash had asked him to. He could see now that he'd gone about it all wrong. He should have insisted on staying. He should have done *something*.

"Is he okay?" Wyatt asked, throat dry.

Noah shrugged. "He seems normal to me. The head witch lady came back last week and said she sensed some evil on him. That it might take him a while to shed it. But hell, I think Ash was always a little bit evil in the first place."

Wyatt raised a dubious eyebrow. He didn't know what he thought anymore. He just knew that night after night of staring at that damn legends and myths exhibition had made him begin to question everything. The bruises on Ash's arms. The coincidences of all the deaths. Finding Ash's keys in that alley. The glimpses of shadowed faces. And the grand finale of Ash's weird behavior last week. He just didn't know what to think.

"If I go with you and hold your hand, will you go see him?"

"Look, after everything that happened, he asked me to stay away," Wyatt said, almost despondent. "Whatever he needed . . . he didn't think it was me. I think I owe it to him to just stay the hell away."

"You know, he asked you to stay away because he really likes you," Noah pointed out. "He didn't want you to see him like that."

Wyatt glared. He'd dangled that tidbit of logic for himself quite a few times over the last week, but he was still going to bed alone and Ash still wasn't answering his calls. Noah nodded, as if he knew Wyatt's inner struggle and was trying to reinforce his point.

"He told you that?" Wyatt finally asked.

Noah nodded.

"When the hell did you turn into an expert on relationships?"

"I know Ash, okay? I know he was falling for you, and I know you were falling for him. It's stupid that you're here and he's there and you're not together."

Wyatt's heart twisted. "It's pretty simple when you put it that way."

"Come with me. Talk to him."

Wyatt exhaled and nodded. He so desperately wanted to see Ash, it wasn't anything but pride keeping him away.

There was a knock on his office door, and he and Noah both winced at the sound. It had an ominous tone to it, as if the fist belonged to a board member with a pink slip. The danger was over, but there was still a Pavlovian response that Wyatt didn't think he would ever shed.

He took a steadying breath and got up to answer the knock. "Here we go," he whispered to Noah.

When he opened the door, it wasn't the squat little toad face of Stuart Lincoln that greeted him.

"Ash," he blurted, blinking in shock at the man's lovely visage.

"Hi."

Noah stood behind Wyatt, and Wyatt knew just from the sound of him that he looked pleased. Ash looked over Wyatt's shoulder and nodded at Noah, giving him a self-conscious smile.

"I'll just go . . . do . . . something," Noah said as he slipped out the door.

"What are you doing here?" Wyatt asked, trying to fight back the flurry of excitement and hope that rose in his chest.

"I . . . I miss you," Ash said with a flop of his hands.

Wyatt felt himself starting to grin. He took a deep breath.

Ash sighed shakily. "What I did wasn't the right move. And I know you're probably still pissed at me. But I really miss you."

Wyatt nodded, not quite sure what to say in the face of such fearless honesty. "I miss you too."

"I figure this is getting sort of ridiculous, the back and forth. So consider this my only move. You're going to have to come after me if you really want me."

Wyatt swallowed and nodded. "Does right now count?" he asked hopefully.

"No."

Wyatt licked his lips and nodded again. "So, if I left and then came back?"

Ash smiled, giving a noncommittal shrug, lips pulling into that old mischievous grin Wyatt had first fallen in lust with. Wyatt pulled Ash into his office by one of his suspenders, turned him and left him standing in front of his desk, and then stepped out of the office, Ash laughing behind him.

Wyatt pulled the door closed, then turned around again to re-enter. When he tried the doorknob, it was locked. He rested his forehead on the cool wood and huffed a rueful laugh; his office always locked automatically. He was destined to be the bumbling professor in this relationship. Thank Christ Ash liked that about him. He cursed under his breath and tapped on the door.

It took a few moments before Ash replied. "It's a good thing you're pretty, Wyatt," he drawled as he opened the door.

Wyatt grinned, elated.

Ash's smile fell and he met Wyatt's eyes. "We need to lay a few ground rules."

"Name them."

"First, the ghost word is off limits. It scares me and I've decided that if I ignore it long enough, it'll go away."

Wyatt nodded.

"Second, I'm not allowed to send you away for being worried about me again. That was shitty of me and I'm . . . I'm so sorry, Wyatt."

Wyatt smiled at the quirky apology. "Agreed." He slid a hand down Ash's arm and stepped closer. "What else?"

"That's all I have. Really, all I had to go on was 'I miss you.' If that hadn't worked, my backup plan was this." He stuck out his tongue to display a stud shaped like a red rose.

Wyatt laughed and met Ash's eyes as delight flooded him. "That's . . . the most romantic thing I've ever seen."

Ash gave him a chipped-tooth grin, and Wyatt pulled him close to kiss him. The rose didn't feel any different than any of the other tongue rings Ash wore, but it tasted far sweeter.

"So, you two made up, I assume," Noah said as he plopped down at the table in the break room.

Ash and Wyatt both grinned at him.

"This poses a problem," Noah said, deadly serious.

"What? Why?" Ash asked.

"Tonight's the Brawl."

"The what?" Wyatt asked.

"The Gravedigger's Brawl," Ash answered.

"Oh yeah, the big scary party," Wyatt said. "Damn, that's going to delay the make-up sex."

Ash frowned as he looked Wyatt up and down. "I see what you mean," he told Noah.

Wyatt glanced worriedly between them. "What? I don't get it."

"The Gravedigger's Brawl is the biggest Halloween party in Richmond," Ash said. "We have to hire extra bouncers and tenders. We open up the upstairs to make room, set up mobile bars up there and outside. Costumes are a requirement."

"Yeah, I remember. So?"

Noah grunted. "Wy, you don't have a costume. You won't be able to get in."

Wyatt studied Ash to see if they were joking, but Ash looked entirely serious. Wyatt grinned. "I have a costume."

"What kind?" Ash asked, looking doubtful. "We hire professional makeup artists to do ours."

Wyatt shrugged. "The gala opening was a costume party, remember?"

Ash's handsome face lit up, and Noah snapped his fingers. "That's right. Wyatt's costume was kickass, too."

"Then you're all set to come tonight?"

Wyatt nodded, though he looked between them uneasily. "You sure you want me there? Parties aren't really my strong suit."

Ash reached out and took his hand, smiling that disarming, sweet smile that Wyatt still dreamed about. "Wyatt, I can assure you that you will fit in better at the Brawl than I do sitting here right now."

Wyatt glanced around the break room. No one was paying them any attention. If Ash felt out of place in the museum, it was all in his head. Wyatt leaned over to kiss him, lingering over the way their lips met, sliding his tongue over the rose, and dragging his teeth against Ash's lips.

When it ended, Ash touched Wyatt's chin with his finger. "It wouldn't be the same if you weren't there. Please come?"

Wyatt nodded, warmed to his very toes. "I wouldn't miss it."

Ash nodded, then glanced at his watch and sighed. "Okay, I have to get back to help set up. I'll see you guys there?"

Wyatt nodded. He watched Ash stand, not wanting to let him out of his sight. He was euphoric, there was no other word to describe it. Noah bid Ash farewell as he made his way out of the break room. Museum workers turned to watch him go, eyeing him not because he was dressed oddly, but because he was a walking work of art with a warm smile and eyes that shone. Wyatt glanced to Noah, unable to curtail the brilliant smile on his face.

"You've got nine lives, my friend," Noah drawled around a smirk. He looked at his own watch. "Time to start getting ready. Go bust out that costume of yours."

Wyatt glanced at the doorway one last time before forcing himself to move.

His costume from the gala was still in his office, hanging in a bag on the back of his door. It probably wasn't appropriately gory for a party called the Gravedigger's Brawl, but it fit and it would do well enough.

He pulled out the Confederate officer's uniform and turned it around, inspecting it for flaws. It was a perfect replica, worthy to be worn by a museum curator in a city that had once been the capitol of the Confederacy.

Wyatt had just buttoned up the brass buttons on the front of his uniform and sat down to tie his shoes when Noah poked his head into the office.

Wyatt looked up at him and burst out laughing. He was dressed in a frighteningly warlike angel outfit. His chest was bare, with leather straps crisscrossing it. He was wearing wings and sandals.

"Oh my God," Wyatt blurted before almost falling out of his chair laughing.

"Hey! It's the Gravedigger's Brawl! They give prizes for the best costume. If I win it, I save Caleb money. He's the one who had the makeup dude come do it."

"You're going to freeze."

"A paltry sum to pay for what Caleb will do to me later."

Wyatt smirked. At least the wool coat of his uniform was warm. He'd probably be singing a different tune when they got to Gravedigger's and found it packed with hot, sweating bodies, but he was too excited about seeing Ash to care.

The sun had set and the streets were full of partygoers in costume as they walked from the museum toward the tavern. Many of the revelers congregated at Gravedigger's, which was the premier Halloween haunt in the city for the third year running. People were clamoring to get in. The line went around the corner of the building and down the alley.

They had hired several bouncers for the event, just like Ash had said. Noah told a large man with a clipboard their names and they were let into the bar without further fuss. The music pounded, vibrating the floor and shaking the windows. The far wall near the stairs had a tiny stage set up but nothing on it. The door to the upstairs was open and, Wyatt was shocked to see, full of people.

"Caleb fixed the upstairs!" Noah shouted above the din. "He's got a mobile bar and lounge areas set up in each room up there, plus one on the patio!"

"Yeah, that's what Ash was saying. I didn't expect . . . this, though."

"I know! It's awesome!"

Wyatt thought maybe he managed to respond, but his words were lost in the sound.

"Hard to think, huh?" Noah shouted with a grin.

Wyatt nodded and looked around the crowded room with what could best be described as shellshock.

"That's the best part, man! Better than drugs!" Noah shouted as he moved with the music. His angel wings moved with him.

Wyatt curled his lip at that and shook his head as he dodged one of Noah's wings. Several people recognized him as "the man who was fucking Ash" and greeted him in a surprisingly friendly manner. He even received a hug or two from inebriated people he didn't know. An alarming number of people saluted him.

Caleb was manning the bar downstairs and he greeted them wordlessly, knowing whatever he said would be lost before it got to them. He had dyed his beard jet black and shaved it into a classic split goatee, complete with pointed ends shellacked with something that made them stick out. They looked sharp enough to pierce armor. His eyes were flat black, an eerie thing since they were usually a gentle green. He had horns that appeared to be growing out of his forehead, not just sitting on a hairband or something, and they curled back and down around his ears like ram's horns. Wyatt couldn't even look at his clothing for being distracted by the brilliance of his makeup.

Caleb spared a moment to leer at Noah's bare chest, and he laughed as Noah reached over the bar and smacked him. Caleb leaned closer and Noah gave him a quick kiss, then they indulged a deeper one. Wyatt didn't look away. They seemed so perfect for each other, he simply smiled and watched. When they were satisfied, Noah said something into Caleb's ear. Caleb answered by pointing upstairs and then pointing left to indicate where Ash was.

"Be back!" Noah assured him, and Caleb nodded as he went back to fixing drinks.

Wyatt followed Noah through the crowd as he forced his way up the stairs. They took the first left and found a little mobile bar set up in one of the small rooms. Ash stood behind it, mixing drinks. He wasn't flairing. It was probably far too busy for that right now. The flairing exhibitions were scheduled for certain times.

When Ash raised his head, Wyatt's heart stuttered. The low light hit Ash's eyes and they seemed to glow like a cat's, only luminescent blue, just like the man Ash had claimed he'd seen. He raised his head higher and the light moved, and his eyes returned to their normal warm brown.

Wyatt stared breathlessly, rooted to the spot as Noah made his way through the crowd.

Ash waved to him as Wyatt remained where he was. Wyatt cleared his throat and forced himself to move.

"Nice costume!" Noah was saying as Wyatt got closer.

"They're pretty kickass, right?" Ash said with a grin.

He had little nubs of horns under his hairline that seemed to be sprouting out of his forehead, just like Caleb's only much smaller, and a long tail that moved with him as he danced to the music. He opened his mouth to show off his elongated canines—without any chips—and the stud in his tongue, a long black strip that held three balls and gave the impression at a glance that Ash's tongue was forked. His clothing had an old, mottled velvet quality to it, and it seemed to fall away from him in strips but still hug close enough not to catch on his bottles. It was a brilliant outfit.

"We're imps," Ash said, still grinning.

"Caleb was the Devil," Noah said, laughing raucously. "I love it."

"Nice uniform, Colonel," Ash said to Wyatt with an approving leer.

Wyatt could hardly answer, he was so preoccupied with Ash's eyes. And tongue. Ash lowered his head to pour and then looked back up at Wyatt from under lowered brows. He was smirking, and Wyatt shivered as his eyes once again glowed a milky blue for a moment. It seemed to Wyatt that Ash knew why he was staring.

"Cool!" Noah exclaimed, leaning closer. "Contacts?"

"Yeah. I warned the guy he wouldn't get them back 'cause I'm going to rip them out of my eyes and toss them away. I can feel them wanting to crawl into my corneas already, but he told me to try them anyway. But they're pretty sick, right?"

Noah nodded enthusiastically and Wyatt found himself staring at Ash suspiciously. Were they really contacts?

"What can I get you?" Ash asked them. "You okay?" he added as he frowned at Wyatt.

"You just . . . you look great."

Ash raised one eyebrow and then smiled at him. "I know what your problem is," he said, laughing as he poured a drink for Noah. Noah toasted him, then dissolved into the crowd, probably going back to find Caleb.

Ash flipped over a sign that said, "Go Next Door, Bitch" and came out from behind the bar. He took Wyatt's hand and tugged him through the crowd, then ducked under a velvet rope that closed off the staircase to the attic.

The thumping of the music grew softer as they climbed, and when Ash pushed open the door at the top of the staircase, the noise had settled to a dull roar.

"Hey, stranger." Ash flicked on the attic lights and turned to face Wyatt.

"Hi," Wyatt said, relieved that it wasn't scary up here. Just messy and full of old paint and furniture and ladders.

"I would kiss you, but it would fuck up the wicked makeup I've got going." Ash smiled. "You want to tell me what's going on?"

Wyatt swallowed and then exhaled in a rush of words, "I'm freaking out a little."

Ash blinked and took a slight step back. "What? Why?"

"You! First the thing with the . . . I'm not allowed to say the word."

"Oh."

"And then finding you on that sheet. Did you ever see those pictures? You looked like you were about to . . ."

"About to what? Paint?"

"No," Wyatt said through gritted teeth.

Ash looked genuinely confused. "What, Wyatt?"

Wyatt bit his lip and looked away, unable to meet Ash's eyes. "You looked like those pictures."

"Meaning? What, you thought I was about to kill myself? Come on, Wyatt!"

"I'm sorry!"

"You know better. You're the one who said you didn't believe in any of it. Hell, I'm not even sure if I do now. It was just a knock on the head."

Wyatt nodded, unconvinced.

Ash gave an almost amused huff. "What happened to change your mind?"

"I found your keys."

"Oh, yeah? Where?"

"They were at the corner of the building, where you said he was standing."

Ash frowned thoughtfully. "That's . . . slightly disturbing."

"Tell me about it. And then I kept seeing—"

"Look," Ash interrupted with a heavy sigh, "I'm scared, okay? But I don't want to dwell on this. It's taken up too much of my damn life already."

"I know. But they said people who are drugged or drunk are more susceptible, and when we did that cleansing you were all drugged up."

"Wyatt."

"And I keep seeing him around you! They said—"

"I know what they said," Ash snapped. He met Wyatt's eyes and shook his head, his expression softening. "I'm sorry. It's just, I think I'd know if I was . . . possessed or something."

"Would you?"

Ash's head jerked up and his eyes flashed in the light of the bare bulb above the door. Wyatt gasped and tensed despite the fact that he knew they were contacts.

Ash examined Wyatt for a moment. "Are you scared of me?" he asked.

"A little. Maybe. Yeah," Wyatt stuttered. "Right now, yeah."

To his surprise, Ash laughed. Softly at first, almost disbelievingly, and then harder.

"It's not funny," Wyatt muttered.

"I'm sorry, but it kind of is." Still laughing, Ash placed his hands on the door on either side of Wyatt's shoulders, careful of his uniform. "I'm nothing to be scared of. I promise."

"Say that to me again without the contacts or the forked tongue or the horns or the fangs, okay?" Wyatt requested, though the knot of tension began to dissipate.

Ash laughed again, and it was the same deep, rich sound Wyatt remembered.

"How about I tell you again in the morning?" Ash leaned closer and brushed his lips over Wyatt's. The chaste touch had the desired effect; Wyatt's entire body flooded with warmth. He cursed the makeup Ash had on that was keeping the man from touching him.

Ash ran the tip of his nose against Wyatt's cheek. "You up for your last chance?"

Wyatt shivered. "Do I deserve it?"

"I'm a charitable imp."

Wyatt nodded and smiled as relief began to seep through him. "It's still not funny."

Ash grinned. "In a year, we'll look back on all this and laugh."

Wyatt smiled as he met Ash's eyes. Ash was thinking long-term. It gave Wyatt the most incredible feeling, and he told himself that he was being silly. Ash was right. There was nothing to be afraid of and everything to gain.

It was past four in the morning when the staff of Gravedigger's finally swept the dregs of the party out of the bar and locked up. The reveling continued in the streets, but Ash, Ryan, Delilah, and Caleb stayed behind to clear away the largest of the messes.

They closed the upstairs, making certain there were no stragglers locked in closets or between couch cushions, and then trudged downstairs to find Wyatt and Noah waiting for them.

"Ready to go home?" Noah asked Caleb with a smirk. He rolled his shoulders and his wings waved. Caleb laughed and, to Ash's surprise, wrapped Noah in his arms, bent him backward, and kissed him soundly. There was something amusing and slightly obscene about watching the devil grope an angel.

"Nice," Ryan snickered. He glanced at Delilah, who was dressed in a feminine version of Ash and Ryan's imp costumes: a skirt that was almost too short, and a corset that displayed her slim waist and highlighted some extremely impressive curves. Her hair fell in soft waves, dyed jet black with purple streaks. Her horns were buried amidst the glitter sprinkled through it.

She was probably the fiercest thing Ash had seen in the Brawl that night, and she'd won the costume contest on the strength of her cleavage alone.

"If I take you home, will you promise to wear that all night?" Ryan asked her as his eyes raked her up and down.

She grinned, showing her fake fangs.

"Everything but those," Ryan corrected.

She laughed and nodded coyly, sashaying toward the door with her tail in hand. Ryan watched her go, biting his lip in anticipation. "I'll be there in a minute," he called after her.

"We're going home," Caleb growled. He pulled Noah toward the door. Noah snickered as he was dragged out of the bar. "We'll clean up tomorrow," Caleb ordered as they left.

Ash glanced at Wyatt and grinned. "Everyone's getting laid tonight."

Wyatt waggled his eyebrows, and Ash laughed.

"You ready to go home, General?"

"Whenever you are," Wyatt said, smiling serenely. Ash could tell that he was slightly tipsy, which was just the way Ash wanted him tonight. The tension had dissipated, and though Ash knew it would take some time, he hoped this was a start to something resembling normal for them.

"Y'all walking?" Ryan asked as he looked into the mirror behind the bar and removed his contacts. He blinked and set them in their containers. His costume was similar to Ash's: horns, fangs, and forked tongue. Ash snickered as he watched him try to pull one of the horns off. There was some serious glue in use.

"You're going to need some WD-40 or something for that," Ash said. He'd discovered as the night progressed that the makeup was pretty damn resilient.

Ryan pulled at the horn again to no avail, and Ash laughed. Wyatt walked up to lean on the bar behind them.

"Did you drive?" Ash asked Wyatt.

"We walked from the museum." Wyatt cleared his throat and pushed away from the bar. "I need air."

"I'll give you guys a ride," Ryan offered. "Just no cock-blocking, understand? Come on, Wyatt, you can help me find my car. And my date." He stepped out from behind the bar and took Wyatt by the elbow.

Wyatt turned to Ash. "You coming?"

"I'll be right out. Just have to take these things out and close out the register 'cause Ryan pretends he doesn't know how to do it."

Ryan smirked and led Wyatt toward the door.

Ash waited until the cow bell dinged and the door fell shut before he began collecting the overflowing glass tip jars. He didn't bother counting the money; he would do that in the morning. He just laid it out on the back shelf and then placed both hands flat on the wood. He looked up into the mirror.

His eyes flashed as the light hit them and he held his head still, looking over his shoulder at the spot where a face had once stared at him. His eyes reflected the same milky sheen as the apparition had. It was sort of funny, now that he'd chosen not to worry about it anymore.

He knew he should be ashamed of the spectacle, but he was still scared and he could blame it all on the head injury and not feel too weird about it. Everyone else had moved on, and he was trying to as well.

He emptied the last jar full of cash and placed a heavy bottle over the stack to keep it from fluttering away. When he glanced up again, his heart skipped a beat and his body went cold as he locked eyes with the man in the mirror, standing at his shoulder and glowering with eyes that glinted a faint blue.

CHAPTER TEN

R yan and Delilah were just barely restraining themselves from groping each other in the car, so it was with intense relief that Wyatt saw Ash leave the bar and head toward them.

When he climbed into the back of the car, he looked shaken.

"Everything okay?" Wyatt asked.

Ash nodded, licking his lips. "It's kind of spooky in there, all quiet."

Wyatt reached his hand out, and Ash slid over and rested his head against Wyatt's shoulder. One of his horns poked Wyatt, and they both laughed. The tension seeped out of them as they headed toward the museum. Ryan weaved in and out of the partiers still crowding the streets, yelling out the windows and tossing Halloween beads from the sunroof.

Wyatt and Ash wished the two lovebirds a good night once they were in the employee parking lot. Ryan burned rubber leaving the lot, and Wyatt and Ash laughed, watching beads fly from the sunroof as the car trundled down Boulevard. Wyatt slipped his arm around Ash's waist, and they walked to his parking spot.

Ash hummed and nodded at the museum. "It looks like it's open."

"It is," Wyatt said with a grimace. "The exhibit is open. They're having an all-night party trying to drum up business."

"How crass," Ash drawled, a smile following the word. "Let's go in. I'd like to see your exhibit again."

"Really?"

"No." Ash stopped and turned to him, his smile somehow foreign with the fake fang covering that chip in his tooth. "But I'd like to go in anyway."

Wyatt raised an eyebrow. "Okay," he said suspiciously. "May I ask why?"

"You'll see," Ash murmured, and the hand he rested on the small of Wyatt's back urged him forward.

"You want to have sex in some unusual place, don't you?"

"And here I thought my subtle hints would go unheeded," Ash whispered into his ear.

A shiver ran down Wyatt's back and he led Ash to the employee's entrance. He held the door for him, watching him as he passed by. Something was different about him, but Wyatt couldn't place what it was.

They could hear the music playing on the floor above, giving the halls they walked an eerie quality.

"Faust," Ash said as he raised his chin.

"Appropriate, if my date is an imp."

Ash turned and began walking backward, holding out a hand. "Dance?"

Wyatt bit his lip. He had the very distinct feeling that he was being seduced. He supposed this was their first real date, though, and he sort of enjoyed that Ash was treating it like that.

He took Ash's hand, laughing as Ash pulled him close and started into a waltz, using the strains of "La Danse Macabre" as their guide through the lower hallways of the museum. As the song came to an end, Ash turned Wyatt and slammed him against one of the concrete walls. He pressed against him to kiss him hungrily, and Wyatt could barely fend him off as he tried to return the kiss.

When they broke, they were both breathless, bodies pressed together, and Wyatt was definitely interested in whatever unusual dalliance Ash had planned. Wyatt stared into his eyes, trying to make out his expression in the semi-lit hallway. When Ash tilted his head, his eyes caught the light and flashed.

Wyatt shivered violently. "I thought you took the contacts out."

Ash's smile was slow as he lowered his head, looking at Wyatt from under lowered brows. "I did."

Noah climbed out of Caleb's '57 Chevrolet Bel Air and grumbled as he tried to pull his other wing off.

"Where did you leave it?" Caleb asked as they headed for the tavern to search for Noah's missing phone.

"I don't know. When we get in, we can call it," Noah said. He finally plucked the wing off, surprised it hurt to rip all that glue off his skin. "Son of a bitch."

"I told you I'd help," Caleb said through a grin as they rounded the corner to the front of the building—

And stared in horror at flames licking at the upper windows. The fire cast a glow on the street below, and a smattering of people had gathered to point and stare, some of them calling the fire department, others merely gawking.

Caleb fumbled for his keys and rushed for the front door.

Noah lunged for him and grabbed at his elbow. "What are you doing?"

"I can't let it burn down!"

"Caleb, no! It's probably an electrical fire, it's already out of control!"

"It's all I have, Noah! Help me!"

Noah watched him fumble to find the right key, his green eyes flickering in the light of the fire raging above. Noah cursed, then bent to pick up the potted plant near the door and swung it at the glass.

Caleb stared for a moment, shocked, and then they both dashed through the shattered door into Gravedigger's.

It took Wyatt too long to comprehend what was going on. He blinked at the face of the man he'd fallen in love with. It was not possible that this wasn't Ash. It just wasn't possible.

"I'm disappointed, Wyatt. I thought you'd be more fun," Ash said. But it wasn't truly Ash's voice. It was deeper, almost resonant.

Wyatt pushed against the wall, trying to step away, but Ash grabbed him and shoved him into it again, pinning him with arms that were too strong.

"You're Vincent, right? Vincent DuBois?" Wyatt asked, feeling stupid despite all the evidence.

"Not anymore. I'm Ash Lucroix." His hand was at Wyatt's throat before Wyatt could flinch, fingers colder than death, squeezing hard. "And all I need tonight is to be rid of you. I'd hoped for some entertainment first, but my dreams have been dashed before."

Wyatt grabbed at Ash's wrist as those fingers squeezed harder.

"He's mine," Ash whispered. "You tried to take him from me, but he's mine now."

Wyatt shook his head, lashing out and knocking Ash in the side of his face. They both toppled sideways, and Wyatt took off at a sprint for the stairwell. A hand brushed at his coattails, and he hit the stairwell door as if the hounds of Hell were on his heels. He was halfway up the first flight when he heard Ash come through the door in pursuit.

He had no idea what to do, but he knew where he was headed. He sprinted out of the stairwell toward the Haunted Hall and the display in the far corner, the one that instructed museum-goers how to get rid of pesky spirits and ghosts who were possessing their boyfriends and trying to kill them.

Noah and Caleb weren't the only brave souls who entered the bar to try to save it. People streamed out of neighboring buildings, houses and businesses alike, to help fight the flames. In a neighborhood like the Fan, if one building went down, all of them went down.

The flames had started upstairs, letting all Hell break loose on old, untreated wood that was dry as kindling.

Smoke swirled and flames licked at the walls as they attacked the fire with extinguishers and damp towels, creating an otherworldly scene in which devils and angels fought side by side with pirates and fairies, cats and vampires, witches, and one very convincing Waldo.

As soon as they extinguished one fire, another would start somewhere else.

"It's like it has a mind of its own!" Caleb called from across the room.

Noah sprayed the nearest wall with an extinguisher, panting, watching the charred remnants of the walls fall to the floor. He caught sight of a shadow at the corner of his eye, but when he whipped his head around, there was no one there. Another shadow danced at the edge of his vision. Was the smoke inhalation getting to him?

Another shadow flitted through the smoke, and Noah saw this one clearly. A little boy dressed in 19th-century clothes. He disappeared into the scorched wall, and Noah stumbled back, running into Caleb and knocking them both to the ground.

"What are you doing?"

"Ghosts!" Noah cried. Caleb's arm was around him, helping him to his feet. Noah pointed toward the wall, just in time for Caleb to look up and see a spark jump from the electrical socket there.

The new fire spread quickly, chewing through the old wood until it neared a crate of unused liquor bottles in a corner of the upper foyer.

Noah hefted his extinguisher and started for the fire, but Caleb grabbed his arm. When Noah glanced back at him, Caleb was peering into the smoke. Faces appeared in its wisps, pleading and desperate. Disembodied hands wrung and sobs emitted over the roar of the fires. Noah gaped, but was too shocked to even gasp a breath.

Caleb stared at the apparitions. Then his gaze transferred to the flames that were inching their way to the liquor crate.

"Caleb!" Noah shouted. The grip on his arm was like iron.

Caleb shook his head, tugging Noah—and the extinguisher that could have saved them—away. "Everyone out!" he shouted above the roar of the fires that still raged above and below. He pulled Noah with him as the crate caught fire. The small explosion sent them sliding down the stairs and tumbling over the new railing.

Noah lay on his back, stunned as fire and smoke swirled above him. Caleb's face came into view, those horns curling around his ears. His hands were gentle on Noah's face. "Darling?"

"Did you see it?"

"I did."

"There's more ghosts. They're trying to burn it down."

"I know. And I'm going to let them. Come on, my love, we need to go."

Noah peered up at the ceiling again. The flames billowed along the wooden slats. "The fire."

"I know," Caleb said as he pulled Noah to his feet. He yanked Noah along, and as they passed in front of the antique mirror behind the bar, Noah saw the devil leading a wingless angel through the fires of Hell. Behind them, an array of men and women in dark, old-fashioned clothes stood, hands clasped in front of them, watching impassively. Waiting to go home.

Wyatt had to force his way through the surprisingly large crowd of partygoers toward the ghostbusting display, and they slowed his progress enough that Ash caught up to him. He tackled Wyatt to the ground, causing an uproar amidst the attendees as those around them parted and he and Ash slid across the floor together.

Ash ended up on top of him, holding him to the floor as Wyatt struggled. He was torn between the very real desire to escape death or dismemberment and the realization that Ash was still in there somewhere. He didn't want to hurt him. But he sure as hell didn't want Ash—Vincent, whoever the hell it was—to hurt him or anyone else.

He scrambled on the marble floor, grasping for anything or anyone that could help him. Ash's cold hands were on his throat again, squeezing, causing lights to flare at the edges of his vision. Wyatt kicked at the floor, pushing at Ash's shoulder, trying to call for help.

There was no way in hell he could be throttled in the middle of a hundred people at a Halloween party. No way.

The people around them started cheering.

The firemen arrived as Caleb and Noah tumbled out of the building. They'd beaten back the progress of the flames, enough that it hadn't reached the main floor yet. Noah thought the fire hoses might be able to save it now, but he was too stunned by what he'd seen inside to say or do anything but stare.

"Are you okay?" Caleb asked, his hands on Noah's face.

Noah nodded and tore his eyes from the flames. "I saw people in there."

"We were the last ones out."

Noah's eyes drifted toward the flames again. "No. I mean . . . you saw all those people."

"Noah," Caleb said, his voice sterner. Noah met his eyes again. "Do you remember what the witch lady said?"

Noah was silent, lost in Caleb's eyes for a moment. Then he nodded. "Sometimes all you can do is burn it the ground."

Caleb looked up at the building, wrapping his arm around Noah to pull him close. "We had more than one ghost all this time."

"All those electrical problems," Noah whispered.

"The victims were trying to burn the place down. They want to go home."

Noah nodded. Flames licked the velvet sky as Gravedigger's burned. "What about the bad one?"

Caleb met his eyes, then they both turned to look down the street to the spotlights of the museum.

Someone gave a shout from the back of the crowd, and it was followed by another whoop. "You show that Yankee devil, General Lee!"

Wyatt scrabbled against Ash's body, trying to find purchase, trying to grasp *anything* that might give him a fighting chance.

His hand finally landed on one of Ash's horns. He grabbed and pulled with all his might, yanking Ash sideways, eliciting a shout of pain and anger. Wyatt rolled out from under him and scrambled to his feet, darting toward the display. He skidded to a halt at the red velvet rope and picked up one of the heavy brass stands. He swung it at the display with all his might, shattering the protective glass.

There were more screams and a smattering of applause. Wyatt realized that these people thought it was some sort of live-action entertainment. Dinner and a show. He reached for the first thing he could get his hand on, a vial of holy water. He turned and tossed the water at Ash's face as Ash advanced on him.

Ash stopped and shook his head. When he wiped at his eyes, his hand smeared his makeup across his face. Then he laughed. "Is that supposed to do something to me?"

Wyatt cursed and grabbed at something else, a shaker of salt sitting on a Plexiglas shelf. He unscrewed the cap as he backed away. The glass underfoot crunched as Ash came closer. His eyes were the most disturbing thing about him, still aglow with that milky sheen. Wyatt tossed the lid to the shaker aside and threw salt at Ash as he neared. Ash dodged most of it, swiping at it as if it burned his chest when it hit him.

"Table salt?" Ash asked with a sneer. "It has to be pure rock salt, Wyatt, didn't your ghostbusters tell you that?"

"You're so up on the subject, why don't you tell me?" Wyatt asked, stalling as he continued to back away through the ruins of the display.

"You can't kill a spirit, Wyatt. I'm already dead."

"Try the iron!" someone in the crowd shouted.

"Yeah, dude, hit him with the frying pan!"

Ash raised an eyebrow, taunting him. Challenging him. "By all means, Dr. Case. Hit your lover in the face with a frying pan while everyone watches. I'd love to see how that goes over."

Wyatt shook his head, glancing at the crowd. Ash took a step closer.

"The only way to get rid of me, Wyatt, is fire," Ash hissed, the enjoyment in his voice making Wyatt's stomach lurch. Ash grabbed Wyatt's lapels and shoved him against the padded wall of the display.

Ash's lips brushed Wyatt's as he spoke. "I have him. He'll never be rid of me now. And you'll never get him back."

Wyatt's hand strained against the display wall, his fingertips brushing the iron handle of the antique frying pan.

The hoses were putting up a valiant fight to save the building that shared a wall with Gravedigger's, but they had given up on trying to save the tavern. The top level was gone, nothing but charred beams and glowing embers left to mark its passage.

The main level, where Caleb had spent half his life making a living, poured his heart and soul into it, was on fire. Flames danced like gleeful imps amidst the tables and the bar, attacked the gleaming new kitchen. They pounded on the wooden floorboards, demanding entrance to the root cellar and the very foundations of Gravedigger's.

Caleb's knees gave out on him and he sank to the curb, eyes rapt on the glow of the fire. Noah sat with him, his arm around his shoulders as they watched the building go down.

"I'm so sorry," Noah whispered.

Caleb gaped at him, then lunged toward him and kissed him almost brutally.

Noah flailed, but then he wrapped his arms around Caleb and returned the kiss with the sort of desperation that came from nearly dying in a fiery explosion.

"I'd rather have you here safe with me than a thousand taverns."

Noah wrapped his arm around him and buried his face against his neck. He had to dodge the horns, but he didn't care.

"Besides," Caleb whispered. "We're going to be rich."

Noah laughed. "How do you figure?"

"I have millions of dollars in insurance," Caleb said, voice wry.

Noah pulled back and blinked at him.

Caleb was grinning again, his green eyes dancing in the firelight. "And at least we'll be done with the ghosts now."

Ash's hand slammed against Wyatt's wrist before he could grasp the handle. Ash yanked him by his lapels and tossed him into the room, away from the useless methods of ghost repellent.

Wyatt slid across the floor, dazed and slowly but surely giving up hope that he or Ash would survive this ordeal. He wasn't cut out for museum brawls. He called out to the crowd for help, trying to convince them this wasn't part of a show, but they merely laughed and clapped.

He pushed onto his elbows, trying to scoot away from Ash as he followed, his feet crunching glass shards. He had the frying pan in his hand.

"Come on Bobby Lee!"

"Kick his ass!"

Wyatt sat up and swallowed hard, looking into Ash's eyes and desperately trying to find Ash in them.

"Ash."

"He's not home." Ash raised the frying pan and Wyatt flinched away, covering his head with both hands. But Ash's body convulsed and he dropped the frying pan with a shout of pain.

Ash's hand burst into flame.

"Ash!"

Ash dropped to his knees, watching in stunned silence as the flames skittered up his arm and enveloped his body.

"No!" Wyatt scrambled for the fire extinguisher near the emergency exit as the crowd began to shout and applaud. They still thought this was some sort of game.

Ash screamed behind him, a blood-curdling, otherworldly cry that seemed to come from everywhere and nowhere at once. The entire room fell into stunned, horrified silence.

Wyatt yanked the extinguisher from the wall, turning back to Ash as he tried to figure out how to turn the damn thing on.

But the fire was gone. Ash lay facedown on the marble floor, and not even his clothing was singed. Wyatt dropped the extinguisher and ran toward him, dropping to his knees at Ash's side as he pawed at him and turned him over. His body felt completely lifeless.

Wyatt slapped his face gingerly and whispered to him. "Come on, Ash, open your eyes," he begged. "Wake up."

Ash's eyes fluttered open, and Wyatt held his breath. Ash stared at the ceiling for a long while, blinking rapidly. Warm brown, no glaze or glow in sight. Wyatt thought he might cry in relief when Ash turned his head, a look of supreme confusion on his face.

"Ash?"

Ash blinked at him again. "Did you roofie me?" he asked, voice hoarse and incredulous.

Wyatt barked a laugh, half sobbing as he pulled Ash to a sitting position and hugged him. The crowd around them cheered.

Ash clung to him, chin resting on Wyatt's shoulder. "Holy hell, Wyatt, where are we?"

"You won't believe me if I tell you," Wyatt whispered. He helped Ash to his feet, unable to keep his hands or his eyes off him. "Come on. Let's get out of here."

Ash leaned heavily on him as they threaded their way through the applauding crowd.

"This is the most awesome museum ever," someone in the crowd said with relish. Wyatt shook his head as he and Ash limped out of the room. A hundred people had just seen him fight to the death with a murderous spirit, and not one of them knew what they'd witnessed.

"What happened to your exhibit?" Ash asked as he looked around, still dazed.

"You did."

"Oh. You're so getting fired now."

"I don't care." Wyatt held Ash tighter.

"I had the weirdest dream."

Wyatt laughed in relief as they stumbled down the stairs together.

"Did you . . . hit me with a frying pan?"

Wyatt began laughing again, shaking his head. "No. But it wasn't for lack of trying."

For some reason, the pile of smoking cinders where Gravedigger's used to be didn't come as a surprise to Wyatt or Ash when they pulled up to the scene.

Ash was gradually beginning to remember what had happened while he'd been "under the influence," as Wyatt insisted on calling it. It was clear now why he'd burst into ghostly flames.

Gravedigger's had burned to its very foundation and taken the house next to it as well.

Caleb and Noah sat on the curb, staring morosely at the hole in the ground. When Wyatt and Ash joined them, both men merely sank to the curb alongside them.

"What happened to you two?" Noah asked.

"Ash was possessed," Wyatt answered, not even trying to sugarcoat it.

"I tried to kill him at the museum."

"In front of everyone there. We crashed the party, destroyed the exhibit."

"Oh," Noah said, voice devoid of emotion. "You're so getting fired now."

Wyatt nodded.

"Thanks for burning down the bar," Ash added. "Killed the ghost. Saved both our lives."

"Yeah," Caleb sounded dubious. "Yeah, because that's exactly what we were aiming for."

Ash nodded, still staring at the burnt remnants of the tavern.

Wyatt's hand slid into his as they sat there.

"Weird first date," Wyatt muttered.

"I feel dirty," Ash added.

"You just got barebacked by a ghost," Noah said. "You should feel dirty."

Ash and Wyatt both turned to look at him. He studiously ignored their evil glares.

"What do we do now?" Caleb asked.

"You just had the most epic Halloween party in existence," Noah said. "The gravediggers can do whatever they want now. You may as well be myth and legend in this town."

Ash leaned sideways and laid his head on Wyatt's shoulder. "I'll settle for being human."

EPILOGUE

"**D**r. Case, do you care to explain what exactly happened on Halloween night?"

Wyatt pursed his lips. "I was haunted."

"This is a serious inquiry, Dr. Case. We would appreciate it if you'd treat it as such."

Wyatt took a deep breath and shook his head. "My boyfriend and I were haunted by the ghost of a monster that Richmond had forgotten. He took hundreds of lives while he lived, and a handful after he died."

"Dr. Case—"

"Gravedigger's Tavern burned to the ground because so many people had died there, and the pain finally overwhelmed the building. The history was buried, and it came back to this museum to bite us in the ass. We were lucky to live through it."

"That's it?"

"I have no other explanation."

"Very well. You'll understand, then, if we ask that you resign your post, effective immediately."

Wyatt nodded, but he was already smiling. "I figured as much."

When Wyatt entered the main lobby of the museum, his friends were all there waiting to hear the verdict. Ryan leaned against a wall in a tattered T-shirt and jeans, and Delilah curled up under his arm, looking entirely out of place in a stunning black lace corset and thigh-high leather boots.

Noah and Caleb sat on a padded bench, their heads bent together, their whispers echoing oddly in the large room. Noah was wearing his square black nerd glasses today, and Caleb couldn't seem to tear his eyes away from him.

Wyatt had to smile. He saw nothing odd about either couple. Caleb had already declared his plan to pick a new city and start fresh, and Noah had every intention of following him. Ryan and Delilah planned to go as well, and Wyatt had a feeling they'd be picking out rings or whips or *something* for each other by Christmas.

His eyes sought out Ash, who leaned against the information desk checking an antique pocket watch chained to his gray vest. When he saw Wyatt, his dark eyes lit up.

"What happened?" Ash asked.

Wyatt shook his head and reached out to snag Ash's vest. He pulled him closer and kissed him until they were both breathless.

"I'm not sure if that's good or bad news."

"It's okay," Wyatt whispered. He glanced at the others, then met Ash's eyes with a mischievous grin. "What do y'all think about Charleston?"

"Big St. Patrick's Day town," Caleb said with a glint in his eye that practically reflected a dollar sign.

"Lots of history," Noah added.

"To haunt you," Ash grumbled. He was smiling though.

Wyatt grinned and kissed him again. "At least the ghosts there just haunt you instead of trying to kill you."

"We hope."

AUTHOR'S NOTE

There's a lot of history included in this book, and with very few exceptions, it's all true. The LaLauries were a real couple, and the things they did to their slaves in New Orleans were so awful that I chose not to include details in this book. You can find out more about them with a simple Google search, or by taking a ghost tour in the city of New Orleans. Their mansion has remained a cursed building over the years, never retaining an owner for more than a year, never successfully hosting a business. The current owner is Johnny Depp, who intends to make it into a hotel. Good luck with that, buddy.

The tales of the Dubois and Fossor families are entirely fictional. No such families ever existed, and neither does Gravedigger's Tavern. But the sights and sounds of Richmond's Fan district are entirely based in fact. The Starlight serves root beer on tap. Monument Avenue is full of Confederate heroes. And Boulevard is a beautiful street to cruise down. Just don't hit a stoner or hipster as you go.

The Virginia Historical Society sits on Boulevard, and the last time I went by there, it was still under construction. Any details of the inner workings, or of the inside of the building, are my imagination. If they've finished all that construction, there's no telling what it looks like now!

The building Ash lives in is based on the one I called home for two years. It will forever be the love of my life, even if I did repeatedly find my knickknacks mysteriously sitting in front of the main door whenever I left.

Noah's facts throughout the book are all true, even his lecture on dueling with hot air balloons and forkfuls of pig dung. You can read about that in *Smithsonian*.

ALSO BY ABIGAIL ROUX

ABOUT THE AUTHOR

Abigail Roux was born and raised in North Carolina. A past volleyball star who specializes in sarcasm and painful historical accuracy, she currently spends her time coaching high school volleyball and investigating the mysteries of single motherhood. Any spare time is spent living and dying with every Atlanta Braves and Carolina Panthers game of the year. Abigail has a daughter, Little Roux, who is the light of her life, a boxer, four rescued cats who play an ongoing live-action variation of Call of Duty throughout the house, a certifiable extended family down the road, and a cast of thousands in her head.

To learn more about Abigail, please visit www.abigailroux.com.

Enjoy this book?
Find more romantic suspense at
RiptidePublishing.com.

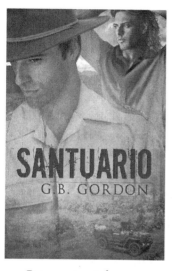

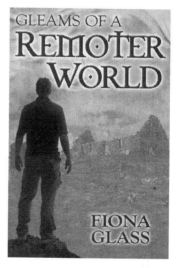

Between two cultures,
love hangs in the balance.

Serving ghosts with the Guinness.

www.riptidepublishing.com/titles/
santuario

www.riptidepublishing.com/titles/
gleams-remoter-world

ISBN: 978-1-937551-65-0

ISBN: 978-1-937551-67-4